BE CAREFUL
WHAT YOU WISH FOR

For Lucas Marshall, temporarily incapicitated by a broken leg, Simon was the kind of son he wished he had—good looking, handy, hardworking, full of get-up-and-go.

For Cat Marshall, feeling unloved and lonely for the first time in her marriage, Simon was a temptation that she knew she should resist, despite the way his touch made her feel.

For Haley Marshall, Simon was the one person who realized she was no longer a little girl but someone who could handle grown-up things, including a guy as hot as Simon.

For Zack Marshall, Simon was everything his dad was not, encouraging him to follow his "weird" interests, no matter where they led.

For the whole Marshall family, Simon was a savior—straight from hell. . . .

SIMON SAYS

SIMON SAYS

by

Gloria Murphy

A SIGNET BOOK

SIGNET
Published by the Penguin Group
Penguin Books USA Inc., 375 Hudson Street,
New York, New York 10014, U.S.A.
Penguin Books Ltd, 27 Wrights Lane,
London W8 5TZ, England
Penguin Books Australia Ltd, Ringwood,
Victoria, Australia
Penguin Books Canada Ltd, 10 Alcorn Avenue,
Toronto, Ontario, Canada M4V 3B2
Penguin Books (N.Z.) Ltd, 182–190 Wairau Road,
Auckland 10, New Zealand

Penguin Books Ltd, Registered Offices:
Harmondsworth, Middlesex, England

First published by Signet,
an imprint of Dutton Signet,
a division of Penguin Books USA Inc.

First Printing, November, 1994
10 9 8 7 6 5 4 3 2 1

Copyright © Gloria Murphy, 1994
All rights reserved

Cover art by Broek Steadman

 REGISTERED TRADEMARK—MARCA REGISTRADA

Printed in the United States of America

PUBLISHER'S NOTE
This is a work of fiction. Names, characters, places, and incidents either are the
product of the author's imagination or are used fictitiously, and any resemblance
to actual persons, living or dead, events, or locales is entirely coincidental.

In loving memory of
Rose Sherry Greenblatt

Thank you

Alice Martell for her passionate pursuit,
Audrey LaFehr for her calm competence,
Laurie and Bill Gitelman for their stinging feedback,
And forever and always, Joe

Chapter One

It was pretty much a ritual—the first Friday after school let out for the summer, Cat and Lucas and the kids would pack up and head for the beach house. But this year nothing was going smoothly. For starters, they were late leaving: Lucas, who always liked to arrive at the shore in time to unload the car while it was still daylight, had been detained at work because of a bogus bomb scare on one of the construction sites. So not until seven-fifteen was the '94 black Bronco packed and ready to leave, a case of Snapple soft drinks the last item in. Then there was the pall thrown on the usual festivities by thirteen-year-old Haley, who in the past few days had been objecting about going to the shore. Though she was now quiet in the backseat across from her brother, she looked as though she were being taken away under martial law.

As they entered the on-ramp to I-91 south, toward the Connecticut shoreline nearly two hours away, the sky clouded over. Had the forecast predicted rain? Glancing in the review mirror, Lucas got Haley's attention. "Once we get settled in, what about inviting a friend up for a few days?" he said.

"It's not the same," Haley said.

"I didn't say it would be. I'm just suggesting it because I thought it might be fun. But okay, if that doesn't sound so hot, maybe you'll want to volunteer to help me out with the dock."

He was sure this would get a rise: reinforcing the eighteen-foot dock was just one of the many items he had decided needed his attention this summer. There was a time when Haley would have found anything at all to do with her daddy exciting, but no longer. The suggestion elicited no response.

"Hold on just a minute. Aren't you the same kid who used to get up at five in the morning to go deep-sea fishing with the old man? Hey, what about that four-and-a-half-pound mackerel you reeled in last year single-handedly? Who knows, maybe this year you'll beat me out—"

"Daddy, stop it."

"What?"

"Trying to trick me into forgetting. Like I'm two years old."

No, cajoling wasn't going to help out here, Cat thought. She had already tried the approach and gotten nowhere. Haley was not about to give up her funk until she determined the time was right. It was, after all, Cat supposed, a fairly effective form of parent punishment. In any event, Cat was relieved to see her hard-charging husband back off before he lost his patience and managed to make matters worse.

Though Haley had always loved going to Kelsy Point, this summer other factors had entered the picture. Leaving Greenfield meant leaving her girlfriends, which meant no afternoons exploring malls, shopping in Annie Sez, stopping for sodas, gossiping and giggling for hours on the telephone about their single most favorite subject: boys. And more specifically, what had brought on this agony to begin with was a boy-girl pool party one of her friends was throwing the next evening, to be followed by other summer parties she would inevitably miss.

Lucas adored Haley, whom he and Cat had adopted when she was fourteen months old, only two years after they got married. Trying desperately for a baby of their own, both of them welcomed Haley into their lives when her parents, Lucas's younger sister and her husband—an army lieutenant stationed in England—were killed in a three-car crash while vacationing in Scotland. Haley, a chubby, blue-eyed imp, in no time became her new daddy's shadow. But now to Lucas's dismay, she was fast changing from a tomboy into a young woman.

"Want to play Yoshi?" Seven-year-old Zack offered his sister his pocket-sized computer, either unaware of her mood or taking his own shot at doctoring it—though more likely the former. Zack, freckled, with his mother's thick auburn hair, had come along three years later when they had just about given up hope of Cat ever conceiving. Very much his own person, Zack sometimes reminded his mother of a professor she'd once had as a freshman in college: thoughtful, circumspect, an incredibly bright and detailed mind—but not always parked in the same universe as those around him.

Cat found Zack's quirkiness particularly endearing. She believed a child was who he was despite his parents' desire to shape him otherwise. On the other hand, Lucas was not as casual with his fathering. Though he was oftentimes a pushover with Haley, he was far stricter and more critical with his son. "It's just a matter of not being able to relate well with the boy," Lucas would complain. And surely that was so, but would that be the case if he wasn't always trying to find his reflection in Zack?

For instance, Lucas was a sportsman—above all he loved boating and fishing. Zack loved to roam the beaches and waters and caverns, discovering new things, often bringing odd-looking plants or little creatures home with him. But get him more than fifty yards offshore on a boat and his complexion turned three shades of green. And though he had tried fishing from the jetty twice at Lucas's urging, he hated it.

Lucas was aggressive, physical, sure, a successful businessman. He was accustomed to making quick decisions and exerting his will on his surroundings. If there were similarities between father and son, they had not yet surfaced.

Zack, having gotten no response from his sister, went back to playing with his Game Boy. Haley, slouched down, her full lower lip in a pout, directed her attention out the window to the passing scenery. As darkness crept in, Cat placed her hand on Lucas's knee, then deliberately and mischievously began to inch it up higher. Out of the corner of her eye she watched her husband react. Though he didn't take his eyes off the road, a vein at his neck began to pulse.

She wondered if there was a law restricting a front-seat passenger from pursuing the driver with intent to arouse and excite. She would be sure to ask Lucas about it later in bed. Certainly it would seem a reasonable law—after all, wasn't there a fine imposed for being without a seat belt? Would she ever grow up? But then, would Lucas like it if she did? She drew her hand away, watching the mixture of relief and disappointment in his eyes. Later in bed, she thought, the anticipation causing a delicious tingling at the nape of her neck.

Sometime later—the earlier threat of rain having never materialized—they reached Route 79, the fourteen-mile strip sandwiched between the lake and Chatfield Hollow, the state park. The road would bring them into Clinton, then onward to Kelsy Point. It was when they slowed to take a hairpin curve that Haley spoke her first words since leaving Massachusetts.

"What does he want?"

At first Cat didn't know what she was talking about. He, who? And from Lucas's expression, he hadn't a clue, either. Then she saw the man, too, rushing out from the darkness between the trees. Not until he had nearly rolled up onto the car's hood did Lucas slam on the brakes.

The car stopped, they lurched forward. Within seconds an enormous man with long, oily yellow hair and a fat, pimply face opened the driver's door and slashed Lucas's seat belt with a steel switchblade. As it snapped free, he brought the knife to Lucas's neck and dragged him from the car.

14

Cat could see mouths moving rapidly and faces and features bouncing in rhythm to them. But the sound resulting was muffled and incoherent, as though she were only a spectator and the audio portion had short-circuited. Then rough, impatient hands forced her up onto her feet.

Now the voices were coming in louder and clearer—Haley's, hers, Lucas's, Zack's . . . other voices she'd never heard before. She could smell the stink of stale tobacco. She looked to her immediate right, then shrank back. Standing beside her was a thin, olive-skinned man with a wiry, black beard and cold, deep-set eyes that were focused on her. Though he was not even close to the size of the man holding Lucas, he was just as repulsive. Just as frightening.

"Don't hurt her," she heard Lucas plead. She had never before heard her husband plead, and it made her so physically ill she had to fight the urge to vomit.

With one hand gripping a switchblade, her assailant motioned for the kids to get out of the car, too. Then, with the passenger door left partially open, the car's light guided them as they followed his instruction to back up from the road.

Once in the woods, Lucas was made to get down on all fours while the knife was held at his throat. She was shoved forward, landing on her bare knees a few feet from Lucas. The dark man backed the kids to thick-trunked trees, then used lengths of rope across their waists to tie them up.

"Look, take the car," Lucas said. "The title and registration papers are in the glove compartment. Give me the title and I'll sign it over. See for yourself, the car's in mint condition. I doubt the odometer registers more than five thousand. It'll bring a good price on the market. No strings attached."

"Did I ask you?" the blond man said, showing a darkened front tooth. He moved the blade a few inches along Lucas's neck, and a red path rose to the surface.

Cat gaped and the dark man came over and stood next to her. Lucas shook his head.

"Then shut your face, okay?"

"Okay."

"Okay, sir."

Cat closed her eyes, wishing she could close off her ears as well. But she couldn't and heard him mimic the required words.

"What's your name, man?"

"Lucas."

"Well, good to meet you, Lucas. My name's Warren, and this here dude is Earl." With his head he gestured to Cat's assailant. "So where're you off to?"

Lucas shrugged. "A ride to the beach is all."

16

"So late? Can't you see it's pitch-dark out there?" When Lucas didn't answer, Warren looked over at Earl. "Or maybe Lucas ain't telling us the whole honest to fuckin' God truth. You gettin' those same sort of vibes, too, buddy?"

Before he answered, Lucas volunteered more lies, "Look, what's to lie about? There's a hotel in Clinton, check it out. Seacliff. We have reservations."

That apparently satisfied Warren because his attention turned to Cat. "Well, so tell me, who's this foxy little redhead here, your daughter?"

The age difference between Cat and Lucas was not something they were sensitive about—in fact, they seldom ever thought about it. But Cat could see the fury now in Lucas's eyes. He remained silent, though, his head twisted in an unnatural angle to accommodate the knife's sharp tip dimpled into his neck. Warren knelt down and, putting his mouth right up to Lucas's ear, screamed into it, "Heigh-ho, mo-ther . . . fuck-er! I asked a question. You in there?"

Lucas jerked back, his teeth gnashing and his features distorting from the pain in his ears. He closed his eyes, then swallowed hard. "My wife," he said.

Both men began to laugh, loud, insane laughter. Then Earl looked at her. "Hey, why's a pretty little lady like you willing to settle for scraps? Especially when you got the prime cut sitting right here. Or should I say standing?"

Earl chuckled at his own joke, then dropped his hand to his pants. Cat heard a zipper being lowered. She remained kneeling, feeling oddly disconnected, as he stooped over and ran his fingers up the front of her blouse. When he reached the top button, his hand sliced downward, tearing her shirt open. The buttons went flying, and in that moment she could feel her throat begin to close.

Her hands, her feet, her body, started to shake. There was a low, deep cry coming from somewhere. Was that her? Earl cupped her chin with his palm, and his fingers on each side dug into her cheeks. He brought her head forward, forcing her to look up at his erect penis. "See that?" he said, smiling. "That's for you." Then with both his hands like lead weights clamping her shoulders, he pulled her toward him.

Lucas lost it. Despite the knife ready to pierce his voice box, his arm swung back, taking Warren by surprise and knocking him off balance. Then he rose to his feet and rammed his fist into Earl's face.

But Warren had regained his balance by then. He rushed from behind and tackled Lucas, sending him sprawling face first to the dirt. Then they both descended on him, punching, kicking, beating him with sticks and rocks and anything they could find, tearing his clothes right off his body. And as strong as Lucas was, he was no match for their assault.

She was aware of screaming—her eardrums throbbing, her limbs rigid, and somewhere in her head she knew she must get to the kids and untie them so they could get to safety. But she couldn't move! They were cornered in the middle of nowhere, and a headline flashed in her brain: FAMILY OF FOUR MURDERED IN WOODS.

Suddenly she heard a loud whistle, then a voice cutting through the thugs' grunting. She clamped her hand flat over her own mouth so she could listen: "Hey, what the hell's going on out there?" the voice shouted. She didn't know whose voice it was or where it was coming from, but it didn't matter. It was the voice of another human being, and he had come to help them.

A wide beam of light was emerging from the woods. The voice now was louder and angrier and more determined. "Okay, schmucks, I've got a semiautomatic shotgun here, fifteen rounds! You tell me, what's your pleasure?"

Warren and Earl straightened up, looked at each other in a silent, anxious moment of communication. They dashed for the Bronco, jumped inside, and slammed the doors behind them. Within seconds the car wheeled around and roared off in the opposite direction.

As the Bronco was pulling away, the newcomer had already reached them. He set down the flashlight and knelt over Lucas, holding his wrist in his hands. Finally he looked up at Cat. "I feel a strong pulse here, I think he's going to be okay. What about you?"

Was he lying? Why would he lie? "I'm okay," she said, still unable to stop trembling. "Please, the kids," she said, pointing. He rushed over to untie them, and within moments Haley and Zack were in her arms crying and hugging her tight and needing much more strength and reassurance than she had to give.

"I don't want to chance causing more injury by moving him myself, so I'm going to go get help. Okay?" She looked up—the person was standing in front of her, talking to her. He was big—and young, though he seemed in control. She nodded.

"You going to be okay, pal?"

He was talking to Zack, who looked like he was going to be anything but okay. But the child nodded his head and the young man was suddenly gone. She and Haley got in closer to Lucas, trying to energize his body with theirs. Zack stayed off to the side, his back pressed against a tree trunk, looking first in one direction, then another as if he expected at any moment someone to spring out.

Cat stroked Lucas's face, arms, hands. With dirty, shaking hands she snatched ripped pieces of his shirt from the dirt, shook them, then covered him. It was a silly gesture, meaningless, but she needed to do something.

"Hurry, please hurry," she whispered, willing the young man to get back to them. Lucas was breathing, she could hear his breathing. Then she felt him move, his fingers, then his hands, his arms ... and by the time the boy returned—followed soon after by an ambulance—Lucas had regained consciousness.

Two hours seemed like minutes, and only after Lucas was treated and wheeled into a private hospital room did a nurse come up to Cat, gesture to her open short-sleeved blouse, and hand her a couple of safety pins. Cat now pulled a tissue from the box on Lucas's bedstand and blew her nose. He would be fine, the doctor in the emergency room had assured her. Bruises, cuts, a broken leg, a clean fracture set in a cast to his thigh. But fortunately, no sign of concussion, no internal injuries. Dr. Robbins, the orthopedist, had given him a shot of morphine to ease the pain and allow him to sleep, and if all went as expected, he would be discharged the next morning to recuperate at the beach house.

Cat studied Lucas's face: the straight, high-bridged nose, the strong chin and jaw, the full lips that would narrow when he was adamant about something. She had come within inches of losing the only man she had ever loved, and her body was still aching with the aftermath of the terror. As she watched him sleep in the sterile hospital room, she thought about how precious he was to her.

The expensive gifts he had bought her at the beginning of their short courtship had actually made her uncomfortable, though there were those who believed she wanted to marry him because of them. She never did understand that: to most nineteen-year-olds, which was what she was at the time she met Lucas Marshall, money was not a high priority when it came to love—at least it wasn't in Calden, New Hampshire, the small town where she grew up.

More impressive to Cat were those marvelous blue eyes that looked at her the way no boy her age ever had and the way he smiled as though he knew things no one else did. One night Lucas had strolled into the 7-Eleven where Cat was clerking while attending day classes at a local college. Since he looked as muscular and fit as an athlete, the fact that he was twice her age was only a passing concern.

She learned that he took a helicopter to Calden twice a week on business: as co-owner of Center Construction and Engineering Company of Northampton, Massachusetts—which Cat later learned was one of the largest operations of its kind in the East—he was in town overseeing repairs to the Ralantano Bridge, which had been found to have major structural problems.

Six weeks later, she was ready to quit her sophomore year of college and follow him to the ends of the earth—or alternatively three hours away to northwest Massachusetts. It made no difference that her landlady had accused her of going after his bucks; her best friend, Monica, argued that having led a bachelor's jaded existence for so long, he was certain to be controlling and fixated; her mother insinuated Cat was marrying the father she always wanted but never had, and her favorite aunt more tactfully said, "You're bright and beautiful, Catherine Ann Demsey. You could have your pick of boys your age."

She didn't care about boys her age, Lucas's money, or even his questionable past. And yes, there *was* some truth in Monica's argument—Lucas did always like to be in charge—but so what? Monica chewed out Cat for admitting such a thing, but she actually found Lucas's arrogance kind of charming. The bottom line was she wanted Lucas Marshall.

And now more than twelve years later, she still wanted him. A little gray had crept into his full head of hair, he was fifteen pounds heavier, yet he was still as handsome and exciting and virile . . . She now sat on the edge of his bed holding his hand. The same lump that had been in her throat earlier had returned. How long would those monsters have kept on beating him?

Their savior's name, it turned out, was Simon Bower. He didn't really have a gun after all, semiautomatic or otherwise. He just said it to scare them. And, blessedly, the threat had worked. She didn't learn that until after they arrived at the medical center in nearby Essex. Cat went with Lucas in the ambulance and because the police were late getting to the scene, Simon offered to follow with Haley and Zack in his van.

She jumped nervously as her mind ricocheted back to the start of the whole nightmare, when they had rounded the hairpin curve . . . She had to make herself stop this: the bad guys were gone—she had to keep reminding herself of that. Disappeared, gone, kaput. And she would never have to worry about them hurting her family again.

Chapter Two

M rs. Marshall?"

Cat looked up—Lucas's door was open and a short, balding man with a barrel chest stood in the hospital corridor. Pinned to his short-sleeved khaki shirt was a police badge. He tipped his wide-brimmed hat.

"Chief Leroy Cooper," he introduced himself.

Though she had never actually met him, she immediately recognized him from seeing him around Clinton Square. The town, containing the library, a town hall/police department, a Stop & Shop, a pharmacy, an automotive repair shop, a Honda dealer, and a couple of dozen clothing and knickknack stores, was where Cat regularly did her summertime shopping.

Though the public beach in Clinton had its own private police force, the town's population—which included the sparsely inhabited area of Kelsy Point—grew from twelve thousand to sixteen in the summer season. So it went without saying that the size of a police force geared for winter residents—a chief, two dispatchers, and nine officers—was sorely lacking once Memorial Day arrived.

Cat leaned over, pressed her lips to Lucas's forehead, then took her purse and followed the police chief into the corridor. "Sorry it took so long getting here," he said, handing her a brown-wrapped package tied with string. "The mister's clothing. One of my men picked them up when he checked the area. So how's Mr. Marshall doing?"

She nodded. "Okay."

He glanced at a clipboard he was holding and said, "I was out at a three-alarm fire— two little kids trapped on the second floor. But we got 'em out okay. I just got back when I picked up your report." He shook his head in disgust and sympathy. "We've been fairly lucky around here till now, not much in the way of crime. Most of our summer troubles have to do with too much booze, disturbing the peace, a domestic squabble now and then, that sort of rowdiness. But nothing one would consider real violent. Of course with you and the mister coming down here all these years, I guess you already know that."

She did know—and apparently he had recognized her as well. He raised his clipboard and led her to a bench at the end of the hall.

"My man, Rudy, the young fellow who came by the hospital to try to talk to you earlier ... ?" He held on to the last word, as though he were waiting for her confirmation, and when she gave it to him, he went on. "Well, he checked the crime site to see if maybe something was left behind. He didn't turn up anything ... other than the husband's clothes, of course. The make and license number of your car have gone out on the radio. Maybe we'll have some luck in that department."

"Where did you get the number?" Cat asked. She hadn't taken time out from Lucas to talk to the deputy. Besides, she didn't even know the plate number.

"Your son knew it. A real smart little fellow you've got there. According to Rudy he was mighty observant, was able to give a detailed description of the two men who terrorized you. I thought maybe you'd want to take a look at what I've got here, check for accuracy or maybe even add something to it." Now he handed her the clipboard—four handwritten pages were secured at the top.

She had just begun to read when he thumbed toward the waiting room next to the nurses' station, "By the way, I didn't notice the kids when I passed by—"

"No, I had them picked up a while ago. Our housekeeper. Maybe you know her, she's

lived in the area for years. Winnie Rawson."
While Lucas was in the operating room having the break set, Cat had visited with the children, assuring them that their father would be okay. Then she called Winnie, who wasn't expected at the beach house until Monday. Winnie had been looking after the beach house on a part-time basis since Lucas had purchased it twenty-four years earlier.

"Sure I know Winnie," he said. "A real fine lady."

Cat nodded. "She agreed to pick up the children, stay with them at the beach house overnight. The doctor will likely be releasing Lucas in the morning."

The chief directed her attention back to the clipboard. She read it through and handed it back. "The only thing I can add is the big, heavyset one, the one who told us his name was Warren, had a rotted left front tooth. You know, darkened."

He jotted the information on the bottom of the top sheet.

"Did either of them look familiar?"

"Familiar? No, why would they?"

He shrugged. "Just wondering if it was something personal. You know what I mean, people angry at you for some reason or another. Seeking revenge."

She shook her head. "No, it was nothing like that. I've never set eyes on them before, and if Lucas had, I would have spotted it immediately. We have no enemies ... actually not a lot of close friends either. We tend not to socialize much. I'm sure most of our neighbors back home would describe us as incredible bores." She smiled, the first one since the attack, and her mouth felt stiff and out of practice. "Besides, remember, those men stopped us at random. They had no way of knowing who was coming down the road."

"No, I guess not. You've got to understand, we haven't had any experience with carjackings in this area. Not that I'm complaining, mind you."

"Well, we haven't either. And you won't see us driving along with our doors unlocked again. If not for that young man—" She stopped, not wanting to say the thought out loud.

"You're talking about Simon Bower, the boy who notified the police for help?"

"Yes. Do you know him?"

"Only what's here and what Rudy tells me. Bower left right after he was questioned. Not that he knew much—apparently the two fellows took off as soon as he announced he had a gun. It was a good ploy, all right. Lucky for everyone it didn't backfire."

She nodded, remembering it. "Could you tell me where I can reach him? I'd like to be able to thank him properly."

"You can't—at least I have no address that'll get him for you," he said as he stood up. "Seems he was camping and fishing over at Chatfield Hollow the past few days. But for all I know, he's picked up and moved on. He's from Arizona originally, one of those drop-out-of-college-to-find-himself people. I suppose if you have to find yourself, better to do it while you're young and fancy-free."

Taking his lead, Cat stood up, wishing again that Simon hadn't been so eager to run off. Or that she had taken a few minutes out to speak with him before he had.

Leroy Cooper tipped his hat. "Oh, yeah, one other thing, Ms. Marshall. Was there anything in the car that might indicate to the fellows where you live. I mean your address out here."

The possibility of those monsters getting a hold of their address caught her by surprise, and her thoughts went quickly to the usual papers kept in the car's glove compartment. But considering it carefully, she was sure the Bronco was registered to Center Construction and Engineering in Northampton.

"No," she said finally. "Nothing."

"Good."

"Are you suggesting they'd come back to find us?"

"I'm not saying that, but you never know about this kind of sick mentality. All I'm trying to do is rule out us being caught off guard again. You mind me asking, Ms. Marshall, you and the mister listed in the local directory?"

"No. Our number has always been unpublished. It's not to be given out."

"That's a plus, too. Listen, maybe once you get a few spare minutes, you can get down to the station and look over some mug shots. Who knows, we may get lucky. Of course, I'll be wanting to talk to Mr. Marshall before he leaves."

She wasn't thrilled at that, and he raised his palm to pacify her. "Now, now, don't be thinking I'm going to upset or tire him. I won't be staying but five minutes. Just enough time to verify what I already have here. And if it all checks with him, which I'm sure it will, well, I'd venture to say you have no cause to worry further."

Then why was she suddenly worried all over again? She went back to Lucas's room, quietly closing the door so as not to wake him. She put down the package of clothes and her purse on the floor near the bed and walked over to the window. She looked out, then raised the window a little to let in some air. It was a carjacking, that's all it was, crazies looking to entertain themselves.

She went back to the bed, sat on the edge of the vinyl easy chair, and looked at Lucas:

swollen and purple beneath his eyes, across his face, lip split and stitched, a lump the size of an egg on his forehead, and twelve stitches along the side of his neck. Dozens of other bruises were hidden beneath his flimsy hospital gown.

Her eyes began to fill again, and she took in a deep breath fighting the tears back. Finally she laid her head back on the chair and fell asleep. For the rest of the night, she drifted in and out of sleep, waking in a panic for the last time at dawn when a hand cupped her chin and fingers were digging into her cheek.

She jumped up, drew in her breath, looked around: no one was touching her, no one was there. She put her hands to her cheeks, which were still tender and sore. Sighing, she leaned forward to check on Lucas.

Seeing that his breathing was strong and regular, she stood up, arms crossed, hugging her chest, trying to get rid of the chill in her bones. She was replaying the conversation with the police chief when she realized that one of her statements wasn't totally true: she supposed someone could have known it was their car coming down the road. Not that it made any sense, of course. But they did always leave for the beach house on the Friday after school let out for the summer, in fact, like clockwork, since Haley started kindergarten. Route 79, though, was seldom so deserted—of course, always before they'd made the trip in the daylight hours. But this time they had left a couple of hours later than usual. Because of the bogus bomb scare.

Now she was being silly, letting her imagination run haywire, not like her. And just because of the chief's questions. The mighty power of suggestion. Enemies? Hardly.

Winnie had made up the second-floor spare room for herself, and though she went to bed right after the kids, she didn't sleep well. First was that telephone call—a wrong number that came at about one o'clock—then she couldn't stop thinking about poor Lucas—and Cat's description of what had happened to them out at Chatfield Hollow.

And the kids had been terribly upset. Haley, as always when she was nervous or excited, had chattered a hundred miles a minute, and Zack had wanted to walk alone on the dark beach. If Cat had been there, she likely would have let him, but Winnie wasn't such a softie as Cat. Darkness wasn't a time for children to be outdoors alone, even if it was in their own front yard.

So to try to take their minds off the terrible events they had witnessed, she mixed up two batches of Toll-House cookies—Lucas's favorites—and while the kids were sampling some, she put on a fifties CD and did a few old

dance steps. By the time Winnie was done, the
kids were laughing and her back was feeling
the results.

Winnie Rawson at fifty-six still looked fit:
five feet two, a hundred twelve pounds soaking wet, and not a bit of cellulite. It was only
her back that made her feel like Methuselah.
Slipping a disc a few years back had put her
out of commission—at least to waitress, the
only work she'd ever done. Besides housekeeping, of course. But that was different.
That was for the Marshalls, and it would
likely take laying her out on a slab before
she'd quit on them.

She worked only three days a week in the
summer, light stuff—Cat Marshall wasn't the
fussy type, in fact far more casual about such
things than Lucas had been before he got married. Still, once Cat had learned about Winnie's back condition, she hired a cleaning
service to come in before the season began to
do the heavy work. Cat never mentioned the
cleaning service to her, of course—Winnie
heard about it through an acquaintance. Cat
wasn't the type to take bows.

Aside for Winnie's cousin Audrey, her husband, and four kids, Winnie's family was
scattered—emotionally as well as geographi-
cally. So the Marshalls soon began to feel like
family, too. Of course, Winnie had been
around long before. When she'd taken the job

twenty-three years ago for Lucus, her only purpose had been to get close to him.

They had gotten to know each other at the Ocean Haven Diner—he'd usually sit at her station when he came in for breakfast or lunch. But it never dawned on him to ask her out. And though she'd never been accused of being subtle—she'd dated lots of men from the diner—when it came to Lucas and telling him how crazy she was about him, forget it.

So when he asked her one day if she could recommend a local person to do housekeeping for him, she volunteered right then and there. And though it took him by surprise, he recovered quickly enough to give her a spare key to the beach house. Since he would usually be gone most of the work week, he told her any weekday was fine.

That's when she started having that silly daydream: it always began with Lucus waking up, turning over to find her lying buck naked beside him. In the first rendition, he was so overwhelmed and passionate, he couldn't get enough of her: in bed, in the shower, twice again in the kitchen, right smack up against the dishwasher—a regular Hercules with a super scrub cycle. In the other rendition, he rejected her, using all sorts of nonexcuses: she was too old for him, he didn't want to mix business and pleasure, he didn't find her attractive . . .

One Saturday at dawn, after weeks of building up her courage, she used her key to let herself into the beach house, then tiptoed into Lucas's bedroom. She found him in bed, all right, but not asleep and not alone.

She hurried out, stumbling over the doorstep. If he had seen or heard anything, he never let on. She thought about quitting, but decided not to be so hasty. Though Lucas was fussy, he was certainly willing to pay for his whims. Besides, what would it hurt to keep up the contact? *Get over it, Winnie, he doesn't own the only dick in town.*

All that had been years back, a fleet of men ago, and a whole army of women come and gone for Lucus as well. During it all Winnie stayed on, doing extra days when he needed her, often cooking and serving when he entertained. Finding mementos: forgotten lace panties under the bed, stretch bras and panty hose tossed in a corner, mascara and nail glue smeared on the bathroom vanity. Often getting a glimpse of the current lady vacationing with him during the work week. Or needing to intercept for him occasionally on the phone to get rid of one who refused to give up. Finding fault and hating all of them, and always a little heartsick at each new face.

She had been prepared to feel the same about Cat—in fact hating her even more when she saw how beautiful, how young she was—

when she saw how serious Lucas was about her. But Cat was not easy to hate.

The phone rang and she jumped up out of bed, forgetting her back until the pain reminded her. By the time she got to the phone Haley answered.

"What about Daddy?"

She listened for a few minutes, nodding. Finally satisfied, she handed the receiver to Winnie.

"Good news," Cat said. "I'm bringing Lucas home."

Between the doctor's and nurses' visits and other early morning hospital routine, Cat didn't have much chance to be alone with Lucus when he first woke. But judging by his abruptness with everyone who'd crossed his path, he wasn't quite ready to be civil. Not that he didn't have ample cause to be bad-tempered. Still, she was hoping all that would change once she got him to the beach house.

Cat had washed her dirty, scraped knees and elbows, and fixed herself up best she could in Lucas's bathroom, then phoned Winnie and the children, followed by Jack Reardon, Lucas's longtime business partner. When she had first met Jack and his wife, Linda, it had been terribly strained—after all, they had three grown children, one son who was close to Cat's age. But as the years passed, they had overcome the age barrier, growing to be their closest friends.

"Do you need me to come up, Cat?" Jack asked after she delivered a capsule version of the story, and he went through all the usual shock and horror and anger at the fouled-up society that tolerated such violence these days.

"No, we're okay. But thanks. Jack, the car was company owned, so if Shirley could notify the insurance people." Shirley was the office manager, had been with the company since it started, and was, according to both partners, irreplaceable.

"Consider it done. When you get a chance, make up a list of what was lost, about what it would cost to replace, and drop it in the mail. No rush on it."

"Okay. One more thing—"

"Go, anything."

"What about that bomb scare yesterday?"

He paused as this idea sank in, then asked, "Why, do you think it's connected to the ambush?"

"No, not really. It's just that the police asked a few questions. And you know how those things go—you sit around with nothing to do, so you try to jam in puzzle pieces that don't seem to fit."

"I can only say, we've had bomb threats before. So have a lot of businesses—a few weeks back there was a bomb scare at the Hampshire courthouse. In any case, as you well know, we've never had one that amounted to anything. Besides, it sounds like you were random victims—at least from what you've told me."

"Oh, I agree. But then I thought, well, we do always leave the Friday afternoon after the elementary school lets out—" She started to laugh nervously, then said, "You know, this is insane. Aside from the remote chance of anyone knowing that kind of information, why would anyone care? Please, Jack, when you talk to Lucas, don't even let on I asked. I don't want him thinking I'm worried."

"You've got it—mum's the word. What kind of flowers does he like? I'll send out a few dozen."

"Forget the flowers. Send him a surf rod, he can use it from the dock or jetty while he's recovering. He'll love it."

She got back to the room in time to see Lucas's temper fly. Chief Cooper had told him the Bower boy was likely back on the road and unreachable. With all the useless information that seemed to be needed to make out the usual police reports, Lucas asked, why couldn't they have gotten the make and license number of the boy's car? He wanted to reach Simon Bower to thank him personally.

When the chief went on to insist his officer

had followed police procedures to a T, Lucas shot back, "It looks to me like damned sloppy police procedure."

Cat put a hand on her husband's shoulder. "Lucas, come on, don't do this," she said, understanding his frustration, but still wanting him to relax.

"Look, Mr. Marshall," the chief said, "I understand you've been through a lot in the past fifteen hours, so I'm not going to hold that comment against you. But maybe you ought to look into the town budget one day, see what we get to run this here force. Considering the swell of population in the summer months—brought upon by transients like yourself—we don't do a half bad job."

A transient paying mighty high taxes, Cat thought and knew that Lucas was likely thinking the same. But to his credit, he held back from saying so. Instead he suggested, "Look, what're the chances the kid's still hanging around Chatfield Hollow?"

The chief's annoyance ebbed as he considered. "Well, I suppose it's possible. But I don't even have a make—"

"I don't know the color or make," Cat said. "But he's driving a van. If that's a help?"

"Well, it is something," he said. "Tell you what. I'll have one of my men drive out there this afternoon and take a look. And if that doesn't pan out, I'll go one better and call Motor Vehicles in Tucson, where the kid's from. If we get his plate numbers, we could put out a local. And if he's in the county, we'd have a shot at finding him. You understand, it's not something we like to do, when it's not a strict police matter."

Lucas reached for the man's hand, and he accepted it. "Sorry for coming down so hard," Lucas said. "I've no doubt you're doing a hell of a job with not much manpower. But I owe this kid—I want to do something for him."

Leroy Cooper left, promising he'd get back to them within a few days. Lucas looked at her. "You okay, babe?"

She nodded, leaned in closer, and they kissed lightly. "It's a beautiful day, Lucas, warm, sunshine, not a cloud—"

"How long was I out, Cat?"

"When?"

"Last night. Cooper filled me in some."

"Not very long. Darling, please . . . Can't we just be grateful that they're gone, and it's over? And won't it be wonderful if the chief does manage to find the Bower boy?"

"Yeah, it will," he said, putting his hand to her cheek and caressing it. Then, sighing, he reached down to open the nightstand beside his bed. "How about finding me something decent to wear and getting me the hell out of here?"

She had picked up a T-shirt for him at the gift shop earlier, and had shaken the dirt out of his shorts. They would do for now. The fact that they didn't have a car to go home in didn't dawn on her until Lucas asked the young male aide wheeling his chair to stop at the lobby desk. Lucas gave the clerk his name and she handed him a tiny manila envelope. From it he took out three keys—one he attached to his key ring, one he handed to Cat. The one remaining he stuck in his billfold.

"A '95 Jeep Cherokee wagon," he said. "Electric blue. The girl I spoke to said it would be parked in the right aisle as we came out the front door of the medical center."

"A lease?" she asked. He nodded. "When in the world did you find time to call?"

"Earlier. When you ran your errands."

"How did you know I hadn't?"

"I guess I figured you had enough to do. Why?"

"Nothing, I just wish you had let me—" That sounded a little foolish even to herself, since she had clearly forgotten about the car. Perhaps it had to do with her wanting to take the burdens off Lucas for a change, something she was rarely able to do. She leaned down and kissed him. "Pay no attention, darling, I'm just annoyed at myself."

She and the aide settled him into the backseat of the Jeep wagon, where he could keep his leg elevated. She set the crutches they'd purchased from the hospital on the floor beside him. Then on to the pharmacy down the block to pick up the medications Dr. Robbins had prescribed: Tylenol with codeine and Valium—both to be used only as needed. Having waited in the wagon while Cat went inside, Lucas was scanning the parking lot when she returned a few minutes later.

She got in the car, put the keys in the ignition, and started the car. "What is it, Lucas?"

"Cat, do me a favor" he said, his voice low and controlled. "Pull the car around to the other end of the lot."

She backed up and headed across the shopping plaza, still waiting for an explanation. When none came, she asked, "Are you going to tell me what we're looking for?"

"I saw them, Cat. Not two minutes ago. They parked near the Radio Shack."

"Who?"

"Those pigs. Driving the Bronco."

Maybe she was dense, but that was the last thing she expected to hear. She felt her chest tighten and her breath caught as she pulled up near the Radio Shack. Now, not a word between them, they looked up and down the car aisles, their search stopping finally at an old model Bronco with Connecticut plates. She turned to Lucas.

"Is that what you saw?"

He scanned the cars again, coming back to the same Bronco. Finally he looked at Cat, shrugged, and gestured toward the road to Kelsy Point. "Let's get out of here. Okay?"

So he saw a similar car and jumped to the wrong conclusion. After what they'd both been through, it was certainly understandable. But now thinking about it, Cat couldn't conceive of those thugs having the nerve to show their faces in the area in broad daylight. And driving the stolen car? They wouldn't be that brazen. Or stupid. Not with the police out looking for them.

Lucas was unusually quiet while they rode, but Cat took up the slack. She found herself chattering about everything from the weather forecast to the public beach news, all of which she'd read in the *Shore Weekly* she'd found in the hospital waiting room, but still he wouldn't respond.

"Well, it was surely a harsh remedy to get Haley's mind off her friends back home," she said finally, trying to get a smile onto his face.

She could sense his eyes on her back before he said, "Okay, so you think we can joke about it, just so long as we don't actually talk about it? Now, have I got it right?"

"What does that mean?"

"Since this morning you've been busy spinning cheer. Trying like hell to stay clear of

44

what happened last night. I assume it means you don't want to talk about it?"

"That's not fair, Lucas. I've talked about it, thought about it, in fact, even dreamed about it. So if I tend to want to concentrate on something a little more pleasant, please try to understand. That doesn't mean you can't bring it up."

"No, you're right, Cat," he said, his tone gentler. "I'm being unreasonable. I just feel as though I've been picked up and shaken and I haven't stopped rattling yet."

Why did it seem like they were spending so much time apologizing to one another? "Lucas, I'm just afraid if we got started—well, I just don't want us to dwell on it." She stopped, took a deep breath. "You didn't recognize either of those guys, did you?"

"No. Did you think I had?"

She shook her head. "I told the chief no. Do you think they used their real names?"

"I don't know." A long silence followed, then Lucas said, "Cat, I want these lousy bastards found. And I'm afraid if we leave it to the locals, it'll get filed away."

Sure, she wanted the men punished, too. If only she had some assurance that it could be done swiftly and they'd be put away for a good long time. But considering that more harm hadn't been done, and from all she'd heard and read about the criminal justice system, they'd probably be out of prison within a few months, if they went at all. She would have been far more relieved to know that Warren and Earl or whatever their names were, were by now hundreds of miles away. And she and her family would never have to set eyes on them again.

"I don't think that's necessarily true," she said finally, referring to the local police. "Why don't you at least give them a chance?" Lucas didn't answer, and though he didn't say so, she knew he was thinking about hiring a private investigator to try to find them. Then she knew for certain every waking minute of their day would be thinking and talking about nothing else.

"You know what I want more than anything?" she said. He remained silent in the backseat, waiting for her to go on. "I want us to try to put all the terror of last night behind us and move on with our lives. I know it won't be easy—emotionally, it's been devastating. But let the police do their job. And let us concentrate on getting healed. Please, Lucas?"

Chapter Three

Anything was possible at Kelsy Point—at least that's how it seemed once they had finally pulled up at the dead end and the children and Winnie ran out to welcome them. Cat had pretty much prepared Winnie as to how beaten up Lucas was, so there was no big show of surprise. Only the full leg cast with the steel walking bar was discussed and joked about—each of them putting their artwork and signature on it.

Lucas had bought the big weathered wood chateau that stood nearly isolated on the northern edge of Kelsy Point long before he and Cat met. But when he first brought her there, she fell in love with it. So along with the Sunfish and sailing lessons he'd given her as a wedding gift, he promised they'd spend summers at the beach house. His business calls could be fielded from there as easily as from Greenfield, and the small private airport outside Clinton had chartered helicopter flights available.

Twelve-foot sliders in the great room, a gigantic, cathedral beam–ceilinged room with skylights connecting the dining area and newly modernized compact kitchen opened onto a magnificent pinewood deck that stood ten feet above the sandy beach overlooking the ocean.

Beneath the deck, two steps below ground level, was the walk-in cellar, where there was a washer and dryer hookup, a bathroom, connecting to a shower and change room that they all used when coming in sandy from the beach, and a separate tool room in back. Though Cat had thought at first of setting Lucas up in style on one of the thick-padded deck loungers, he looked already tired and in pain, and when given the chance, he opted to be off by himself.

Because the master bedroom was on the second floor, she had asked Winnie earlier to make up the first-floor spare room for them. Now she settled him in with half a dozen pillows, set up a tray with juice, tissues, the TV remote control, and the pain medication that she offered him but he refused.

"I wish you'd take something," she said.

"When I need it, I'll take it."

She began to putter around the room, arranging things so they'd be within easy reach.

"Haven't you got something to do?"

"What is this?" she said, stopping, smiling. "Are you trying to get rid of me?"

"Look, I don't need you hovering over me, I'm fine. You go off and do whatever you need to do."

"Hovering? Since when do I hover?"

"Why don't you go change your blouse."

She looked down—surprised to see she was still wearing the same dirty buttonless blouse with the safety pins holding it together. Realizing it, she felt the fingers again digging into her cheeks, but she shook the feeling, hurrying to one of the dressers and hunting up clean shorts and T-shirt and underwear.

Though they all kept a small wardrobe at the beach house, a lot of clothes and other items they'd intended to use had been packed in boxes still in the Bronco. If the car wasn't found soon, she'd have to go shopping to fill in the missing spots. "I could use a shower," she said. "Winnie picked up a few items last night, but I really need to do some food shopping. Actually I was thinking—" She was going to say she could call the Queens Market, a family-style grocer whose high prices included delivery. But he didn't give her a chance.

"Good idea," he said, grabbing at the opportunity to get her out of there. "Winnie's here to watch over things. Why don't you get me one of those little salamis? Hebrew National."

She paused, then smiled. "Okay. What else?"

"Surprise me."

"Want something to read?"

"Get me a *Playboy*."

"Sorry," she said, busting on him. "You get your own *Playboy*."

Hugging the clean clothes to her chest, she knelt on the mattress, leaned over, and kissed him. "I love you, Lucas."

Winnie agreed to stay and watch things until she got back, and Zack, who normally hated shopping, decided to tag along. And any success she might have had in avoiding thinking about the incident quickly began to unravel. Whistling some tune she couldn't make out, Zack's glance went up and down every street they passed.

"They're not going to come back," she said finally.

"Who said?"

"I do. What those men did is called carjacking. It's been in the news a lot lately. A criminal stops a motorist, tosses him out of his car, and takes off with it."

Zack looked at the Jeep's doors that weren't locked. Despite her declaration to the police chief last night about locking her doors, it all looked different in the light of a lovely summer day. What were the chances of such a thing ever happening again to them? Besides, she couldn't let herself think that way, because if she did, she might never let the kids step out of the house. Still, Zack pressed down his door lock, then getting to his knees, leaned over and pressed hers, too.

"You've heard the saying, 'Lightning never strikes twice in the same place,' haven't you?" she asked.

"Yeah."

"Well, I think that's what applies here. It's not as though we were doing something foolish that put us in the line of danger. It was simply bad luck, a matter of being in the wrong place at the wrong time: one of those awful, senseless, random things that occasionally happens to people. But it's over with. We've gotten through it, and it's never ever going to happen again."

There was a long pause, then he asked, "If carjackers only wanted the car, why did they stay to beat up Daddy?"

She didn't want to talk about what happens when sick minds suddenly go out of control, escalating the original plan. What was the point? They were the lucky ones. "Because of me," she said finally. "Daddy thought they would hurt me, so he swung at one of them."

"The man Earl, the one with the black beard?"

"Yes?"

"Did he want to do sex with you?"

She glanced at him, surprised. She hadn't really talked about sex with Zack, though maybe she should have. She had talked about it with Haley when she was even younger than Zack. But Haley had come right out and asked her questions. So far he hadn't.

"What do you know about sex?"

He shrugged. "I know about *that*."

"Yeah? Who told you?"

"Kids are always talking in school. Is that what Earl wanted to do to you?"

She nodded, calmly. But she was beginning to feel the same cold clamminess at the back of her neck, the same panic of last night ... She took a deep cleansing breath—she couldn't allow herself to go into some kind of crazy anxiety attack out here alone with Zack.

She willed her mind to other things: the food shopping she was about to do, the surprise she'd bring home for Lucas ... She would get him *Playboy*. She tried to think ahead to moonlit nights, the sound of waves lapping the surf, she and Lucas alone on the deck, long walks or runs on the beach, taking out the Sunfish ...

And, oh, yes, she mustn't forget to tell Lucas to talk with Zack about sex.

She had already picked up a couple of crossword puzzle books for herself and a half-dozen sports and business magazines for Lucas. The *Playboy* magazine she would need to buy in the pharmacy. She never got the chance. As Zack was helping her put the grocery bags into the back of the car, he looked up and pointed excitedly.

"Look, Ma, there's Simon!"

She stopped what she was doing and looked, not quite sure if she would have recognized him in broad daylight without Zack's help. But it was him. With a bag of groceries in one arm, he was heading toward a green van.

"You stay here. Okay?" She ran across the parking lot, just getting within shouting distance as Simon began to back up. "Wait, don't go!" she called.

He heard and turned—a red stretch sweatband cut across a full head of sun-bleached hair. He had blue eyes, scraggly blond brows, and a great smile. He was wearing a gray, hooded sweat jacket, the jacket open and the hood loose against his back.

"How's your guy?" he asked with a gravelly quality to his voice.

She nodded. "Lucas. Bruises, bumps, a broken leg. But he's going to be fine. I took him home today."

"Great."

"Well, not so—"

His eyes narrowed, waiting.

"He's upset he didn't get to see you. To thank you."

He shook his head. "Hey, tell him to forget it. I didn't do much more than shoot off my mouth."

"You risked getting hurt yourself."

"Did I do that? I oughta watch myself, not be so quick on the trigger in the future."

He was teasing her, but she wasn't about to drop it. "Please. It's important to him."

He sighed, looked upward as though pleading to the gods, "Let this lady get lost." But when his eyes came back to Cat, they were still smiling. "Where to?" he asked.

She pointed at the Jeep Cherokee wagon— Zack had gotten into the passenger seat and was waiting. "I'm right over there," she said. "You follow."

Simon's eyes widened when he got out of his van and looked over the territory at Kelsy Point: the house, her Sunfish, Haley's Catamaran, and Lucas's thirty-three-foot cabin cruiser anchored at the dock, the miles of sandy beach and coastline. A quarter of a mile up the coastline was a jetty that stretched about two hundred feet into the water. She could easily relate to how he felt—she had experienced much the same awe when Lucas first brought her here years ago. Simon finally shook his head as though to clear it.

"Wow. I grew up in the desert," he said. "And I never got to see much of the beaches out west. Here in the East I've seen some, but not a setup like this. Get many sunbathers up here?"

"Well, we're pretty isolated. But we do get runners and young people passing through."

Simon carried four of the bags on the trip inside and would have gone back for more, but Cat insisted he leave the remainder for Haley and Zack. She was anxious to bring him to Lucas, and wouldn't have held off long enough to introduce him to Winnie if she hadn't made a pest of herself by standing right in front of him, wiping her hands on a dish towel tucked in her waist, and gawking as though she'd never seen such a good-looking young man before.

"You from around here?" she asked after the formalities.

"No, ma'am."

"Family from here?" When he shook his head, she said, "Funny. You look familiar . . ."

"Maybe. I've been floating around town for about ten days. Camping mostly at the state park."

Winnie reluctantly moved aside and Cat hurried him off to the bedroom and pushed open the door. "You asked for a—" But she was the one surprised. She naturally knew about the revolver Lucas kept in a wooden box on the shelf in the downstairs bedroom closet, but he never so much as took it out. Now he was sitting on the edge of the bed, it in one hand, a rag in the other.

"What're you doing?"

"What does it look like?" he said, but looked over her head to the boy and returned the gun to the box that was on his nightstand. "Well, are you going to introduce us?" He seemed surprised, but pleased.

She put her hand on Simon's arm. "Yes, of course," she said. "Lucas Marshall, Simon Bower."

"Good to meet you, Simon," he said.

Simon moved around her, went up to Lucas, giving him a high-five. "You sure look like hell, man."

Lucas smiled. "Sonofagun, you notice that, too? Funny thing is, around here people don't seem to see much of a change. I was beginning to think I was using a bad mirror."

Clearly that remark was directed at Cat. If he wanted her to remind him of how beat-up he looked, she would try to accommodate him in the future. But meanwhile, her thoughts were still on the gun. "Lucas, answer me, please. What are you doing with that?"

"Cat, we have company. You have something you want to discuss, we'll do it later." He lifted his glass, lightly swirling the pale liquid. Then he turned to Simon. "What would you like, son?"

The boy shrugged.

"Beer?"

"Yeah, okay." Simon looked up at her. "If you don't mind."

"Of course not," Cat said, taking Lucas's glass. The poor boy was feeling awkward, and it was her fault. She shouldn't have brought him here. She checked her watch, then said, "It's nearly one, how about some lunch?"

Haley had put away the groceries without being asked—she was finishing the last bag when Cat got back to the kitchen. "Thanks for the help, honey," she said.

"No problem."

"Where's Winnie?" Cat took fresh vegetables from the refrigerator and set them on the counter.

"Down in the cellar trying to get the dryer to stop shaking. You know how it sometimes goes into spasms?"

"Right." One of the things Lucas was going to get to. "We're going to have to get someone in to fix that," she said, then turned to Haley. "A dirty washload already?"

"Zack peed his bed last night. But no one but Winnie is supposed to know."

"Oh," she said. Zack hadn't had one of those accidents since he was five, but thanks, of course, to last night ... Everything was held in such damn delicate balance. Turning back to the counter, she took out a salad bowl and began to wash the lettuce. She felt her daughter's eyes on her and paused. She finally asked, "You want to talk about last night?"

Haley shook her head, shrugged. "What's to talk about?"

"I don't know, that's for you to tell me. How you felt, I guess."

"Scared, of course. Weren't you?"

"Of course."

"But it's over. Isn't it?"

Cat dropped what she was doing and went over to Haley. She stooped down and hugged her. "It is, of course it is. And Daddy's fine. I know he doesn't look it now, but—"

Haley pulled away. "I don't really want to talk any more about it. Okay?"

Cat stood up, watching her daughter as she hurried out to the deck and down to the beach. Each of them seemed to have his or her own private hell. Cat's was having stood there, watching her man get beat up and not able to lift a finger to help. What was Haley's?

* * *

Lucas motioned Simon to a seat next to the bed. Though it had been too dark the night before to really make out the boy's features, he realized as soon as he walked in the room that it was Simon. "So where'd she find you?"

"In the shopping plaza in Clinton, near the Stop & Shop. I came to town to get a bike part. So while I was there, I thought I'd pick up a few rations."

"What kind of bike?"

"Oh, it's not much—a Yamaha XJ600. An '85. I got it cheap. It needed work, but I'm pretty good with my hands. It runs—" He smiled. "At least it usually runs. So how're you feeling?" he asked, turning the subject from himself.

"Okay. It seems I have you to thank for that. You did quite a heroic thing."

The boy put his hands in his sweatshirt pockets and shook his head. "You're making more of it than it was. Like I tried to tell your lady earlier, I didn't really do anything but shoot off my mouth. The guys took off by the time I got to you. I never even saw them."

"Don't be so modest. The first thing you did right was use your head. The threat of a gun— How did you know they didn't have one?"

"I didn't, I was just guessing. Or maybe hoping. From what I could hear through all that shouting . . . Well, I figured there must be more than one of them. So I thought it might be easier to sucker them rather than try to go one on two."

Lucas had no trouble remembering the formidable appearance of Warren, the one who had pulled him from the car. Lucas was six feet, a hundred ninety pounds. Yet Warren had to have had four inches and sixty pounds on him. Simon was far from puny himself—and certainly in better shape than Lucas . . . But still, that was one big motherfucker for anyone to deal with.

"Fortunately, it wasn't necessary," Lucas said. "Just the fact that you were willing is what matters." Simon pressed his lips together, looked down at his sneakers, and Lucas asked him, "How old are you?"

"Nineteen. Why?"

"Just curious," Lucas said, thinking he was pretty young to be so bold. "So, Simon, what can I do for you?"

He looked up. "What do you mean?"

"I mean, last night you really put yourself on the line for me and my family. I can't very well return the favor, but I'd like to do something."

Simon shook his head, his shoulders rolling like big loose sockets, and his eyes wary as though he weren't sure if he were being put on. "Look, man, Mr. Marshall—"

"Call me Lucas."

"Okay. Look here, Lucas, I don't really want anything. Can we just leave it?"

"What do you do for money?"

"I take a job now and then when I'm low. It's not like I need a lot, though."

Lucas sat back—this kid was making it difficult, all right, in a day and age when a lot of kids would rob you if you made the mistake of wearing sneakers they liked. In fact, because of all the vandalism and thievery occurring on the construction sites, the company had started to use attack dogs at night.

"The police chief tells me you're hanging out at Chatfield Hollow." Simon nodded. "Done any fishing?"

"Yeah, sure. Excellent bass."

"Ever do any saltwater fishing?"

"Uh-uh, only fresh water. I was telling your lady before, I've never seen a setup like this. I mean, the big house and all, and a private beach. Movie star kind of stuff. It's great."

"Yeah, we enjoy it. Ever operate a boat, Simon?"

"Some, I've used a Bow Rider. A buddy of mine from Detroit let me run it out on his lake."

Lucas nodded toward the window. "Go on over there and look out. You'll see a thirty-three-foot Cutty Cabin anchored at the dock." Though Lucas kept the boats at a local marina through the winter, he always had them brought over to the house a couple of days before they arrived for the summer.

"Yeah, I saw it coming in," Simon said, going to the window. He stood with his fingers stuffed in his sweatshirt pockets, staring out. "That's quite a boat."

"Think you can handle it?"

He nodded. "Sure." Then turning back to look at Lucas, "Why?"

"I thought maybe you'd want to use it."

He looked at the boat, then back at him. "You mean it?"

"I don't make offers I don't mean."

A long pause, then he asked, "When?"

"You tell me. What about tomorrow?"

He nodded, smiled. "Okay, you're on."

"And don't worry about equipment. I've got a bunch of boat poles, plenty of tackle and bait. In the shed. Haley will show you. She's quite a fisherman herself."

"You mean, woman."

"Pardon?"

"I said, you mean fisherwoman."

Lucas nodded. "I stand corrected. Haley's forever catching me on those female issues. Born in the wrong era, I guess. Fortunately for me, Cat overlooks it."

Simon's eyes suddenly grew more serious as he looked over at the box on the nightstand, the one holding the .38-caliber Smith &

Wesson. "You afraid those same guys are going to come after you?"

Was he afraid of that, and if he was, would
he actually admit it to himself? But Simon's
question was a good one. Rationally he knew
better: pigs like that just move along to their
next victim. And he told Simon so, too.

Though Chief Cooper insinuated it could
have been a personal vendetta, it was unlikely. Actually, his life was not all that complicated. It centered around Cat and the kids,
the rest of the world having been booted to
the bleachers once he went into that 7-Eleven
years ago. No more women, no more all-night
poker games, no more shuttles to Vegas or
long nights at the track.

It wasn't just those big chestnut eyes or the
slender nose with the flare at the end, the
sprinkling of freckles that, unlike most
women, she never thought to cover with
makeup, or even those long legs and sensa-
tional body. Cat was natural and trusting and
exuberant about everything she did.

Professionally, though Center Construction
was constantly in competition with other out-
fits for job bids, that was the nature of the
beast. But none of his competitors bore the
kind of grudge that would have prompted
last night's assault.

Ever since he'd come to, his skin had felt
like it was crawling. Like those sonsofbitches

were still circling around him. His wife was threatened—he'd been humiliated in front of his family: stripped and kicked around like a fucking basketball.

Winnie—bless her heart—unsuccessful at trying to win over the clothes dryer, helped Cat prepare an antipasto before she left. To serve with the tuna salad. Though Cat planned to serve their lunch in the bedroom, Lucas suggested that since he hadn't had much chance to be with the kids, he and Simon join them on the deck.

"You're sure of this?" she asked, thinking he looked even worse than before.

"No problem."

"What about something for the pain?"

"I'm fine."

The kids seemed to like Simon and he in turn opened up with them, mostly because Zack asked a lot of questions that were really none of his business. It turned out Simon had been brought up by an aunt, and though undecided about his future, he'd gone along with his aunt's wishes, entering the University of Arizona on a scholarship. But he had dropped out in his sophomore year to travel the country, still not certain if college was what he wanted. Since then he'd been bouncing from state to state, and to hear him tell it, having a merry ol' time.

"Simon's going to take the cabin cruiser out fishing tomorrow," Lucas announced, surprising not only the kids but Cat. Lucas barely trusted her to take it out alone.

"Oh, excellent, can I go, too?" Haley asked.

Lucas smiled, clearly pleased that she was again taking an interest in boating and fishing. Though if he had been paying stricter attention, he would have noticed the way Haley was looking at Simon. Definitely flirtatious. But to Simon's credit, he was not responding in kind.

"I think not this time," Cat said.

"Why not, what's the big deal? I could operate the boat myself if Daddy would only let me. I earned my senior lifesaving badge like you wanted me to. Why did I even bother if you won't trust me out there?"

"I trust you. You take the sailboat out, don't you?"

"Only if I stay near shore," Haley sulked.

"Look, honey, there'll be lots of other days to go fishing. What about off the jetty?"

"Yuck."

"Hey, look," Simon said, "I don't want to get in the middle here. But if she wants to come along, I have no problem with it."

"I don't think—" Cat began again, but Lucas overrode her. "She does know what she's doing out there. She might be able to help with the controls."

Haley was in seventh heaven, kissing her father, then tactfully kissing her mother, though she knew she hadn't really gotten her vote. Then she began talking to Simon about fishing in her best rapid, convoluted teen-speak. Simon looked a little overwhelmed. Cat began to laugh.

"What?" Simon said.

"You just look like maybe you were thinking it wasn't such a wise offer."

Haley looked up apprehensively, and he met her eyes. "Don't sweat it, I'm not backing out. But hey, do you think maybe you could lower the speed of that motor?"

The laughter came to an abrupt stop when Lucas stood up. "What's wrong?" Cat asked.

He held up his hand, indicating for her to stay put, but he suddenly started to sway. Simon got up immediately, grabbing his elbow at the same time Cat put her hand to his back. They both helped him into bed, over insistent pleas to be left alone. Once he was in bed, Simon tactfully stepped out of the room.

"You're in pain, aren't you?" Cat said anxiously.

"A little. I'm mostly tired."

Tired was hardly the word for it. Five minutes after Lucas swallowed the painkiller, he was asleep. Not even the telephone on the nightstand could wake him. One of the kids picked up before the second ring, and Cat quickly pushed the ringer switch on his extension to off. She took the gun box from the stand and returned it to the closet shelf, then quietly left. The kids and Simon were out on the porch chatting, and Simon, looking concerned, stood up when she came out.

"What's wrong with him?"

She shook her head. "Tired and hurting. I gave him medication for the pain, and it knocked him right out. He's one of those macho men who refuses to give in without kicking."

"Mommy!" Haley scolded, surprised at hearing her mother say such a thing about her father, and in front of Simon.

She smiled. "Okay, who was it?"

"What?" Haley asked.

"The phone rang a few minutes ago, who was it?"

Haley shrugged. "Oh, that, they hung up without saying. A wrong number, I guess."

Simon left soon after, promising Haley he'd be back by eight the next morning. As Cat cleaned up in the kitchen, she wondered what she would have done if Lucas had actually fallen. Winnie was there three days a week, but with her tricky back she wouldn't have been much help in lifting him. And that's when the idea first struck her: there were chores around the beach house that had to be done, things Lucas intended to take care of but despite good intentions would be unable to do with his leg.

She wondered if Simon might consider taking on some work from them.

Lucas slept until eight o'clock, and Cat prepared a late dinner for just the two of them on the deck after the children were in bed. As they headed to the bedroom about eleven-thirty she decided to broach the subject of the gun.

"Lucas, I don't want a loaded gun in the house. It makes me uncomfortable."

"It's loaded and it's staying that way."

"Don't I get a say?"

"There's nothing to say. We're living in a dangerous time. There's sick people out there who would sooner slice your throat than step over you. Just pick up the newspapers, read them, Cat—there are decent, sane people out there building walls around their homes, around their entire neighborhoods."

"Dammit, why're you trying to scare me like this? It's over, Lucas, isn't it? Please! If we'll just let it be—"

Her eyes filled, and he put his arms around her. "I'm sorry, babe. The last thing I want to do is frighten you. You know that. But wanting something doesn't always make it so. We need to be prepared for next time, if there is a next time."

She sank her head against his chest, trying to capture the well-being she always felt when she was in his arms. Twenty-four hours ago her world had been perfect. Sure, she had known there was violence out there—and a lot of it—but it never seemed to have much to do with them. Not until her family had become victims.

The night wasn't over yet though. About one o'clock in the morning a horn bleating woke her. Startled, she sat up and got her bearings. Lucas, who had apparently heard it first, was already out of bed and on his way to the kitchen.

"Wait, Lucas," she said, grabbing a light robe and getting out of bed, but she didn't catch up to him until he got to the kitchen window, by which time the horn was silent. Lucas was leaning forward, looking out—one hand against the wall, the other stuffed firmly in his white terry robe pocket. She peeked over his shoulder. A vehicle was parked in the middle of the dead end, but she couldn't see much with the bright headlights directed right at them.

"Who do you think, Lucas?"

"I don't know."

"Could be just kids clowning," she said, looking to Lucas for reassurance. But he wasn't giving any. Finally, gratefully, she saw the tightness leave Lucas's face as the car slowly began to back up. Once it got about a hundred fifty yards from the house, it changed directions and drove off. It looked like a Bronco.

Chapter Four

The Cliffs were a fifteen-minute walk from the beach house. In a two-hundred-foot area where waves had dislodged gigantic rocks along the beach, turtles and toads navigated, shelled creatures hugged wet stones, and tide pools swelled with mystery. Best of all and unknown to anyone but Zack was the hideout, a nine-by-six-foot oval cavern the surf had gnawed out of rock. The year before, to discourage intruders, Zack had rolled two boulders in front of the entrance, camouflaging it.

When he got there at dawn the next morning and climbed the slippery rock, the boulders were still right in place. He pushed them aside, then crawled in and looked around—it was just as awesome as he remembered from the year before. Not as big as Mommy and Daddy's bathroom with Jacuzzi at home. But way better.

It was a place where he could store things

he found, play with them or study them. Here he could just be alone, all by himself to think.

Lucas woke early when he heard the kitchen phone ring. He grabbed the extension instantly before it woke everyone in the house. But whoever it was had misdialed or changed his mind and hung up. Lucas sat up slowly—cringing as he did—every body muscle in him aching and sore. Passing on the Tylenol and codeine prescribed by the doctor, he went to the bathroom medicine cabinet to get aspirin. He disliked taking a drug—at least anything beyond a few beers or aspirins.

His father had been a fall-on-his-face drunk, retreating from society and leaving Lucas at eleven to take over as the man of the house. From that time on he had decided he liked his feet on the ground. Never was it more apparent than when he first tried marijuana at a party in the sixties. Uncomfortable with the numbing effect, he took off from the party and ran about five miles through the January cold to get his head straight. Lucas liked control of his world; something, he admitted, he hadn't possessed in the past thirty-six hours.

Had he overreacted last night? Maybe. When the car horn blasted like that, he had already been awake, mulling over the assault, getting more and more angry at those bastards the longer he thought about them. So it wasn't surprising that they were the first ones that came to his mind. He immediately had gone for the gun. Gratefully, Cat hadn't noticed it in his robe pocket—at least, she hadn't said so.

Now he poured three aspirins into his palm. Shutting the cabinet door, he moved closer to the mirror and appraised his face. He looked tired, old. The bruises emphasized heavy eyelids, sagging skin he hadn't noticed before, even a few wrinkles. He swallowed the aspirins, splashed cold water over his face, toweled it. Then placing his crutches under his arms, he headed out to the kitchen.

A few minutes later, a quart of OJ snug under one arm, he went to the deck. He looked up one end of the beach—he could see a couple of runners off in the distance. Once the leg was healed, he would start to jog again, get back in shape.

He had just opened the juice carton and begun drinking when he heard the voice: "What're you doing?" Lucas's hand jerked, causing juice to spill. He set the carton on the table, shaking the liquid from his hand. Turning, Zack had come up from his left. He was wearing a sweatshirt, swimsuit, and sneakers, and carrying a pail. "Sorry," the boy said. "Didn't mean to scare you."

"You didn't," Lucas said. "What I want to

know, though, is what you're doing out so early."

"I was out at the Cliffs," Zack said, gesturing to the pail. "I got a rock crab. Want to see?" The Cliffs, more than a half a mile away, with its sharp, uneven rocks, broken beer bottles, and stinking seaweed, was not Lucas's favorite place. By day it was relatively deserted; by night it was a place where kids liked to party.

"I don't like you going out there without your mother's or my knowledge."

"Mommy says I can go as long as I wear sneakers and watch out for the glass."

"Without telling her?"

A pause, then staring at the sand Zack said, "She didn't say."

"Well, I say. I don't want it to happen again. Did you eat breakfast?"

"Uh-uh."

Lucas pointed to the pail. "Get rid of that thing and go have something to eat."

Zack complained he wasn't hungry. So what else was new? Lucas thought irritably.

Haley got up before seven—excited about going out on the boat, since the first time of the summer was always best. This time, though, it was even better—she was going fishing with Simon. Nineteen years old and drop-dead gorgeous! Haley spent thirty minutes fiddling with her long, ash-blond hair, deciding finally to wear it in a French braid. Once it was fixed, she applied mascara and eye shadow. Makeup was off-limits—that was Daddy's rule and on this one Mom agreed with him.

"For gosh' sake, Haley," she'd say, "why bother tampering with what's good?"

Yeah, right, easy for her to say, Haley thought. Mom never wore a stick of makeup, and if Haley's eyes were as big and dark and awesome as hers, she wouldn't either.

Haley was finally ready, prancing in front of the mirror. After four tries, she had settled on a pink and white checkered bikini and, for Daddy's benefit, a long navy-blue sweatshirt and sunglasses. She now peeked around the corner, looking at the wall clock in the great room: it was already ten to eight.

She hurried to the kitchen, pulled out a thermal jug from under the counter, and filled it with Gatorade and ice. Then taking out the picnic hamper, she tossed in napkins and plastic utensils, and, in a helter-skelter fashion, a dozen or so items from the refrigerator.

She was done and waiting impatiently on a stool at the counter when Simon finally knocked at the kitchen door. She jumped off, went to the door, and opened it. He was wearing jean cutoffs, a sweatshirt, and sneakers, and had another one of those sweatbands on his head. "I thought you weren't coming," she said.

"I said I was."

She pointed to the clock. "You're more than fifteen minutes late."

He shrugged. "You want to go or not?"

If she didn't watch it, she would squeal like a pig with its leg caught . . . and then what? She didn't answer him. She just picked up the lunch and led the way to the tackle and poles out in the shed. Wait'll her friends heard about this . . .

Awakened several times by nightmares triggered by the strange car and its glaring headlights from the night before, Cat didn't get up until nine-thirty—and then only because the doorbell rang. She quickly slipped on shorts and a T-shirt and started to the door. But Lucas was already there, a crutch under one arm: a messenger was handing him a large flowering plant with colored pebbles and tiny figurines.

Hearing her behind him, he turned, "Morning, babe," he said, then gestured to her purse lying on the counter. "Want to toss a couple of bills over here?"

She quickly took out money and handed a tip to the messenger on his way out. Then taking the plant from Lucas's arms, she carried it to the dining-room table to set it down.

"It's a European garden, Lucas. It really is magnificent, isn't it?"

"You shouldn't have gone to the trouble. You know I'm not a plant per—"

"I didn't," she said, thinking Jack and Linda must have sent it. Who else knew? Lucas had no close family to speak of, and she had seen no need to upset her mother or other family members in New Hampshire with that kind of frightening story. She plucked the little card from the plant and held it out.

"No," he said, his voice short. "You read it."

She pulled the card from the envelope. " 'Feel better,' it says. Signed, 'The guys.' "

"The guys at work know? What did you do, Cat, send out memorandums?"

"Well, I had to tell Jack . . ." She hadn't thought to tell Jack not to mention it to the others, though. She hadn't known it was an issue for Lucas. Apparently it was.

Haley directed Simon to a place near Mirra's Island, a tiny island about two miles at sea. It was a good place to fish; sometimes the mackerel were so hungry and plentiful, they nearly jumped onto the hook on their own. Well, she had never really seen that happen, but that's what Daddy always said. Anyway, the fish weren't biting at all today—by eleven o'clock neither she nor Simon had gotten a nibble.

A warm wind was making the water choppy, but the sun was strong and hot, and though she'd been dying to get her sweatshirt off all morning, she hadn't worked up the courage. Talk about a ninny, didn't she wear the bikini around dozens of kids at home at the club pool without one bit of embarrassment? But somehow with Simon, she felt different. Not that she really had much to worry about—he hadn't really looked at her once since they'd left. When she had tried to make small talk earlier, he quickly shut her up, saying she was scaring away the fish.

So she was surprised when he turned, gestured toward the picnic basket, and asked, "What'd you bring?"

"Food," she said with a slight edge, deciding to act as cold and disinterested as he was.

He smiled. "It was a real feat you staying quiet all that time, wasn't it?"

She didn't answer—it was the kind of put-down question that didn't deserve one.

"See? I bet if you practice it more often, you'll get better at it."

"Maybe I don't want to get better at it."

He shrugged. "You want guys to like you, don't you?" Of course she did, but she hated the way he was trying to make her feel like a kid. He gestured to the island.

"Ever go there?"

"Uh-uh."

"Want to? I thought maybe we'd have a picnic there."

Though she was still annoyed at his behavior, the idea was intriguing. So romantic. She wondered how long he'd been thinking about taking her there. Who knew, it might have been on his mind all along. Maybe he had been up all night, unable to sleep. *Yeah, sure, right, Haley, dream on.* She smiled, though, feeling a lot better as she began to pull up the anchor.

While Lucas sunned himself on the porch, Cat prepared sandwiches for lunch. When the telephone rang, she picked up. It was Linda and they spoke for the better part of a half hour before Jack got on. "Cat, how's Lucas doing?"

"Hi, Jack, okay. He's a little on edge still, I was telling Linda. We both are, I guess."

"It's to be expected—shrinks' offices are filled with people who have gone through such traumas. Give yourself a while. Any progress in finding those men?"

"We haven't heard any word, so I assume it's negative."

"Oh. Listen, is he close by? I want to say hello."

"Wait, I'll tell him to pick up on the deck." She started to put down the receiver, then remembering Lucas's comment earlier brought it back to her ear. "A favor, Jack. Try not to mention anything about the plant the employees sent."

"Easy to do, I didn't even know they had. Why, what's the problem with it?"

"No problem, at least not with the plant. It's just Lucas. He doesn't like the idea of people knowing about what happened."

"Afraid to show he's not invincible, that's our Lucas, all right. I suppose I should have kept my mouth shut, but I was upset when you told me the news. Greg Fielding noticed how preoccupied I was and asked what was wrong. Not thinking—"

"Please don't apologize, Jack. Just so you know how hard Lucas has taken this. Wait, I'll put him on."

By the time she brought the lunch to the deck a few minutes later, he was off the phone. She set the plates of chicken-salad sandwiches and glasses of iced tea on the table, then sat across from him. "So what did Jack have to say?"

"Nothing much. Business is fine."

She always found it odd—no matter how close men were, aside from business and sports or something specific, they seemed to have little to say to one another. Not like women, who always seemed able to find a topic to chat about. She took a bite of sandwich, and as she did, remembered her conversation the day before with Zack. "Lucas, I think you ought to have a talk with Zack about sex."

"Yeah, why?"

"Because what he's learning is only what other children tell him. He needs an adult to talk to, and I think it's more appropriate if that adult is his father. Don't you?"

He agreed ... reluctantly. "What do you want me to tell him?"

"I'll leave it to you."

"Where is he now?"

"He met a boy—Andy Canter. Apparently the Lansings rented out the house this year." The Lansings were their closest neighbors— this was the first time there had been any children within close proximity to the beach house, and she was happy for Zack. "In any event," she said, "the boys took a lunch to the jetty."

Lucas frowned. "Don't you think you ought to keep a closer eye on him?"

"Why, what's wrong?"

"He must have been up and dressed and out of the house at dawn. He was already on his way back from the Cliffs when I got out on the deck at about seven o'clock. I don't know what he finds so fascinating about that place."

"Come on, Lucas, can't you remember

when you were a little boy? Surely you liked to explore."

"I don't know, I can't remember that far back."

Something so wistful in the way he said it made her smile. She went over to him and stooped in front of him. "Yeah? Well, I can remember." With practiced fingers she undid his shorts, then slowly slid her hand inside, caressing him. "In fact, I wouldn't mind a little exploring right now."

He sighed—his penis was growing hard in her hand and his arousal excited her. "God, Cat, out here?" In reply, she ran the tip of her tongue over her lips. He groaned, then no longer caring about where they were, put his hands to her face, guiding her down on him. Then just as suddenly as it appeared, his erection wilted.

Though she wanted to bring it back, he wouldn't let her try. Instead he pulled away, ending it. He fixed his shorts, stood up, and reached for one of his crutches, which was leaning against the railing.

"I'm sorry, Cat, I'm tired, I guess. Christ, I've been up since before seven . . . even the doctor talked about me getting sufficient rest. Hey, what kind of wanton woman are you anyway, trying to seduce a man in my condition?"

It was a lame joke, and neither of them

laughed. Dammit, again those bastards pulling apart their lives—she didn't have to ask Lucas to know what had killed his arousal.

They anchored the boat a little ways offshore, Simon tying it to a boulder jutting out of the water. When Haley got out, the water came past her waist. She took the jug, Simon took the picnic basket, and together they went onto the sand.

Putting down the basket, Haley ran around, looking at it all—the island was small and untouched and excellent, the sand warm and silky soft. Still, though, she felt a little shy and awkward being alone with Simon. Maybe he was feeling much the same way because he was kind of quiet.

"Oops, guess what? I forgot to bring a blanket," she said, breaking the silence.

"No big deal." Simon plopped down in the sand, closed his eyes, tilted his face toward the sun. He was so handsome, she thought, tracing his strong chin and jawline with her eyes. But then he happened to turn and catch her looking—and she quickly pulled the food hamper over to open it. "I kind of just tossed some things in—" she began, and he put his hand over hers, stopping her.

"Wait, hold it," he said. "No rush. Or is there?"

"No, I guess not."

He lifted his sweatshirt a little—beneath it he had a belt bag—he unzipped it and took out a bag—in it were sticks and stuff. "What's that?" she said.

"Ever see pot?"

She shook her head. Though she naturally knew all about it, she had never actually seen it. The truth was, no one in her junior high school dared do drugs while on school grounds. Two years ago, some kid had been expelled for carrying pot, and though the kid's parents sued the school committee to get him back in and won, the kid missed three months of classes and had to repeat the eighth grade.

Oh, there were kids she knew who did it, but not in school and not kids she hung out with. Of course, next year was high school—everyone said that was different.

"Don't be afraid, it's not going to bite you," Simon said and laughed.

"I didn't say it would." She looked closer. "It looks gross," she said. "What're those clumps?"

"Buds." He put his hand in the bag, took out twigs and little seeds, tossing them, then with his fingers broke up the buds. He tilted his head, his eyes narrowing as they studied her. "Hey, this isn't going to be a problem, is it?"

"No, of course not," she said. After all, he

was nineteen years old—not some little high school kid who could get grounded if he got caught. After all, he'd even gone to college! He could do what he felt like, he didn't have to ask permission. Certainly not from her.

"Good. I was beginning to wonder for a second. I didn't take you for being all that young when I first met you. But, hey, people make mistakes. I find it tough to tell sometimes, a lot of girls look and act older than they are."

"I'm going to be fourteen in October," she offered, though he hadn't really asked.

"Really? If I had to try to guess, I would have said sixteen, certainly fifteen."

Lots of her friends had told her she looked older, even sophisticated. Once a high school junior had tried to pick her up at the movie theater. She was sure it was because of her long neck—there was definitely something chic about a long neck. She had ignored that junior boy, of course, though it felt good knowing he wanted her. It felt good now, too. In fact, with Simon, it felt especially good. She wanted to say something in response, but what? Thank you?

She watched him as he took out a thin white paper, folded up the bottom like a pouch, then poured the greenish tobacco stuff into it. He shook it, distributing it, then rolled it. With his tongue he licked along the edge of the paper so it would stick, then put each end of the cigarette in his mouth, licking it again.

"Gross. Why do you do that?"

"To keep the joint from coming apart."

"Oh." She was quiet for a few moments, then said, "My folks think it's bad to do drugs."

"Pot's really no big deal—that is, if a person's old enough and smart enough to know what he's doing. Kids, for the most part, don't—at least kids I've seen. See, the trick is to handle it, not abuse it. Here, watch." He put the joint to his mouth, sucked in smoke, held it a long while, then let it out. It had a funny, sweet smell. "You know how to drag, take in smoke to your lungs, Haley?" he asked after she had watched him do it a couple of times more.

"I don't know, I never tried."

"Not even a cigarette?" She shook her head, hoping he wouldn't decide to make fun of her, but he didn't. "Here, try," he said, handing her the joint.

"Uh-uh," she said.

"One hit's not going to kill you. Look at me, do I in any way look dead?" He crashed back onto the sand, spread-eagled, lightening up the conversation a lot, making them both laugh. Finally he sat up. "Hey, look, sorry, I don't want to scare you."

"Who says I'm scared?"

"Yeah, well, whatever. Smoke is supposed to be fun, not work. Besides, I like you, Haley. I don't want you to feel uncomfortable around me."

"I don't," she said, though she wasn't being entirely honest. And she did feel a little tempted—at least, just to try it. But she kept thinking about her parents. She looked away from him, pretending to be really into the scenic view, but finally she couldn't help but turn back to him. "If my folks ever found out—"

"Hey, hey, wait," he said, touching her arm. "I have no intention of telling them. Do you?"

She put her hand to her chest. "Me . . . tell them? You're putting me on, right?"

They both started laughing, and he handed her the joint. She tried to copy what she'd seen him do, but she couldn't get the knack of taking the smoke in. She tried again . . . and again. Finally he took the joint from her. "You've got to loosen up. You're way too tense. Ever get examined with a stethoscope?"

"Of course," she answered, though her mind was not on that at all. She was thinking about that adorable deep, scratchy voice of his. Gazing into those incredible green eyes. But he stuck strictly to business.

"Okay, good," he said, reaching with his other hand for a shell in the sand. "I want you to pretend this is a stethoscope, okay? I'm going to hold the joint to your mouth, and when I press this shell to your chest, you take a deep breath."

Chapter Five

Lucas had gone off to the bedroom, and Cat went after him trying to convince him he was making too much of his momentary impotence, particularly after what he'd just been through, but he wasn't listening. Finally, she left him alone in the bedroom and went downstairs to the laundry.

Yesterday she had strung a clothesline across the width of the cellar, a place to hang Zack's washed sheet and pajamas. Now she pulled them off the line and folded them—they felt stiff. She carried them upstairs, then went to the phone and opened the directory. She had to find someone to fix the dryer.

But before she was able to dial, Chief Cooper called and promptly told her that though his man hadn't found Simon at Chatfield Hollow, he'd managed to get the information Lucas wanted on him. She took down the license and registration number and slipped the paper in her shorts pocket. "It all checked out fine, like the kid said. The aunt is Hazel Bower, the Tucson address is 225 Welmont Road. Now if the mister wants, what I can do is—"

"Wait, Chief," she said. "We really do appreciate the help—thanks. But it won't be necessary. I ran into Simon yesterday at the shopping plaza. I convinced him to come back to the house to meet Lucas. Well, to make a long story short, he's out in the boat fishing with our daughter as we speak. I should have called, I'm sorry."

"Forget it, I'm sure you have your hands full out there. I'm glad Mr. Marshall's happy, though. Listen, I also want to let you know that we found an abandoned car ditched near the lake. A wreck, no plates or papers. We figure it could be what the carjackers used to get over to the area."

"Oh? Then you might be able to trace them—"

"Not really. As I say, they had stripped the car first. That doesn't mean we've given up, though."

"What about our Bronco? What do you think are the chances of that turning up?"

"It's hard to say. Some of these cars get painted over, parts sold, things like that."

Though it was about the last thing she wanted to do, she agreed to go down to the police station to look at mug shots the next day. She had promised herself she'd cooperate with the police, and she wouldn't be able to look herself in the mirror if she backed down on that. And as far as the practicalities were concerned, Winnie would be there to watch out for Lucas and the kids.

Later she'd go shopping—Haley needed a little of everything. In addition to the losses, many of her things left behind from last year she'd outgrown. Cat, Zack, and Lucas all needed swimsuits. She'd get Lucas a few more pairs of shorts, too—a larger size with wider legs—the ones he had being snug over the cast.

For the next half hour she put her energies into locating an appliance serviceman. After five inquiries, she found a repairman in the next town who worked out of his home and whose soonest opening was in eight days. It wasn't exactly the speedy service she had in mind. Still, she made the appointment and hung up, then went to the sliding screen doors and looked out. From there she could just make out Zack and his young friend on the jetty.

She looked out to the ocean. Haley was out there somewhere with Simon, hopefully reeling in a big one. Well, at least the kids were having fun.

* * *

Lucas woke at about two, the rumblings in his stomach making him aware that he hadn't eaten his lunch. When he remembered why, his frustration and anger started up again. As much as he had wanted Cat earlier—he couldn't remember a time he hadn't wanted her—Earl had suddenly popped into his head, captured in the act of trying to force her down on him . . .

But he had stopped Earl, hadn't he? Sure, temporarily. But how much longer would it have been before those sonsofbitches had finished with him and gone back to what they had begun? Earl raping Cat, the other likely taking his turn at her, too. And Haley, what about her? Who knows what else if not for Simon?

Using one crutch, he walked into the bathroom, took a leak, splashed cold water over his face, then toweled it and headed out to the great room. He cleared his throat, looked around the room. Where in the hell was everyone anyhow? Finally he went to the kitchen, opened the refrigerator, and began to search through the shelves for that salami Cat had promised to get. Unable to find it, he settled for a boxed pizza from the freezer which he microwaved.

He took the finished product to the sofa, put it on the coffee table, then turned on the television. The pizza was doughy and tasteless, but he ate it anyway—at least, until the kitchen door slammed, and Zack came rushing by, whistling on his way upstairs.

"Hey, wait, where're you going?"

Zack stopped on the first step. "Oh, hi, Dad. I'm going to get my magnifying glass."

"What for?"

"Me and Andy want to study some rock scum. I'm taking him down to show him the Cliffs. Andy's a new kid—"

"I know, Mommy told me. You got a few minutes to spare?"

"Yeah, I guess."

He came hesitantly toward him, and Lucas stared at his young son: a blue and white baseball cap sitting lopsided on his head, big questioning brown eyes. Those eyes often peered at Lucas as though they didn't know who the hell he was. How did a father go about getting close to a kid he couldn't even pretend to understand? "Mommy tells me you have questions about sex," he said finally.

"Uh-uh," he said.

"Then she was wrong?"

He shrugged.

"You talk about it with the kids in school?"

"Some."

"So you understand that the sex act is called intercourse, sometimes coitus. And it's the way a man and woman show their love for one another?"

"What about the F word?"

Okay, great. Why the hell couldn't Cat have handled this one? "Where'd you hear that?" he asked, mainly to give himself more time to prepare a response.

"In school."

"Well, you already know, it's not a word your mom or I like you using. But you want to know where the word fits in ... right?" Zack nodded, and Lucas plodded ahead. "Yeah, well, it's used to refer to the sex act as, well, sort of a crass way to say it, though. Maybe putting a different perspective on sex, too—the kind of sex you might hear guys wisecracking about in a boys' locker room."

Shit, a different perspective on sex, did he really say that? Or believe it? Better still, how in the hell did he expect a kid Zack's age to relate to what went on in a locker room? But not knowing where to go from there, he said, "Get it?"

"I guess," Zack said, shrugging. Then, as if changing to a new thought, "What about Earl?"

"What do you mean?"

"Earl wanted to have intercourse with Mommy. Does that mean he loves her?"

Lucas felt the muscles in his neck tense. Why did the boy have to bring this up now? "No," he said, trying not to let his anger get the best of him. "That's different."

Zack paused, then as if something clicked, his eyes narrowed and his voice lowered almost to a whisper. "I think I get what you mean now, Daddy. Earl didn't want to have intercourse with Mommy—what he wanted to do was fuck her."

Lucas brought his hand down hard onto the coffee table. "Dammit, I don't ever want to hear you say that again!"

Zack looked as though Lucas had struck him. And though Lucas tried to think of something to say, he wasn't much up to it, and neither was Zack.

"Look, why don't you go upstairs and get your magnifying glass? You're keeping your friend waiting."

When Cat came in—she had been out washing her sailboat—the first thing he thought to hit her with was, "Where the hell is that salami I asked for?"

She went to the refrigerator and looked through the shelves. Finally she faced him. "I don't see it anywhere, Lucas. Someone must have gotten to it first."

"I ask for one stinking thing—"

Her jaw dropped. "What is the matter with you? It's only a salami. But if it means that much to you, I'll gladly go out and get another." She reached for her handbag.

"No, don't."

"Lucas, I'll be back in twenty—"

"Dammit, Cat, I said no!" And right then he was hating himself for doing this to her. He somehow had to pull himself together. He went out to the deck, leaned against the pine railings, looking out at the water. What was driving him? Sure, the other night, but that was done with—and like Cat said, they were lucky to walk away, albeit with the help of a bit of plaster for him. Then what was freaking him?

The Bronco he had spotted on the way home from the medical center? But as it turned out, not his Bronco. And what about the car parked outside the house last night . . . Was it just another case of him making something out of nothing?

After many fits of coughing and three solid hits, Haley took off her sweatshirt, not even embarrassed when Simon did a double take on her swimsuit. In fact, she found it funny. While she was having the giggles, Simon, who had taken off his own shirt and rolled it in a ball for a pillow, was lying back, quiet.

"What's the matter with you?" she said, swiping at his face with a strand of seaweed, teasing him and sounding so sure of herself, she couldn't believe it was her.

"Nothing, just mellowing out."

"Talk to me, I want to talk."

"Sure, what about?"

"Anything. What's your favorite color?"

"White."

"Silly, white's not even a color. I remember that from art class. In sixth grade we had an art teacher who used to give us weekly quizzes. Can you imagine, quizzes in art? I mean, like what major thing could she ask—what colors do you mix to get blue?"

"So what colors do you mix?"

"Um, let me see. Red and purple? No, no, red and green." She began giggling again and he shook his head. "Am I being an idiot or what?" She knew she was, but couldn't seem to stop—and he was polite enough not to agree.

"You like games?" he asked.

She shrugged. "I guess. I used to play games with friends, but most of them now think it babyish—you know, like playing with toys. My mom and dad like to, though, so lots of times we play together, especially here at the beach. Why, do you?"

He nodded. "Yeah, I like games. I used to play 'em with myself a lot. Monopoly solitaire on the cellar floor, ever try it?"

"How come in the cellar?"

"I didn't have a Monopoly board. So that's where I drew it with chalk."

"Oh, well, I guess that makes sense." She started to giggle again. "Okay, I've got to ask, who won?"

His expression turned cocky. "Me every time. I'd get on a winning streak and there was no stopping the kid. The faster I'd win, the sooner the bank would run dry. So I had to improvise, make my own money. I'd cut up old newspapers: the comics were five hundreds; classifieds, hundreds; entertainment, tens; the stock market, five; and the obituary, ones."

"You are nuts. Why didn't you play with someone else?"

"I couldn't find anyone who could play as well as me."

"Are you for real?"

"I doubt it," he said, smiling. And she couldn't tell if he was putting her on or not. He turned over, facedown, and with his finger started to draw weird faces in the sand. "Actually, all I am is an aberration, just some joke weed that sprouted in your imagination."

"I haven't a clue as to what you're talking about, Simon."

"Ever hear that philosophical theory about the tree falling in the forest?"

"Uh-uh."

"Well, the question goes something like this. 'If a tree in the forest falls and there's no one there to hear it, does it make a noise when it hits the ground?' "

"Of course."

"How do you know?"

98

She must have looked confused because she was—her arms waved through the air. "Well, I don't really. I mean, I never watched a tree come down. But other people have. Besides, everything makes a sound when it falls—at least, anything heavy."

"Maybe. But the real question is, can we count on our senses to tell us the truth? Who's to say it's not just that a person imagines something is there? In other words, without someone like you to imagine me, would I be real?"

"That's the dumbest thing."

"Yeah? Not so dumb. But even as a kid, I had the feeling I wasn't real."

"Well, you are. I see you. And hear you."

"Only because you want to. If I wanted to see a great white shark out in those waters," he said, his hand gesturing to the ocean, "I could do it in a snap."

"What about if you didn't want to see it, were scared to see it, but you saw it anyway?"

"People don't see what they don't want to see."

"Well, suppose the shark bit you? That would for sure prove it was real."

"Don't you get it? It couldn't. People do all sorts of things with their minds, they bend them to fit their own fears and anticipations and needs. First off, you have to believe that reality is based in the head—it originates there and dies there."

Haley was just sitting there, listening blankly, trying hard to focus on what he was saying.

"Ever hear of halitosis of the brain?" he asked.

Was he putting her on? "I've heard of halitosis," she answered cautiously.

"Good. Then just apply it to the brain. It's when meat rots due to lack of use. That's when the maggots crawl around inside your brain, making it stink."

She sat up, grossed out, making a face. "Simon!"

Without another word of explanation, he stood up and raced toward the water. He dived in and began swimming. She called out to him, but he didn't turn back—at least not until he'd gone a good long distance. And though she finally settled herself on a rock and stopped calling to him, she was still mad by the time he got back. "Why did you do that?" she asked, getting up.

"Why not?"

"You didn't even say anything. You just ran off."

"So?"

"Suppose you had gotten a cramp?"

"What are you, my mother?"

Had she really sounded like a mother? Suddenly she felt foolish, like she ought to be the one to apologize. "I'm sorry," she said. "I didn't mean to sound so nagging. It's just that I was scared, Simon. I thought maybe I'd have to go and rescue you. At one point while you were swimming, I thought you were having—"

"So what'd you say you put together for lunch?" he asked, closing her off.

She hadn't even realized it until he brought up the idea of food, but now that he had, she discovered she was starving. Both of them dug in and pulled apart the basket: cheese, yogurt, pickles, granola bars, raisin bread, bananas, Doritos, Winnie's Toll-House cookies, and a salami. Taste testing each item and rating it with a number, one to ten—Simon's idea. It was the best time.

Simon demolished the salami—she only got one bite.

It was four o'clock—Cat and Lucas were on the deck, playing gin rummy. Though she was competitive, she wasn't nearly as cutthroat as Lucas, who refused to be a good loser. Or for that matter be a loser at all. Clear thinking, he would brag openly to get her goat, was what cinched a game for him, though she was sure it had much more to do with determination.

But this afternoon he wasn't really into the cards, his glance was wandering toward the water. "Haley's a good sailor, sweetheart," she said. "And Simon's clearly quite capable. I'm sure they're fine. Oh, by the way," she said, pulling out the paper that she'd written the information from the police chief on. She handed it to him. "Not that we need it any longer, but it's the license and registration number of Simon's van. Chief Cooper said it all checked out."

Lucas looked out at the water, then back at Cat. "Go out to the van, see if those numbers match."

"Lucas, why?"

"No reason at all. Just that it would make me feel better."

"I won't. I can't go snooping in his van."

He began to stand. "Okay, then I will."

She did it. She only needed a few minutes—actually, everything was quite orderly. Shelves along the top portion held clothes, a tent, rope, a few pots and pans, kitchen items, a dozen movie videos and tape cassettes, envelopes of photographs; there was a toolbox and two large closed cardboard boxes in the corner on the floor.

The registration and insurance papers were right together in a plastic envelope in the glove compartment. Everything matched exactly, even the aunt's name and Tucson address the chief had mentioned earlier. She quickly put the papers back, feeling uncomfortable and sneaky and imagining Simon would appear and catch her there.

As she closed the glove compartment, she thought she heard a noise in the back of the van and jumped up, nearly hitting her head. A guilty conscience—definitely not detective material. But at least Lucas's touch of paranoia was satisfied.

Fifteen minutes later they spotted the boat coming in. They watched from the deck as the kids anchored: Simon helped Haley out, though she'd been doing it by herself since she was four. Nonetheless, she didn't resist. Looking sunburnt and happy—Simon carrying the picnic basket and jug, Haley, her sweatshirt and sunglasses—they made their way up the beach to the house.

"What's for dinner?" Lucas called out, teasing them. It was quite apparent they were carrying no fish. "All afternoon my taste buds were screaming for salmon."

Simon played along, flinching. "Gee whiz, Lucas, I feel like a real spoiler. Listen, I could go pick up some if you want. I passed a snappy fish market over on Route 80—"

"Sorry to disappoint everyone, but dinner is flounder," Cat said. "Corn on the cob, too, Simon. And you're welcome to stay."

Though Simon complained he was still full from the great lunch Haley had packed, Cat assured him that dinner wouldn't be until seven. And though she didn't ask, putting two and two together, she felt confident that she had found out the salami thieves. She also sent Haley straight to the shower room to wash the runny eye makeup off her face before Lucas spotted it.

Not until after dinner, when Simon was talking to Lucas about fixing his bike, did she even think of her plan again. She had gone to answer the phone—another wrong number—and when she came back she said, "Simon, just how good are you at fixing things?"

He shrugged. "I've always taken things apart, put them back together. Why?"

"Well, I have a dryer that sort of has fits of shaking—"

He was already up. "Let me take a look."

But Lucas wouldn't let him, at least not then. First off, he had to promise he'd accept payment. Besides, tomorrow was soon enough, Lucas insisted, insuring that the boy would be back. And Cat understood his motivation—with Lucas out of commission there was something quite reassuring about having Simon around.

Simon left soon after dinner, and Cat and the kids settled into a game of Scrabble. Lucas, unable to concentrate, bowed out, getting up from time to time to wander around the house. If anyone were to ask, he would have said it was only by chance that he went to the deck doors at the particular moment someone was out on the beach. But in retrospect, maybe he heard a sound that had triggered him to investigate. In any event, it was nearly nine o'clock, had already gotten dark, and Lucas was only able to get a glimpse of the man's back as he ran through the sand. He looked husky and tall, too big to be a serious runner, and ... was he imagining it, or did he have that same light, long hair Warren had?

Lucas hobbled onto the deck. By the time he reached the railing, the runner had turned up toward the street, across to the dunes beyond. And though he was long gone, it was several minutes before Lucas was able to look away.

As his glance dropped, he spotted the small empty bottle on the deck. He stepped over, picked it up, and read the label: Snapple kiwi strawberry cocktail. His thoughts went immediately to the variety-flavored case he had packed in the Bronco, one of several cases that the CEO from Snapple Beverage had sent to Lucas and Jack: an appreciative gesture for a job the company had done.

Though the night was cool, Lucas felt a line of sweat rise to his forehead. One thing wasn't necessarily connected to another, in fact, it wasn't likely connected at all. The empty bottle might have been left there by a couple of kids passing through—with no trash cans in sight, Lucas's deck might have looked like a good dumping place so as not to litter the beach. It could have been a Coke bottle, of course . . . or even a Pepsi bottle, but it wasn't. It was Snapple. Though why not? Certainly, the soft drink was all the rage.

Had Lucas's perceptions been off, had his mind distorted the runner's size or the color and length of his hair? Was there even a resemblance to Warren?

Surely Cat would think he was overreacting.

"Lucas."

Startled, he swung around like a kid caught in the john smoking a butt. Cat was standing at the sliding screen door. "Are you okay?" He nodded, and she asked, "Coming in?" He had started toward her when she noticed he was carrying something in his hand and asked, "What's that?"

"Just something someone left." Once inside, Lucas went to the kitchen trash and dropped the bottle in.

Chapter Six

Despite Cat's fussing the next morning about not leaving Lucas until Winnie arrived, he insisted she go. Zack went off to see his new friend; Haley tagged along after Cat, eager to shop for new clothes. Lucas, not much in the mood for sunshine, headed back to his bedroom, and soon after, Simon arrived. He let himself in, then stuck his head in the room and gave Lucas a salute.

"The tools, nuts, bolts, are in the little room at the back of the basement," Lucas told him. "Look around, help yourself to whatever you need."

"Didn't see the Jeep. Where's your lady?"

"Off looking at mug shots."

He nodded, then went downstairs. For a while Lucas poked around with the television remote, switching from a talk show paneled by gay bashers to a game show with giggling contestants. Finally switching it off, he took the morning newspaper off the nightstand.

Winnie came in at about ten and appeared in the open doorway.

"Where's Cat?"

"Hi to you, too. Looking at mug shots, shopping."

"Where're the kids?"

"Haley's with Cat. Zack's with the boy whose family is renting Lansings' place."

"Have you tried the cookies yet?"

"They're great, Winnie," he lied, aware of them, but not really in the mood.

"I saw the green van out there," she said. "So what's he still doing here?"

Lucas was as fond of Winnie as the rest of the family, but sometimes she thought her three days a week entitled her to run the whole shebang. And though he was perfectly willing to tell her to mind her own business, Cat got pissed at him when he did.

"He's not *still* here," he said. "He came back today to fix the clothes dryer. Have you any objections to that, Winnie?"

"Why should I object? What I really want to know is what you're doing holed up in a dark room. It's beautiful out." She marched over to the window and drew the blinds, letting the sun in. "Out," she said, "I've got cleaning to do here."

Lucas sat up, grumbling, considering he insist she do upstairs first, but concluding it wasn't worth the flak. "You know, Winnie you get bitchier and battier the longer I know you. Why don't you get your ass out of here so I can dress?"

It was almost noon when Simon showed his face again.

"How'd it go?" Lucas asked.

"A piece of cake. I found a tube sock stuck in the fan. You shouldn't have any grief with it from here on. And, oh, yeah, while I was there, I happened to spot the air vent was blocked with lint. Any new lint would have bounced right back into the basement. So I took it apart, cleared it."

Lucas nodded—the lint-blocked vent was the sort of thing that if let be might have sparked a fire. The kid was not only bright and able, he had initiative. He had dealt with employees for years, and it was something he didn't see often these days. "Take a seat," he said, gesturing to one of the chairs.

Simon sank down, silently admiring the landscape. "I bet you never want to leave this place," he said.

"Winters get pretty cold."

"Yeah, I hear," Simon said.

"So how do you like the Northeast so far?"

Simon nodded. "It's pretty decent. Of course, I haven't been through a winter yet. That may change my mind."

"There's always skiing, snowmobiling, to-bogganing, ice hockey, frostbite. Watch out, you might like it." Then moving forward on the chair, Lucas said, "Simon, you mentioned the other day that you worked when your funds got low enough. Well, I don't pretend to know your finances, but I might be able to boost them a little. I'd like you to consider working for me."

He looked a little surprised, but even more apprehensive. "Where?" he asked.

"Right here."

"Doing what?"

"Just odd jobs, much like what you did today. Though I usually handle the upkeep here, the last year or two I've been admittedly lazy. This year despite plans to get a number of things done"—he put his hand on his cast—"well, as you see, it doesn't look promising."

Simon screwed up his expression, shrugged. "The thing is, I don't really plan ahead. Sometimes I wake up in the morning, and on a whim I'm history—off to another town."

"I get it, and I'd expect you to operate no other way. You feel the itch, just give me fifteen minutes notice—enough time to try to change your mind, or alternatively, give you your pay." Simon still didn't look all that convinced, and Lucas went on. "Before you say no, I want you to hear me out on the perks."

Simon smiled, nodded. "Okay, go ahead."

"Now, the idea of being a wandering

soul—at least so they tell me—is to be able to dig your feet into the earth, find out all about it. Not just work the environment, play it as well. Am I right?"

He laughed. "Yeah, I guess."

"So to facilitate that play, my idea is for you to work half a day—the rest of the day, you're on your own. In fact, I'll make a list of what needs doing—you figure out how or when you want to fit it in your schedule. Meanwhile, use the beach, the boats, the house. Camp out on the beach if that's what makes you comfortable. If not, there's a spare bedroom upstairs that's yours to use. In other words, enjoy this." Lucas swept his arms, encompassing the view.

Lucas could see in the boy's eyes that he was relenting. "It's quite an offer," he said finally.

"It's meant to be. Now, while you think it over, go in my bedroom, get my wallet out of my top dresser drawer. Then tell Winnie to make us lunch."

Cat had done her duty—she had stared at a computer screen for more than an hour, scanning hundreds of strange, vacant faces and the physical statistics that went along with those faces. She didn't spot either Earl or Warren, in fact sat in horrible anticipation and fear of actually coming across their faces on the screen.

The night before, she had made up the insurance list Jack had asked for, and now on the way to JC Penney's she stopped at the post office to mail it. Haley had three letters of her own to send out. "Looks like you were up late last night," Cat said.

"Sort of. I couldn't get to sleep, the sunburn on my back was killing me."

"Next time use sunscreen. There's nearly a full bottle in the boat's cabin—with skin so fair, you mustn't forget. And remind me to pick up something soothing for your burn. So tell me more about your fishing trip yesterday."

"Well, as you saw, we didn't catch anything. But we stopped at Mirra's Island and had a picnic."

"Really? That sounds nice."

"It was. We were so starved by then, you should have seen us go at the food. We were being real pigs—Simon accidentally snorted, and we couldn't stop laughing." Which reminded Cat immediately to pick up another salami for Lucas. Maybe two. "Oh, yeah, that reminds me," Haley said, "can I buy a camera today?"

"But you have one, Haley—"

"I *had*. It was in the Bronco."

Another thing to replace. Fortunately, the

movie camera hadn't been in the car—when they had come to the beach house for a weekend in the spring, they left the camera. "Okay. Be sure to pick up lots of film. We have to get some pictures of Daddy with the cast." Though Lucas hated both movies and photographs taken of him, it was always a challenge to get a few good ones in while he wasn't paying attention.

"Pictures of Simon, too."

Cat smiled uncertainly, then glanced at her daughter. "He's very good-looking, isn't he?"

"Oh, is he?" she said, straining her act to appear nonchalant. "I really hadn't noticed."

Haley of course didn't mention anything about the pot. Simon was right about it, too, it was no big deal. It didn't turn your brains inside out or backward or upside-down or anything else that adults would have you believe. In fact, it was fun, it made her feel good. What was so wrong with that?

She didn't mention their conversation either. Not that she had anything to be ashamed of—in fact, Haley felt kind of complimented that he thought she was smart enough to talk about such complicated things. It was just that she was getting older and couldn't very well go on telling her mom and dad every single thing.

That's what friends were for, she guessed.

She had written her friends about Simon, about their picnic on the island, about the deep and philosophical things they talked about. She even told them how she did some pot. They would never be judgmental. In fact, they were more likely to be impressed.

Of course, Simon hadn't tried to kiss her or hold her hand or even put his arm around her, and though she had been disappointed at the time, the more she thought about it, the more she began to see it as positive. It showed he was sensitive.

Though he was older and obviously more worldly, he was being extra careful not to come on to her too strong. He didn't want to scare her, not that he ever could, of course. Once she got some snapshots of Simon, she'd send copies to her friends.

Winnie had just finished the kids' rooms upstairs and was coming down to check on the vegetable soup she had begun earlier when her attention was caught by noises in Lucas's bedroom. Was he burying himself indoors again? She went to the doorway, peeked in, and that's when she saw the dresser drawer wide open and the Bower kid standing there, casually sifting through Lucas's things.

"What the hell are you doing?" she asked.

He jumped back, as well he should have,

then laid his palm to his chest and smiled. "Christ, you scared me," he said.

"Caught you is what you mean, isn't it?"

He looked at the drawer, then back at her, then seeing she was waiting for an explanation, he said, "It's not what you think. Lucas asked me to get his wallet."

Did he really expect her to believe that? So okay, he had done a good deed the other night and now Lucas was giving him work, but even a house guest didn't get to go through the dresser drawers. Which it sure looked like he was doing.

She went over and shut the drawer, then headed to the door. "Why don't I ask Mr. Marshall about that?" she said, expecting him to follow after her. Maybe even take an unexpected hike. But when she saw he wasn't budging, she went to the bedroom window, where she could still keep an eye on him and called out to Lucas on the deck. "Lucas, did you ask the kid to get your wallet?"

"The kid's name is Simon, Winnie. And yes I did. Is there some difficulty?"

"No, no difficulty." She turned around, egg all over her face. But the kid didn't gloat like she thought he might—he just opened the drawer and took out Lucas's black suede wallet. So why hadn't he done it that quickly and easily the first time around? she wondered. Because he was also snooping, that's why.

When she reached the door, he called out her name, and she stopped.

"Where're you off to now?" he asked.

"To do the laundry. Why?"

He flashed a cocky grin. "Tell you what, why don't you hold off on that awhile? First, bring me and Lucas some lunch. That soup you have going on the stove sure smells good."

At first Simon fought Lucas, not wanting to accept money for the work he'd done. Only after he realized how determined Lucas was going to be about it did he finally take it. The phone rang when he and Simon were eating lunch, and when Winnie came out carrying dessert, Lucas inquired about it.

"Oh, that," she said, shaking her head. "No one was on the line. A wrong number."

Lucas remembered the call the day before—no one had been on the line then either. His irritation switched from that thought to another. To no one in particular he said, "Where the hell is Zack? Doesn't he even bother to check in?"

"I was wondering that myself," Winnie said. "But then again, who am I to wonder?"

"What does that mean, Winnie? If there's some deeper meaning to that, say it."

"Just thinking out loud."

"Where should he be?" Simon asked.

"According to what he told me earlier, he was going to play with the boy in the Lansing house." Lucas pointed to a large white clapboard colonial about an eighth of a mile down the beach.

Simon took his napkin off his lap, put it on the table as he stood up. "Why don't I go get him?"

"I would really appreciate that. You don't mind?"

"Hell no. It'll give me a chance to run on the beach—I've been wanting to do that since the first day here." He started down the stairs, stopping a moment to address the housekeeper. "By the way, Winnie, I just wanted to say, the soup was good. I can always tell the difference between the poison in the cans and the real stuff."

She said nothing, and when Simon had taken off, Lucas looked at her. "You got a bug up your ass today?"

"It seems we're discussing my ass way too often these days, don't you think?"

Lucas smiled. Sooner or later, one of her comments always got to him. But he wasn't getting waylaid on this. "Okay, what is it, why don't you like him?"

"Who?"

"Cut the shtick, Winnie."

She thought about it a moment as though it were the first time she'd taken the trouble to question her lousy attitude toward the kid. "I think he's slick is all," she said finally. "Good-looking and slick. I just don't trust that type."

Winnie finally went back to the kitchen, and Lucas turned to catch a glimpse of the boy. Simon was already a couple of hundred yards along, his head held high, running like a deer. Strong and proud and healthy. But slick? He'd run across a lot of bad-news nineteen-year-olds, but none he'd consider slick.

In any case, this one had checked out. He was who he claimed he was, and had come from where he said he came from. No lies, nothing unusual or misleading either in his story or manner. No, in fact, Lucas himself would vouch for him.

A soft touch, Cat had buckled under Haley's charm more than once, buying her much more than she needed. By the time the two came in carrying a dozen shopping bags, Zack was being bawled out by Lucas. Apparently the child had left Andy's house and gone with him to the Cliffs to collect snails. Zack, bravely holding back tears, ran right past her and Haley when Lucas sent him to his room.

"Why on earth are you making such a big issue over this?" Cat asked.

"I'm not making it anything it isn't. Dammit, Cat, pay more attention to the kids! Zack runs around loose and you're either oblivious to it or think it's okay."

Though annoyed at Lucas's accusations, she went out of her way to take his precarious emotional state into account. "I do think it's okay," she said calmly. "He doesn't go anywhere you or I don't know about. Besides, I trust him. He's smart, careful ... and quite self-sufficient in case you haven't noticed."

"He's also two months short of eight years old. And I don't like it. I want him home when he's supposed to be, and if he can't manage it, I'll set up some tight boundaries for him."

She walked into the house, leaving Lucas on the deck with Haley, who with total sisterly disregard was eager only to show her father her new purchases. Simon had slipped away, apparently not comfortable being around Lucas during his tirade.

She filled a bowl with vegetable soup and put it on a tray with crackers, milk, and pie. She was about to bring the tray upstairs to Zack when Lucas called out to her. Though she felt like ignoring him, she wasn't good at those kind of games. She went over to the screen door.

"What is it, Lucas?"

"What about the mug shots, any luck?"

She shook her head. "Nothing."

"Any other leads?"

"I told you about them finding their car."

"No, you didn't."

She shrugged. "Well, it's not really important. Chief Cooper mentioned it when he called about Simon yesterday. Anyhow, they think they found the car, but the license plates were gone. No papers. Nothing to link anyone to it."

His mouth tightened to a fine line. "I want to know these things right away, Cat. I don't like the idea of you screening out information, deciding whether or not it's important enough to tell me."

"But I didn't mean—" She stopped, sighed, then did what she occasionally did to avoid an argument. "I hear you," she said. "Anything else?"

He gestured with his head to the tray. "What's that for?"

"Wasn't that part of the difficulty, Zack missing lunch? Or are we deciding to forget about that?" She turned and went upstairs, thinking unhappily that the carjacking had really done a number on her family.

After Haley finally went inside to change into one of the new swimsuits, Lucas sat alone on the deck, feeling off kilter. Cat had a way of putting him on the defensive with just a look or tone, even when to anyone else she seemed to be agreeing and he was clearly in the right. And this time was no exception.

Two bogus phone calls, hardly a big deal. But what about those men he'd seen at the shopping plaza? He would have sworn it was those two misfits driving the Bronco, that the car was his car. And what about the runner he'd seen last night, the empty Snapple bottle left on his deck? Sure, he had managed to reason it all out in his head, but did he really believe his own reasoning? The fact was, it was dangerous out there, and Cat was refusing to acknowledge it. Despite the torment they'd been put through the other night.

With respect to Cat's inability to identify either of the two men, he hadn't expected more, but he supposed, he had hoped. Maybe he should have hired a private investigator. He'd thought of it then, but hadn't recovered enough to think straight. By now the trail was already getting cold . . .

"If you want, I can come back," the voice said.

He turned in sudden alarm. Simon was standing there, apparently having been waiting for a while. "No, it's okay," Lucas said. "Stay."

Simon nodded his head, looked down at his sneakers, then back at Lucas. "That offer you were talking about earlier? Well, if it's still open, I'd like to take you up on it."

Lucas smiled with pleasure. He liked the boy, and though he hadn't lived the same footloose life at his age, he might have if he'd had the right circumstances. Simon was a boy he could relate to, a boy he wouldn't mind doing something for.

But Lucas was pleased for other reasons as well. He experienced a great sense of relief—it would be nice having a strong, able young man around the house. At least, until he was back on his feet.

When Haley got down to the beach—wearing a white shirt open over her new yellow bikini—she looked around for Simon. The van was still parked street-side, so she knew he hadn't gone far. She'd wait for him to find her, she decided as she unfolded her blanket, spread it, then set down the 35-millimeter Kodak and portable radio. She turned the radio to a station with rock music and lay down.

Fifteen minutes later she sat up and looked around again. She still didn't see Simon. A little while later, Zack headed over to the blanket. "I thought you had to stay in your room," she said, hoping he wouldn't be around by the time Simon showed up.

He took out his Game Boy and started playing with it. "I can't go past the house for the rest of the day."

"Oh. Too bad. Have you seen Simon?"

"No, why?"

She shrugged. "Just wondering where he is."

"You like him, huh?"

She knew what he was asking, but she certainly had no intention of opening up that kind of information to her little brother. So she made her voice casual, "Sure I like him, he's a nice guy." He didn't say anything and she said, "Why, don't you?"

"I think he's kind of bossy."

"Why, what'd he do?"

"At the Cliffs. Just the way he acted—saying I'd better come home or else."

"What'd you expect him to say? I'm sure Daddy made it clear you'd be in trouble if you didn't get right back. Simon was trying to save you from being punished worse."

He was silent a long while, playing with his game, then he started whistling a tune that sounded like "Farmer in the Dell." "Will you stop that," she said, "I want to hear the music."

"Haley, are you scared for Mommy?" he asked.

She sighed. "Why, should I be?"

"Because that guy Earl wanted—"

She raised her hands. "Look, squirt, I don't want to talk about this, okay?"

He continued anyhow. "Well, suppose he decides to come back? Ever think of that, huh? Mommy says no way, but how can she know something like that?"

"I don't know, Zack, and I told you already I don't want to talk about it!"

"Why not?"

"Just because I don't!"

She made the music louder, then turned away and shut her eyes, closing him out. Though Zack was clearly a weirdo, he was kind of a cute one, and she really didn't mind putting up with him. Not like most of her friends, who would have gladly strangled their little brothers or sisters. So right now she didn't like herself much for being so mean to him. But it was partly his fault, too. Why did he always have to ask so many questions?

If she didn't talk about the carjacking, she wouldn't have to remember. And the last thing she wanted was to remember that awful night. How would she ever be able to really face Daddy again? Her whole life she'd thought of him as some kind of handsome superhero: fearless and strong and smart, able to do anything. But all that was a lie.

And that made her angry. Not at those pigs either, but at Daddy.

Chapter Seven

Cat had changed into a swimsuit and gone down the beach, and Lucas had moved himself in front of the television in the great room. So when the doorbell rang, Winnie went to answer it. She took the package from the delivery man and brought it to Lucas.

"Want me to open it?" she asked

"Go ahead."

She tore open the cardboard and took out two pieces of a fishing rod and a large aluminum tackle box. He took it from Winnie, put the rod together.

"A ten-footer, not bad," he said, giving it some wrist action in a cast. "Who's it from?"

"I don't see a card."

But when he opened the box—packed to capacity with just about every fishing item available—he came across the card. He pulled it from the envelope and read: *You know us, Lucas, don't know a house fly from a worm, but*

*we left it to my experts. Hope nothing's left out.
Love, Jack and Linda.*

Winnie left Lucas fiddling with the rod and
went downstairs to change over the laundry.
It wasn't until she had the clothes inside and
the dryer turned on that she even noticed Simon. Standing, his back to her, he was leaning
against the doorjamb, looking out at someone
or something on the beach. Winnie moved a
little, to get a better line of view. Cat was lying back in her chaise lounge nearby, her new
white two-piece suit shown to its best advantage on her long, lean body-to-die-for.

Suddenly Cat got up, walked to the deck
stairs, and climbed them—with Simon's stare
following all the way—then she went toward
the sliders and disappeared into the house.

"Oops, looks like the show's over," Winnie
said loud enough to be heard.

Surprised, Simon turned, smiled when he
saw her, not even bothering to protest.

Cat found him in the great room—a fishing
rod lying over the coffee table. Apparently
Jack had taken her suggestion. "A surf rod,
it's a nice one, Lucas."

He turned, lifted the tackle box to show her.
"Compliments of Jack and Linda. Every gad-
get on the market's here."

She nodded, went up to the chair across
from him, and sat on the arm. "Lucas, I don't

want to fight, please. You know, I can't bear being angry with you."

"Come here," he said, paying more attention to her new swimsuit than what she was saying.

She moved over to the sofa beside him, and he lowered his head, his mouth dipping into her cleavage, cool lips against her skin, while one hand slipped down to her hip, caressing it. "By the way, the swimsuit's dynamite. And you, too."

She sighed, a sensuous ache settling deep in her abdomen, though a part of her mindful that Winnie was somewhere in the house and could at any moment appear. But before she exerted the necessary discipline to push away, she heard the sliders close.

Lucas jumped, as did she. It was Simon, standing there, his hand flat on his crown, looking somewhat startled.

"Hey, look, sorry. I didn't mean—"

"Forget it," Lucas said.

"I just wanted to ask you if you had any other work you wanted done today."

"Nothing, Simon. You're now on play time." Cat was looking curious at their exchange, and Lucas said to her, "Meet our new hand, Cat. Simon's going to be working here. Rooming here, too."

"Really? That's great."

"Yeah, we thought we'd make it a combo—part work, part play."

Simon stood there, now looking happy.

"Have you got a swimsuit, Simon? she asked. He shook his head. "Well, go into the bedroom and take one out of Lucas's bottom dresser drawer." He started to protest, but she insisted. As he went to the other room, she called out, "Take in your belongings whenever you want, Simon. Upstairs, the last bedroom on the right. I'll have Winnie make up the bed for you." Then she looked at Lucas and whispered, "I think it's a marvelous idea."

"Yeah, why?"

She shrugged. "It's nice having him around, I don't know." Then slapping his arm playfully, she said, "What kind of foolish question is that?" She put her head against his chest, then pulled back some, smiling up at him. "Did you see his face, Lucas? I think it might have embarrassed him to see a couple of old fogies so preoccupied."

He kissed her forehead, then his glance strayed to her swimsuit. "Why don't you go like a good girl and put on something decent?" When she opened her mouth to protest, he put a finger to her lips. "Do it for me, babe. Okay?"

As he picked up his new rod, at first she thought it was her teasing comment that had upset him, but he wasn't upset—at least not that she could see. In fact, he seemed in fairly good spirits. Then why was he dismissing her like a child, sending her off to cover up? And for whose benefit, his or Simon's?

It was Zack who saw Simon heading to their blanket, and he nudged Haley who had been lying there for the past half hour as though sleeping. "There he is, Haley," he said.

Her eyes opened, and she turned. Then she stood up and waited for him to get there. "Where were you?" she asked as he came within hearing distance.

"Around."

She looked at him, noticing he was wearing her father's old blue and white striped swim trunks tied tight, but still big around the waist. She looked at the water—it had gotten windier and the waves were getting higher. She liked them that way.

"Want to go swimming?" Simon looked out at the water, not answering. "Simon?"

He turned toward her, and at first she thought he was going to say something about her swimsuit, but he didn't. Maybe because Zack was sitting there, all big ears perked up to hear everything being said. "What?" Simon said.

"Swimming. Want to go?"

"Okay." He took off his shirt—he had chest

hair, not lots, but just enough to look sufficiently sexy. He sat in the sand, pulled off his sneakers and socks.

She hadn't noticed it the day before, and she might not have noticed now if Zack hadn't opened his big mouth, but he did. "Hey, what's wrong with your toes, Simon?"

"What? Oh, that," Simon said, holding up his right foot for better viewing: two of the five toes on his right foot were bonded together by a thin layer of skin, only separate at the very tip. "Webbed toes, the Simon Bower trademark."

"Wow, like a duck's foot," Zack said, looking close, examining it. "Does it help you swim better?"

"Zack!" Haley scolded, trying to shut him up.

But Simon didn't seem to mind—in fact, he laughed off the question. "Maybe," he said. "But having never swam any other way, I don't know for sure."

"Does it hurt?"

"Only if you take a razor to it to try to separate them."

"Oh, gross, I'm going to be ill," Haley said, then took his arm and pulled him in the water. Zack followed them, suddenly interested in Simon because of his strange toes. Mom was always saying Zack was so smart, and

Haley supposed he was—but why couldn't he see that she and Simon wanted to be alone?

Cat decided not to make an issue of it. She simply slipped on one of her beach gowns over her swimsuit and began to prepare dinner. After making up the bed in the spare room for Simon, Winnie—who normally loved to stay for barbecues—refused Cat's invitation to join them and went home.

Dinner was simple—Cat made up hamburgers, put together a tossed salad, and set the table. With Lucas unable to do the usual honors, Cat had fully intended to handle the gas grill. But as it turned out, Simon stepped in and took over the job. "I figure I might as well do something useful for my room and board," he said, coming up behind her and taking the spatula from her hand.

"Room and board?" Haley said, looking at him.

"Simon's going to stay here awhile, do some work for us," Lucas said, reaching into his pocket. "Oh, before I forget." Taking out his key ring, he detached three keys—cellar, shed, and sliding doors—and handed them to Simon. "You're likely going to need these." Simon pulled out his own key ring and clipped them on.

Haley watched, her mouth open. "That is so excellent! Why didn't you say so before?"

Simon shrugged.

"For how long?" Zack asked.

"As long as he wants," Lucas said.

"Could he take out the Ping-Pong table?"

"I'm sure if you ask him," Lucas said. Then to Simon, "It's folded in the shed. We usually keep it out all summer."

"Guess what, Daddy, Simon has two toes webbed together. Right, Simon?"

Cat could see Lucas just about to scold Zack for his lack of tact when Simon cheerfully nodded, apparently used to the to-do over his peculiar toes, and Lucas, thank goodness, backed off. Cat watched as Simon laid the hamburgers on buns, put them on a plate, and set it on the deck table.

The kids were excited, happy, talkative. Was the food especially tasty? She wasn't sure. But even Zack's appetite seemed heartier than usual. And for the first time since the ordeal, Lucas looked almost relaxed. The bump on his forehead was beginning to go down, the bruises on his face and body fading. Even the soreness in her cheeks where the man's fingers had dug was almost gone.

Taking his van, Simon left soon after dinner. Though Cat spotted it from the kitchen window at ten parked right in back of their Jeep, he hadn't come inside by the time she and Lucas locked the doors at midnight.

The only real letdown to the evening was

when she and Lucas got into bed and she nuzzled up to him. Though she naturally understood he couldn't be as active sexually, there were—after all—other ways. But Lucas didn't seem at all interested. "Tired, sore, tense, not really much in the mood with my leg in this condition, babe," were his excuses. "Please try to understand."

Of course she would understand. What kind of wife would she be if she didn't?

Winnie's house was a neat five-room Cape with a sunny postage-stamp yard in Clinton. She never would have been able to swing the purchase without the extra money she earned cleaning the beach house. Even for the twenty-five-thousand-dollar down payment required at the time, she had come up five short and after much stalling and deliberation worked up the nerve to ask Lucas to lend it to her. She had it all worked out to the penny— the monthly payments she would send him, including interest and possible late fees, but he turned her down flat: nothing personal, he didn't believe in giving out loans, he said. The next morning he stopped at the diner and handed her an envelope containing five thousand dollars in cash—an early house gift.

She loved the house—the mortgage paid up, it was now all hers. So when she came home all upset over Simon, she retreated to her inner sanctum: herself and Luke, a rude and talkative parrot that was smarter than most people; a family portrait of the Marshalls on one end of the fireplace mantel, a picture of her cousin Audrey and her family on the other end. And all kinds of bit and pieces of Lucas around the rooms. Nothing could invade her world here.

Not until late that night did Winnie even bother to think about Simon again. At first when Cat had asked her to make up the spare bedroom for him, it really stuck in her craw, so much so that she'd refused to stay for the barbecue. Thinking about it now though, she was able to think a little more clearly. Still, what was the matter with Lucas and Cat? In this day and age, letting a stranger move into the house? Or was this just a matter of her being jealous seeing this kid suddenly step in like a newly self-appointed member of the Marshall family?

He had surely made a fool of her when she accused him of rifling through Lucas's dresser drawer, though it still seemed that way to her. And of course as payback, he had laid it on thick and nasty, cavalierly ordering her to serve him and Lucas lunch. And what about when he stood in the cellar doorway, watching Cat sunbathe? Come on, Winnie—Cat is gorgeous, a real sexpot, Winnie chided herself. What red-blooded male wouldn't take the time to stop and look at her?

So what was it about this kid that had set her teeth grinding right from the start? Was it something about him that reminded her of someone? A guy she had once dated? A guy who had come on strong or weird? Certainly she had run into enough of those. She started to go through her cluttered past, finally giving up forty-five minutes later when she succumbed to sleep.

Simon must have been sitting there awhile, but Zack didn't spot him until he got close to the Cliffs the next morning. The older boy was sitting high on a pile of rocks, knees up, eyes watching. "Hi, Simon," he said. "What're you doing over here?"

"Just taking an early run. I figured I'd see what's so hot about your place."

Zack climbed the rock and sat beside him. For a few minutes they sat silently, then Zack said, "Once I found a pine lizard on one of the dunes. I called him Frito. He was about this big." He held his hands about four inches apart.

"Yeah? What did you do with him?"

"Played with him, watched him. He was real fast and could climb just about anything I put in front of him. I fed him insects—he liked water bugs best."

"Where is he now?"

Zack shrugged. "That was last year. When I went home, I let him loose."

"I had a bull snake as a pet once—I named him Rex. I kept him in the cellar."

"Wow, a bull snake! They're as big as diamondback rattlers!"

"Nearly nine feet."

Zack had picked up plenty of green snakes and milk snakes, but they were different. A bull was one of the largest reptiles in North America. And they had a way of inhaling and exhaling that made them sound fierce.

"Did he ever bite you?"

Simon shook his head. "Not really, he got to know me. You'd be surprised how smart they are."

"What did you feed it?"

"Rats, mice. He'd find them in the cellar and swallow them whole. He was like a built-in exterminator."

"Neat. Didn't your folks—I mean, didn't your aunt mind he was down there?"

"She would have had a stroke if she knew, but she didn't. She was afraid of cellars anyway—you know, darkness, spiders, rats, and all the other bogeymen the old girl carried around in her overworked brain. If anything needed to be brought up or downstairs, she'd send me to do it." Simon smiled. "I probably should add—just between you and me, Zack—my aunt was off her rocker."

"Oh," he said, thinking he had never really met anyone crazy and wondering how a person like that would act. Kids of course said that a lot about other people, but only to put them down. But Simon wasn't exactly a kid, so he likely meant it. "What did you do with the snake when you left home?" he asked.

"Well, that was kind of a problem. I mean, I couldn't very well let it loose. Rex was used to being in captivity, having its meals more or less jump up on his plate. I thought about maybe giving him away to someone. But who? Hey, Zack, did you ever try to give a snake to someone as a birthday gift?" He shook his head, then sighed hopelessly. "So I did the most humane thing I could, I killed it."

They jogged back together, Simon reminding him he'd be in big trouble if he wasn't back in time for breakfast. Zack, though, couldn't keep up with Simon's speed. The best he could do was follow after him, and ended up about a hundred fifty paces behind Simon by the time he reached the beach house.

Zack kept thinking about the snake. He agreed—Simon had been in a real bind, but it sure couldn't have been easy to kill a pet snake. Simon was smart and interesting, way more interesting than he thought he'd be. With him getting along so well with Dad, Zack had never expected Simon to be his friend, too.

Geez, rats and a nine-foot snake crawling around loose in his cellar, maybe jumping out at you when you weren't even expecting it. Zack didn't say so, but he wondered if—like Simon's nutty aunt—Mom would have been scared, too.

Cat had just carried out a big breakfast tray as Simon returned from his run. She put a plate down for Lucas, herself, then Simon. "Come, have breakfast," she said, handing him a tall glass of juice. "Did you by any chance see a darling little redhead?" she asked, but before he got a chance to answer she saw Zack running toward the house. She set another place, and when he got closer to the deck, she called out, "Good morning, honey, you're right on time."

"I thought you were going to stay clear of that place," Lucas said, though Cat recalled Lucas's bottom-line demands were that Zack check in frequently and get home in time for meals.

"He was out running with me," Simon said before Zack could even answer. And by the way her little guy smiled up at him, Cat noticed that Simon had made himself a friend.

"Hey, Lucas, you get a chance to make up that list of chores?" Simon asked.

"I did, a nice long affair. You'll find the paper on my nightstand." Simon immediately began to get up, and Cat smiled: there was something dear about him, maybe because he so wanted to satisfy Lucas. But Lucas put his hand on his shoulder, stopping him from going anywhere. "Hey, slow down. Eat first."

The phone rang—Cat leaned over and picked up the cellular phone. She said hello a few times, but when there was no answer, she hung up. Lucas's brow furrowed.

"You know, that's happened a couple of times since we've been up here."

Cat shrugged. "Wrong number. Or else kids fooling around." Lucas didn't look convinced. In fact, he looked even more concerned, and she suddenly realized what was going on in his head. "Lucas, you can't possibly think it's—"

"I don't know what I think, I just find it odd is all."

Simon looked from one to the other, then entered his hat in the ring. "Listen, I don't mean to butt in or anything, but if you want to know how I see it . . ."

He stopped there, and Lucas looked at him. "Go ahead. How do you see it?"

"Well, I think those creeps are long gone. They'd be scared not to be, unless, of course, they're some sort of masochists, looking to get snagged. Besides, if they wanted for some crazy reason to pursue you guys—risk getting caught with your car and all—wouldn't they have shown their hands by now?"

It was the right thing to say, at least coming from Simon. Logical, not emotional. Lucas considered it, then seeming to agree, he nodded. And Cat breathed a sigh of relief.

Zack was careful on the way downstairs to make sure no one spotted him carrying the pillowcase. So when he reached the cellar and Simon stepped out from the tool room—a towel around his shoulders and his hair wet as though he'd taken a shower—Zack jumped about a foot. "Wow, I didn't expect you down here."

Simon gestured to the pillowcase, now behind his back. "So I see. What's that?"

"Nothing."

"It looks to me like something." He reached out his hand. "Let me see it, Zack."

When Zack didn't respond, he moved up closer. But Zack moved the other way. Finally turning, he set the bag over in a corner. "Just some laundry I was leaving down here for Winnie."

Simon went up and opened the pillowcase, and when he took a whiff of the contents, he pulled back. Zack felt like he would die, and

140

he might have, too, if not for the look on Simon's face. "Jesus, I thought it was a nuclear bomb or something. Why didn't you just come out and say what it was?"

He shrugged.

"The fewer people who know, the better, huh?" Simon said, dropping a hand to Zack's shoulder. "I guess you tend to forget that feeling. The thing is, you really shouldn't have to explain any of this to me, Zack, I peed my bed till I was eight."

"Really?"

"Yeah, really. But that information is confidential, stays strictly with me and you. Okay?"

Zack nodded, agreeing immediately. And in view of Simon's startling admission, he didn't feel quite so sick or ashamed as he had before. After all, if Simon peed his bed, there was hope for him, too. Look at Simon now: strong and smart and brave, no one, not in a hundred years, would ever guess his secret.

"Good. And you know what I'm going to do, *kemosabe—*"

"What's that mean?"

"Ever hear of the Lone Ranger?" Zack shook his head. "Well, he used to be on TV; he was a masked dude who helped the good guys. He had an Indian sidekick, Tonto, who called him *kemosabe.* It means friend in Indian." Simon pulled out the smelly sheet and pajamas from the pillowcase. "I'm going to take care of this wash personally. That way nobody, not even Winnie, gets to dig into your business. What do you say, *kemosabe*?"

"You would do that?"

"Sure. What are friends for? But I need one small favor in return."

"What is it?"

"No need to look so uptight, Zack. It's nothing bad and, for sure, nothing hard. What I want is for you to see that there's no more secrets between us."

"What do you mean?"

"I mean what it sounds like. You tell me what you're thinking or feeling, or anything else that's going on around here that I ought to know about. The thing is, I need to be kept well informed. Because there's no way I can do a good job of protecting you people if I'm kept in the dark."

Zack nodded. "Is that what your job really is here, Simon? To protect us?"

"Let's say, a little of everything."

"Why? Does my father think that something bad is going to happen again?"

"I didn't say that, did I? It's just that you never know, Zack. Better to be safe than sorry."

So that's what he was here for. Zack should have figured it out himself right off, the way a special guy like Simon was suddenly so

concerned about all of them. Mom especially—he saw Simon watch her a lot. Zack
doubted she even knew about the arrangement his father had made with Simon.

But he wouldn't let out his father's secret.
Why should he? It was for the good of them
all, wasn't it? Especially his mother. And con-
fiding in Simon wasn't so hard—he never
looked at Zack like he was a freak like Daddy
sometimes did. Besides, Simon knew how to
handle things. Just this morning he had
steered the conversation away from the Cliffs
so Daddy wouldn't end up mad.

Zack thanked Simon for taking over his
laundry, and Simon kind of ruffled his hair,
the way guys do in the movies to younger
guys they really like.

"Okay, now get going," Simon said. "I've
got to get busy, earn my keep."

Zack was already at the top of the stairs
when he thought of something, so he came
back down a few steps and leaned over the
railing. Simon was just tossing the sheets and
pillowcase in the washing machine, adding
detergent. "Hey, Simon, I looked in your room
this morning. You know, to say hi?"

Simon looked up at him, waiting.

"Well, it didn't look like you slept in the
bed."

"Is that right? Some reason you were
snooping around in my bedroom?"

Zack hadn't been really, but he guessed anyone listening in would have thought it looked that way. Sometimes he said dumb things or asked questions he shouldn't, embarrassing people or making them mad. It was something he should try to watch. At least that's what Haley was always telling him.

Chapter Eight

Haley couldn't believe she had slept so late. By the time she got up, everyone was finished with breakfast and out of the house. Simon—shirt off, muscles glistening under the sun and looking foxy in torn, grungy jeans—was kneeling on top of the shed, hammering shingles. She walked closer to watch. She could tell he saw her, but when he didn't acknowledge her, she said the first thing that came into her head. "Where did you get those shingles?"

"At the barbershop," he said, underlining how dumb a question it was. She was just about to walk away when he said, "Hey, you always sleep so much?"

She stopped, turned, wondering if that could have meant he missed her at breakfast. "Not always. But I couldn't get to sleep last night."

"Yeah, why?"

She shrugged. It wasn't that she couldn't

get to sleep as much as she hadn't. And the reason was simple, though she couldn't very well tell it to him. She had been waiting for Simon to get home. But he never did—at least, not before two o'clock when, no matter how hard she'd tried to stay awake, she couldn't. Had he been down at the public beach where all of the older kids hung out?

"So, what'd you do last night?" she asked, not believing she actually had the nerve to ask.

He could have told her to mind her own business, but he didn't. Instead he just looked at her. Like some super wonderful movie hero zeroing in on some groupie—his eyes laughing, his head shaking at the pathetic sight of her. Until suddenly he lost interest, and his eyes dismissed her totally.

She ran in the house—got her camera, loaded it, and came out. Standing only a few feet away from the shed, she called out. "Hey, Simon, look what I've got!" He looked up, his mouth dropped partially, caught by surprise.

She guessed she did it to embarrass him, she wasn't really sure. Simon made her think strange and act goofy. She wondered if anyone else had noticed that.

For the first time this season Cat had gotten into the water. It was unbearably cold until she got used to it, then finding it marvelously invigorating. When she came out, she spread a blanket on the sand and lay down on her belly.

Though she hadn't said so to Lucas, his newly acquired habit of tossing and turning all night, banging his leg cast against her, was cutting into her sleep time. Not that her nightmares these days hadn't already ruined her sleep. Now alone, soaking up the warmth of the sun, she fell off within minutes.

When she woke later, she lifted her watch from inside her leather sandal, checking the time, surprised to see she'd slept through lunch. Leaving the blanket, she hurried toward the house. She looked up onto the deck—Lucas, she noted, was no longer there. He was probably inside trying to put together a meal. He was competent and intelligent in so many areas, but in the confines of a kitchen, the man couldn't seem to manage anything more complicated than a plate in a microwave.

She passed the table tennis—somewhere between last night and now Simon had gotten it out, and judging by the piece of new wood at each of the legs, he took the initiative to cure the wobbling.

She grabbed shorts, underwear, and a top from the clothes dryer and hurried into the shower room. It wasn't until she stepped out of the stall and opened the linen cabinet door that she realized Winnie had forgotten to fill it with towels.

Dammit. She threw back the changing room curtain and without hesitating rushed to the dryer. She stopped only when she realized Simon was standing there. Her mouth opened, her arms went to her body in a hopeless attempt to cover her nudity, and before she could manage the awkward retreat, Simon pulled a fresh towel from the dryer and whipped it at her. She caught it, held it in front of her, then backed up into the shower room, finally yanking the curtain closed.

She stood stock-still a few moments, feeling foolish, embarrassed. Did her face look as hot as it felt? Okay, so he saw her in the raw, so what? Get over it, Cat, you're a big girl. She toweled herself dry, slipped on underwear and shorts and a tank top, then brushing her auburn hair into a ponytail, stepped out of the shower room. Simon—a load of clothes folded neatly on the utility table—was transferring a wet load into the dryer. He looked at her, stopped what he was doing, then said, "Look, Cat, about what just happened here—"

He seemed stuck for words, and she took over. "My fault, I should have looked first. But thanks for the towel." She would just have to get used to having another male animal around the house—one that wasn't family.

He sighed as though he'd been expecting a reprimand and was relieved not to get one. She quickly rinsed her swimsuit and tossed it over the clothesline.

"I saw you sleeping on the beach," he said. "Did you get in a swim, too?"

She nodded. "Yes, it's great. You ought to try it." She started upstairs. "I've got to make lunch. Lucas is likely to be on the warpath." As she got to the top stairs, she stopped, looked down. "By the way, Simon, there's no need for you to bother with laundry. Winnie comes three times a week. So put whatever needs washing either down here or in the bathroom hampers. It'll keep until she gets to it."

"Thanks." He gestured to the clothes now in the dryer. "This is a little different, though." She waited, and though he went on, he did so reluctantly. "You see, Zack wet his bed last night, and I guess he was embarrassed. Winnie wasn't around, and he didn't want you or his father knowing, so he kind of recruited me. I'd appreciate it if you didn't say anything, or at least not mention I did."

"No, of course not." Cat was a little surprised that Zack had so readily confided in Simon, particularly about so delicate a subject. And Zack ought to know better than to be embarrassed around her. But she guessed around Lucas he was a little different: Zack was always trying so hard to impress his father. In any event, it was admirable of Simon to come to his rescue.

What about Zack's bed-wetting? It was the second time since they had arrived here, at least that she was aware of. It was of course a natural reaction for a young child to experience after going through the kind of trauma Zack had been through. But she felt sure, as the memory of the abduction faded—and of course it would fade—the problem would go away.

It was after two when she walked into the kitchen—no one was around. Pinewood cabinet doors closed, the sink, dining-room table, and ceramic tile counters all spotless—no sign that Lucas or the kids had rifled through the kitchen, trying to come up with their own lunch. She found Lucas lying on his bed, his right, bad leg high on pillows and reading *Playboy.* "Found an old issue, huh?"

He looked up. "Hi, babe." Then looking at the magazine, "Oh, this? No, actually it's a current one. When Simon went to the lumber yard this morning to get shingles, I asked him to stop at the drugstore and pick it up for me."

She folded her arms over her chest, pressed her lips together in mock scolding. "My, my, aren't we sneaky?"

"How else am I to survive?"

She smiled. "Speaking of survival, you must be starved. The kids, too. How about I send Simon to hunt them up while I make us all some lunch?"

"Don't bother, we ate. Simon and the kids put out a superb spread while you were off on the beach. Salami, hot Italian bread with garlic and cheese, and a salad put together with close to everything not nailed to the refrigerator shelves, including that fried eggplant. *And* they cleaned up after. Winnie better watch her step around here—that boy is invaluable."

"Don't you dare say that to Winnie."

"I'm saying it to you, and I'm only joking. Winnie's a goddamned fixture here."

Cat went out to the kitchen to fix herself a sandwich or, if she got lucky, maybe some of those salad leftovers. All the while she was thinking about Simon. There was no doubt about it, the boy was multi-talented. Athletic, bright, as good in the kitchen as out—one of those new generation males she had heard so much about, the kind who apparently could do it all. Sensitive yet still very much a man. She could certainly see why Haley was attracted to him.

There was some salad left after all, right in front in a covered plastic bowl. Just waiting for her.

"I'm a game freak," Simon bragged to Lucas that night after dinner. It started with Zack taking out his 2100 chess computer and Simon offering to sit in for the computer. Simon was quite adept at chess, and after beating Zack solidly, he gave him a blow-by-blow analysis of their moves. Moves which somehow both Simon and Zack had kept filed in their heads in perfect order.

"Your first and fatal error was moving your knight out of the playing action," Simon said, picking up the piece and putting it on the fourth row at the edge of the chessboard. "A powerful center is what you're aiming for, *kemosabe*, and this won't hack it. Ergo, a knight on the rim is dim."

Zack grinned. Cat had never played chess, and Lucas knew only the basics, so on Zack's last birthday, Lucas had come home with a chess computer that could adapt to the skill of the player. And Zack truly loved it. But now he had someone who could talk to him about it, and he was clearly delighted.

"Do you have a rating from the Chess Federation?" Zack asked once the analysis was complete.

"I played in postal tournaments when I was a kid. You'd play a few games simultaneously, sending off your moves on postcards. I was sort of a natural, not really into studying games from books. I reached a rating of 2000, then sort of leveled off, never quite making it to a master I guess. That's why I quit."

Lucas nodded, clearly able to relate to that need to be number one. He was always initiating family tournaments of some kind or other: board games, fishing, swim meets, badminton, table tennis, volleyball, nothing too insignificant to be overlooked. "All right, game freak," Lucas said, "my real game is poker, but since we don't have enough players for that, how's your gin?"

"Not so bad," Simon said, a smile lodged and hiding somewhere between his lips.

"Yeah?" Lucas, hopping along on one crutch, headed toward the cabinet in the great room where trophies and cards and numerous board games were kept. Simon had gotten Lucas's competitive juices flowing, and before Cat knew what was happening, the two of them were sitting across from each other heavy into a game of gin. They each won two hands, and if not for Haley getting angry, arguing that it wasn't fair to choose something they couldn't all join in on, Lucas would have demanded the tiebreaker then and there.

As it was, he relented and told Haley to go choose a game. She went for the Balderdash. She was just beginning to hand out the pencils and papers, and Zack had gone back to the cabinet to fetch the dictionary, when they heard a noise from the cellar. Like something had dropped. She looked at Lucas, who sprang to his feet.

Listening . . .

The next noise came, which sent Lucas heading to the bedroom to get the gun. "Call the police," he said to Cat. Looking at the kids, he hissed, "Get upstairs, both of you!" Seeing their father in such a state, they scurried upstairs, stopping when they reached the landing. There, they huddled together to watch.

"I'm scared, honey," Cat said.

"Dammit, Cat," he shouted from the bedroom. "Call!"

She picked up the receiver, pressed in the operator, and though her mind felt fuzzy, the right words managed to come out. "This is Cat Marshall, 12 Shore Lane. At Kelsy Point. Please send someone out here, we have an intruder!"

Even before she put down the phone, she started yelling at Lucas, who was already heading with the revolver to the cellar door. "Are you crazy, Lucas? You won't make those stairs! And the gun . . . No, please, wait for the police!"

But already Simon was standing in front of him, blocking him from going forward. "Hey, Lucas, there's steep stairs, you've got a bum leg, you'll end up face first," he said, trying to keep his argument reasonable and calm. "Come on, it's likely a loose shelf that fell, something like that. Put the damned gun away, will you?" As he was saying the words, he reached down, lifted one of his jeans legs, and, shocking Cat, pulled a black-handled knife from a small sheath strapped to his leg. "Let me go see," he said.

"Let's wait—" Cat began, but she got no further than that in trying to hold him back and neither did Lucas. Simon opened the door and, without switching the lights on, slid through and closed the door behind him. They both stood still, waiting while it got so quiet, she thought she would jump out of her skin.

He was alone down there, in the pitch-dark, unable to see where he was going. Suppose he got knocked out or killed? Oh, dear, why couldn't he have waited for the police? But she had to admit she'd rather have Simon down there than Lucas.

Suddenly there was a loud squeal, then a bang, another louder bang, another squeal, then Simon shouting up, "Hey, someone upstairs turn on the lights!"

Simon emerged from the cellar, a dead raccoon hanging like a hideous trophy from his knife.

In fear, it had attacked Simon, and he'd

grabbed it, clenched it in his fist, smashing it against the cement wall. Then as the creature got ready to spring once again, Simon stopped it with his knife, cutting it down to its bloody miserable death. Lucas should have considered the possibility of an innocent animal getting trapped in the cellar accidentally—raccoons were known to come out from their hiding at night and walk along the water's edge in search of food.

But that fear of being attacked again—those men coming back to finish the job they'd begun—was what had put Lucas in such a state. And once he had panicked, Cat had, too. And the kids, what kind of fear trip was he laying on them? Chief Cooper—when he showed up at the beach house a good thirty-five minutes after Cat's telephone call—admitted that though they hadn't given up the search for the men or the automobile, the possibility of now finding them was flimsy.

"Besides," Cooper said, "if they were going to make a move toward you or your family, Mr. Marshall, I would have thought they'd have done it by now."

Exactly what Simon had said, and it still made sense. What made no sense was the fear. The irrational fear that was becoming worse rather than better.

"I guess I really screwed up a good evening," Lucas said after Simon and the kids had gone off and he and Cat were getting ready for bed. The doors were all locked and doubled bolted. Lucas had asked Simon to make it a habit to check the cellar door every evening after everyone was in from the beach.

"Not your fault," Cat said. "After all, there was a noise."

"But the kids." He stopped, sighed. "And Simon going through that. Raccoons are strong, vicious, too, when threatened. He could have been bitten."

Cat nodded, pulled the blanket up over them, looking tense and tired. "I was astonished when Simon pulled out that knife. Did you see the blade on it?"

"It's a hunting knife, Cat. A perfectly reasonable tool for him to be carrying."

Besides, it's dangerous out there in the world, Lucas thought. Very dangerous. He'd said it once before, probably more than once . . . But Cat didn't want to hear.

Zack still felt as though his mouth were full of cotton, though he had drank two full glasses of water before finally turning off the overhead light in his bedroom. After the last trip to the bathroom, Simon came in and sat on the edge of his bed.

"How you doing, kid?"

Zack nodded. "Were you scared. . . . you know, going down into the cellar alone?"

"Not really. I didn't think there was anything dangerous down there."

"But the raccoon, that could have bit you."

"I'm pretty fast."

"What if there had been a man down there? Maybe those same men?"

"I had the knife. Besides, better me than your father. He could have hurt himself. His leg and all, then carrying that gun. I wouldn't want him to fall, shoot himself accidentally."

"You know what I thought, Simon?"

"What?"

"That we were all going to get murdered. I once saw a movie where the bad guy cut the telephone wires from outside before he broke into the house. The mother and kid ran upstairs to hide in the closet. But there wasn't any safe place in the whole house, the bad guy hunted them down and shot them." Tears filled his eyes, and as a couple started down his face, he swiped them away with his fists.

"Hey, that doesn't say a hell of a lot for me, does it?" Simon said. Zack just looked at him, not quite getting what he meant. "Do you think I'd just sit back and let that happen? Don't you think I'd step in—spread my hands around the person's neck and snap it?"

"Could you really do that?"

"What do you think?"

"What about my mother?"

"What about her?"

"Suppose someone tries to get her?"

"I told you, *kemosabe*, I'm here. And I'm not going anyplace."

"Are you stronger than my dad?"

Simon stood up—as he did, Zack reached up and wrapped his arms around his neck. Simon let them stay a minute, then disentangled his arms, placing them back on the blanket.

"Go to bed, Zack."

Simon was talking to Zack real soft, and Haley didn't want to interrupt. Poor Zack hadn't been having an easy time of it lately, and she hadn't been much help to him. But right now she was hurting, too, and it was seeming like forever until Simon came out of Zack's room. "What were you telling him?" she asked when he got to the hall.

"Nothing. Why, what do you want?"

"Can we go in your room?"

He hesitated, then went in there with her. Other than a green duffel bag sitting on the dresser, there was no sign that it was Simon's bedroom. "I'm scared," she said.

"Of what?"

"Of everything, I don't know."

"I saw your dad try to talk to you after the cops took off. But you turned him off. Why didn't you lay this fear on him?" She shrugged. "So what do you want from me?"

"I don't know." Her hands were shaking, she felt like she was going to vomit. She probably shouldn't have bothered him. But then he stuck his hand in his pocket and brought out a joint. He lit it, sucked in deeply, then holding it in, he blew the smoke out the open bedroom window. Finally he gave it to her.

"You're a quick learner, aren't you?" he said, watching her, then taking it back.

"Why is Daddy so scared?" she asked, once she had calmed down a little.

'Those guys beating on him. Not being able to protect his family. A tough thing to go through."

She took the joint again from his hand and took another hit. "It's never going to be the same again. Is it, Simon?" It was almost a joke her asking him that. How would he know what the same was anyway? He hardly even knew them. Still something about Simon made you believe he knew. They finished the joint and she did feel a whole lot calmer.

The next morning Zack was awake, dressed in swim trunks, and waiting forty-five minutes on the top-floor landing before he heard Simon come up from the cellar shower. By the time Zack got to the kitchen, Simon was already pouring himself orange juice. When he saw Zack, he took down another glass from the cabinet.

"Want to go down to the Cliffs with me?" Zack asked. "I've got something real neat I want to show you." He had never shown his secret hiding place to anyone, not even his new friend Andy. But he had thought about the promise he'd made just yesterday to Simon, and wanted to keep to his bargain.

Simon finished his juice, then looking toward Lucas and Cat's closed bedroom door, walked closer to the outside kitchen door. Zack followed. "Did you pee last night?"

"Yeah. Want me to get the sheet?"

"You didn't plan on leaving it there, did you?"

Zack hurried down with the wet sheet and Simon stashed it temporarily in the tool room. Then Simon sent him back to his room to make his bed and take a shower. And it wasn't until after they had run all the way to the Cliffs, collapsed on a rock to catch their breaths, that Simon brought up the subject again.

"From here on, don't drink a lot before you go to bed?" he said.

"Why?"

"You want to pee your bed forever?"

He shook his head.

"Then listen to what I say." He gestured to his wrist. "You have a watch?"

"Yeah, why?"

"I want you to wear it from now on. That

161

way you'll know what time it is, and what time you'll have to start back to make it home in time for meals."

"So I won't get in trouble with my dad?"

"So you won't get in trouble with me."

But Simon had a smile on his face when he was saying it, and Zack took it to mean he was fooling around. So he came back with, "You're not exactly a boss, you know."

Simon sat forward, grabbed him by the shoulders, and glared at him, and Zack gasped. Then just as suddenly as the hands grabbed him, they pulled away. "Hey, take it easy, Zack," Simon said. "For a second there I thought you were taking me seriously."

Zack didn't bother to tell him he had. If he admitted that, Simon would take him for the biggest wimp on two feet. It's just that Simon moved quick as lightning, flitting from one thing to another, and a person had to keep his brain going at top speed to keep up.

Simon dropped his arm over his shoulder, and his tone became very somber. "Zack, ever hear the game Simon Says?"

"Sure."

"Good," he said. "Then I don't have to explain that when Simon says to do something, he really means business. I have to be able to count on you to obey orders. For instance, in case an emergency crops up. Not that I expect one, but who can tell about these things?"

Zack was studying Simon's intense expression, trying to analyze what he meant, when suddenly a big grin spread across Simon's face and he asked, "Now, where the heck is that neat hiding place you were going to show me?"

He hadn't even said it was a hiding place, but Simon knew these things.

Irritable from the moment he woke, Lucas refused breakfast and stayed in bed. So while Simon and Zack ate on the deck, Cat brought in a tray with his newspaper. "Just in case you get hungry," she said. He looked at her, nodded, then returned his attention to the television.

"If you want to get out of bed, I can move the nightstand and easy chair closer to the window. That way you can get some sun on you."

"If I wanted sun, I'd go outside."

She set the tray down, then sat on the edge of the bed. "Are you hurting, sweetheart?"

He picked up the remote, pressed in another channel, then picked up the newspaper. "I'm fine, Cat."

"Then this is about last night?"

He whipped the paper against the mattress, making her jump. "Look, is this going to be twenty questions? Because if so, I ought to warn you now, I'm not in the mood."

He opened the newspaper, drew it to his face, closing her out. She sat for a few moments, waiting. But when there was nothing forthcoming, she made another attempt. "Would you like me to join you? I could bring in another tray. And we could read the comics out loud. Lucas, remember how we used to do that Sunday mornings?"

He lowered the paper slightly, only enough so she could see his eyes. They were bloodshot, indicating too little sleep. "Look, do me a favor, Cat. Go outside and eat with the kids. I'll be fine here alone. I just need a little time. Okay?"

She had her coffee sitting on the stool at the kitchen counter, no longer much in the mood for company herself. But when Winnie came downstairs to clean the kitchen, she found herself describing the commotion from the night before. She told her the entire story, right down to Chief Cooper showing up.

Then she backtracked. "There was a noise in the basement, of course. All of us heard it. It's just that Lucas panicked. And then we all panicked along with him." She thought about it a moment, then corrected herself. "Actually, that's not completely true—Simon didn't. If not for him going down to investigate, I'm afraid Lucas would have gone down himself. Broken leg, gun, and all."

"What is the kid doing carrying a knife?"

"You haven't heard a word I said."

"Not true, I've heard everything. I was just curious about the knife is all."

"Actually, I was, too. Lucas says it's a hunting and fishing knife. And considering Simon's been living outdoors, it makes perfect sense he would carry it."

"Isn't Davy Crockett sleeping in now?"

"Winnie, you're bad."

"Just asking a question."

"Well, actually, I don't know if he's sleeping in. For all I know, he sleeps on the beach. You'd know better that I. What does his room look like?"

"A duffel bag, that's it. The bed is always made."

She studied Winnie's expression, then said, "You don't like Simon, do you?"

"No. And if you're going to ask why, don't. I'm not certain myself—other than it occurs to me, he looks or maybe acts like some slippery character out of my past."

Cat smiled. According to Lucas, Winnie in her younger days had been quite the swinger. "Might we have to line up all the men in the state to find out which one?"

"The county ought to do just fine," she said, always sticking to her straight-character routine. She wiped the counter down, hung the wet dishrag over the faucet spout, then lifted a full laundry bag off the step stool. "I'm off to the wash. Anything of yours or Lucas's not there that needs doing?"

"It's all downstairs in the basket. Winnie, did Zack wet his bed last night?"

She shook her hear. "I checked the hamper—no sheets. The bed was made, but I double-checked, and it was dry."

Cat nodded, then raising her finger to stop Winnie. "Oh, yes, before I forget. Please see to the linen cupboard in the shower room. It's out of towels."

"That's impossible. I just filled—"

"Trust me. I was caught yesterday without one."

Winnie shook her head, grumbling as she made her way downstairs. "What are we running here, some kind of swim club?"

Cat poured herself another cup of coffee. After the traumatic episode last night, she had expected Zack to be agitated. But this morning, coming back from his run with Simon, he looked in good spirits. And she supposed it was a good sign, too, that he hadn't wet his bed.

Haley, though, was another story entirely. Cat looked down at her watch—it was nearly ten-thirty. What in the world was she doing still sleeping?

Chapter Nine

She hadn't gotten to sleep until late. Simon had taken only a couple of hits—the rest of the joint she had smoked herself. Once she had gotten out of that silly, weepy state, she'd been eager to talk, and she begged Simon to stay. But he couldn't stand being cooped up, he said he wanted to get out into the fresh air. So with his arm draped over her shoulder, he walked her to her bedroom, then took off. Out of her bedroom window, she could see him walk down the beach, then disappear into the night.

She thought of all this as she was being awakened now: she thought at first it might be Simon at her side shaking her shoulder and fought furiously to open her eyes. But when she did finally open them, she saw her mother.

"What do you want, Mom?" she asked, annoyed.

"Are you feeling ill?"

She shook her head. "I was tired is all." Exerting a lot of effort, she pulled herself up. "What time is it anyhow?"

"Nearly eleven. Everyone's been up for hours. I was afraid to let you go on sleeping."

"Lots of people sleep late, Mom. It's not exactly a disease."

"Maybe not, but it could be a symptom of illness. What time did you get to bed?"

"Not till real late."

"Then I suppose that explains it. Because of what happened last night?"

She shrugged—her head was pounding. The last thing she needed now was a ton of questions. "I guess, I don't know. Some. Mom, would you just leave me alone?"

"Haley, it dawned on me a little earlier . . . Well, remember how Daddy promised that you could invite one of your friends to come up for a few days?"

She nodded. She hadn't even thought about her friends. They seemed so far away, so distant. And so young, too. Like if she ran into them, she wasn't sure if they'd have anything to talk about. "Yeah, I remember," she said. "Why?"

"I was just thinking, maybe now would be a good time to take him up on it."

She lied to her mother, told her she would consider the idea, but she had no intention of asking anyone to the beach house. Right now all she wanted to do was concentrate on Simon. Look at him, talk to him, be with him. It was so weird how a person's entire life could change so much so quick.

She hadn't used her catamaran or surfboard once yet this year. But she wondered if she asked real nice, Simon might take her out on the cabin cruiser this afternoon.

He was just finishing up the roof on the shed, nailing up the drainpipes, when she got there. But he looked up right away. "Where have you been?"

"Sleeping." He shook his head, looking almost as upset by it as her mother. But she didn't find his concern at all annoying. "Why, what's wrong?"

"I need to talk to you," he said.

It couldn't have been better had she planned it, he opened it right up for her. "Okay," she said after consideration. "How about taking me out on the boat?"

He didn't take long to agree. "Okay. Go inside and make us lunch." She started to run, but he called her back. "Ask your folks if it's okay."

"They won't mind."

"Did you hear what I said?"

"Okay, okay, I'll ask," she said, only to make him feel better. Daddy being the first one she encountered in front of the television in the great room, she asked him.

"Sure, no problem," he said in a voice that sounded weak and kind of flat and not at all like him.

Cat came in from the bedroom wearing her new white bikini. "Sounds like fun, Haley."

Naturally, of course, they approved—Simon was taking her. Simon was super bright and perceptive about lots of things, but when it came to her parents he was a numbskull. Couldn't he see how much her folks liked and trusted him?

Only an hour ago, the child had seemed like she needed a dose of vitamin B12, but now she was raring to go deep-sea fishing with Simon. Cat headed to the water, leaving Haley busy putting together a picnic basket. Maybe a swim before lunch would pick her up. Maybe a walk along the beach.

As she reached the surf, she turned and noticed Simon looking her way. She waved to him, then glanced toward the deck to see if Lucas had come outdoors—he hadn't.

Was he going to sulk forever because of an animal in the cellar? So it had frightened him, so what? Even Simon had thought enough of the danger to take out his hunting knife. For God's sake, why couldn't he come to grips with it?

Deciding to get that first shock behind her, she turned back to the water, ran, and dived in. Once her body adjusted to the cold, she swam along the coastline, not stopping until she'd gone about a quarter of a mile, ending up not far from the Lansings' beach house.

She waded to shore, seeing if she could spot Zack, who was more than likely nearby playing with Andy. But she didn't see either of the boys. Out of breath, she sat on the sand, her arms stretched back, balancing. She looked toward their property. In the distance she could make out Simon and Haley carrying the picnic basket and drink toward the boat, him helping her get on board.

This time they headed straight for the island. When they got there, Haley leaned toward him to put her hand in his pocket. "Did you bring the smoke?"

He raised his arms, then pulled away. "Whoa, take it easy. Okay? Not so fast." He sat down, leaning back on one elbow, looking at her and frowning.

She stood over him, glaring at him with impatience. "What is wrong?"

"You're sleeping way too much. You're going to make your folks suspicious."

"What do you want me to do? Not sleep?"

"I want you to wake up at a reasonable

171

time. If you can't, maybe it means you shouldn't be fooling around with this stuff."

"You turned me on to it. So it's no big deal, and I like it. Now you're saying, don't?"

"I'm saying, learn to handle it. Or stay away from it."

"Okay, okay," she said, making an exaggerated bow. Then falling to the sand beside him, "If it'll make you happy, I won't stay in bed so late. Now, your kingship, can I have some?"

They were on their fourth hit when Haley got to feeling talkative. "You know, Lucas and Cat aren't my real parents," she said, and could see surprise show in Simon's eyes. "They adopted me when I was less than two years old. Daddy's my real uncle, though. My mother was his kid sister."

"Yeah?" he said, thinking about it. "Well, you'd never figure it by the way they treat you."

"She and my real father were killed driving through Scotland. They were on vacation. I was supposed to go with them, but then at the last minute they decided to leave me with a sitter. Do you think maybe they had a premonition?"

He shrugged, and they sat for a little while not saying anything. He was right, of course. She never felt like she didn't belong with Lucas and Cat. She couldn't even remember her real parents. When they died, she had been too young to feel sad or lonely or even scared. The kinds of feelings she was having these days.

"He's different," she said finally.

"Who?"

"Lucas. My father. Ever since he was beat up."

"Yeah. How?"

She shrugged, looked down at the sand, then picked up handfuls and let the grains trickle through her fingers. "He used to be so sure about everything. I thought he could be or do anything. You know what I mean, don't you? And now, well—" She sighed, then looking at Simon. "It scares me."

"What scares you?"

"I don't know," she said, then suddenly out of nowhere, she began to giggle.

"What?"

It took her a full minute before she could get a hold of herself enough to explain. "I was just remembering that look on my mother's face when you pulled up your pants leg and took out your hunting knife. I mean, there's Dad, all wild-eyed and looking possessed like he was ready to smash through the door, leap downstairs, and shoot up the place. But still your silly old fishing knife shook her!"

He began to laugh, too, and as she watched his handsome features contort and his laughter intensify, she realized something that was even scarier: the only time she felt really safe these days was when Simon was around. She grabbed his hand with both her hands and squeezed it so hard, her hands hurt.

"Promise me you won't leave us, Simon," she said. "Please."

A while later, Simon started asking her a bunch of questions. He had gone swimming—and she had snuck out his wallet, looking for pictures of girls, but hadn't found any. They had taken snapshots of each other, dug a huge sand castle and deep moat. He had carried her piggyback around the whole island, and they had ended up moosing out on all the food in the picnic basket. Now she was ready to take a nap, and let herself fall back onto the sand.

"Uh-uh, no," she replied to about his fourth question. "Would you believe I don't even want to talk?"

"Haley doesn't want to talk? Whoa, I'm calling a doctor!" Simon said, cupping his hands over his mouth like a bullhorn and shouting. "Attention, attention, is there a doctor in the house?"

The scene was too funny and she started to giggle again. Then he put his finger on her waist and began tickling her. "Stop it!" she pleaded between spasms of laughter.

"Only if you'll answer my questions."

"Okay, okay, I will."

Finally catching her breath, she said, "Okay. What do you want to know?"

"Everything. Tell me about your other house in Massachusetts. In Greenfield."

"It has twelve rooms, two acres of land. A pool, a tennis court, a weight room, a sauna."

"You're lying."

She shrugged. "Why would I lie?"

"I don't know. Were you always so rich?"

"I don't know, I guess."

"What does it feel like being rich?"

She shrugged. "It really doesn't feel like anything. I mean, what should it feel like? What was your house like?"

"Not like that."

The way he said it made her decide not to follow up on that question. It was funny—most of the kids she knew, she guessed, were rich, though she never really stopped to think about it before now. "What happened to your folks?" she asked.

"They took a powder."

"What does that mean?"

"My father didn't care if I lived or died. My mother cared, at least long enough to see me born. Though once that was done, she decided to slit her wrists."

Haley drew in her breath—she'd heard of people committing suicide, but never anyone she knew. And though she'd never known Simon's mother, in a way it was like she did because she knew Simon. And the idea of her doing such a thing was shocking.

"I usually don't tell anyone about that," he said, looking as though he had said something he shouldn't have.

"Don't worry, I won't tell. Honest."

He seemed to relax at her saying that and she realized he had confided in her. No one else but her. And maybe because of that one little bit of sharing, he started to tell more. "I was six months old when it happened. Want to know why?"

Haley nodded, and he said, "Because one day she got a whiff of my diaper." He began to laugh, and though she knew he wasn't really laughing deep down, she could understand him trying to turn it into a joke, pretending it didn't matter. But with the drugs in her system, she easily joined in with his laughter.

He continued to ask more questions about her family. As boring as the subject was, he seemed to be really interested in it. But she did not want to talk about what it was like growing up with Lucas as a father—the nice houses, good schools, vacations . . . She came back at him with a question: "Simon, do you think I'm pretty?" Suddenly he fell silent. If she could have fallen through the sand and landed in China, she would have gladly done so. But of course she couldn't. So all that was left was to sit and wait for an answer that didn't come.

Finally, leaving everything, she raced back to the boat and climbed aboard, sitting at the stern with her knees up to her chin and waiting while Simon took his sweet time in picking up their junk and bringing it back on board. He deposited the picnic stuff on the floor, then lifted the anchor. She heard the motor start.

Dammit, she had spoiled everything. Why had she gone and opened her big mouth? She knew she had no right to be mad at him either. After all, it wasn't like he had come out and said she was a dog or anything. Only his silence said that.

Once Simon anchored at the fishing spot—she had expected he'd head straight home—he said to her, "Hey, I didn't mean to hurt your feelings, Haley."

"Don't worry, you didn't," she shot back, not wishing to be humiliated more.

"Well, you sure are acting like it."

"Am I?"

A long silence, then he said, "Look, Haley, you're beautiful. Is that what you want me to say?"

"Do you mean it?"

"I said it, didn't I?"

It was what she wanted to hear—and though he seemed annoyed at her for pushing him, suddenly everything was okay, in fact, it was wonderful. He didn't have to say anything else, and he didn't. And she didn't get up the nerve to look at him either.

They fished silently, exchanging only a couple of words here and there when Simon reeled in three good-sized flounders. She caught nothing, but even that couldn't spoil the compliment. Even when Simon later decided the boat was a pigsty, it was her fault, and she should clean it. She would rather have taken a nap, but she cleaned instead—it wasn't worth getting him mad.

He took a few more hits of smoke, but kept the joint to himself, saying she'd had enough. Before they headed back, he took out a bottle of eyedrops from his pocket, used it on himself, then made her sit still while he dosed her.

The next night, everyone—with the exception of Lucas who was barely civil these days, much less sociable—was congregated around the dining-room table playing the board game Risk. A car horn began to honk. Immediately Cat was reminded of their first night at the beach house. She saw Lucas put down the newspaper, tense up. Before he could get to his feet, Simon intercepted.

"Hey, no problem, Lucas," he said. "You read the paper, I'll go see to it."

But still they all followed him to the window: again the scenario was the same—the horn had ceased, and with the brights on and the distance it was from the house, it was impossible to see the car clearly. "This happened our first night here," Lucas said. "I think maybe this time we ought to call the police."

"Wait, give me a few minutes to check it out," Simon said, already heading for the door.

Lucas's halfhearted plea didn't stop him. Using a crutch, though, he headed to the telephone. "I don't like this, Cat, it's far too much of a coincidence."

"Maybe we should just wait and see," she said, wanting to look at Lucas but intent on keeping her eyes on Simon through the window. Simon had just gotten to the car when Lucas began dialing. "Wait, don't!" she said, finally turning to Lucas, and he held the receiver away from his ear. "Whoever it is, Simon is standing there talking to him. Everything seems—" A voice came through the phone, and Lucas hesitated a moment, then hung up.

Cat heard a motor start, and she looked back out the window. Simon stepped away from the car, and it backed down the road.

"It's all okay, Lucas," she said, turning. "They've—"

But he had already gone into the bedroom.

A minute later Simon was back, "Well, they're history," he said, looking around the room for Lucas. When he didn't see him, he looked at her.

"He went to his room," she said.

"What's wrong? Is he okay?"

"Oh, yeah, sure. He's just tired," she said. She was lying, and Simon knew it.

"Well, who was it?" Haley asked impatiently.

Simon walked toward the game table. "Just a couple of kids wanting to park. They thought it might be a good spot. I told them to cross it off their list."

"I bet they about died when you caught them," Haley said.

"Let's go back to the game," Zack snapped, as though he wanted to end all the talk.

Simon looked at Cat, who was still thinking about Lucas and the young parkers Simon had just chased away. She thought it was odd that parkers would beep the horn at all, but with all the comments circulating, she didn't bother to say so. Besides, what did it really matter?

The kids hadn't begun to play the game and she realized they were waiting for her to join them. "You guys go ahead and play. Count me out, though, I have a headache."

She went to the bathroom and took some aspirin. Refilling the glass, she took the water and aspirin in to Lucas. She set the glass on the nightstand and handed the pills to him.

"Will you leave me the hell alone!" he shouted, his arm coming down and his hand swinging, knocking the bottle and loose aspirins out of her hand and across the room.

Her mouth dropped. She stood there, staring, flabbergasted. He'd never done anything like that before, or had even come close. And though he now looked as stunned as she felt, it wasn't nearly comfort enough. She bolted out of the bedroom. Past the children, out of the house, running down to the sandy beach, not letting her tears start to fall until her bare feet reached the water.

God, what was happening to them?

Under the full moon, she walked for miles along the beach, not getting back to the house until much later. By that time the lights were off, all but those on the deck, the bathroom, and a dimmed one in the great room. Everyone had gone to sleep. No, not quite everyone. She didn't see Simon at first—he was standing at the dock, apparently having been watching out for her for some time.

When he saw her look in his direction, he

quickly turned away to face the water. Not
wanting to be conspicuous. Not wanting to
invade her privacy.

Chapter Ten

Lucas tossed and turned more than ever that night, or maybe Cat's own inability to sleep was what forced her to notice. Every foghorn, every crick and croak and yawn that normally vanished into the night, she heard, and Lucas heard, too. She would see his head lift a bit from the pillow to listen. And because she always so relied on Lucas's strength, his fears were becoming hers.

They received another phone call in the next few days, and it put Lucas on edge all over again. Though she encouraged him to take a tranquilizer more than once, he refused. Simon even tried to get him to go to the dock to try out his new fishing rod, but he declined, preferring to sit in the house quietly and watch television.

When Cat took Lucas to Dr. Robbins's private office in town to have his leg checked—the cast would need to stay on another three weeks as it turned out—she finally asked for help. While Lucas was in the waiting room, she excused herself, claiming she needed to fill out some insurance papers with the secretary. Instead she got to see the doctor alone, and did her best to explain what was going on.

Dr. Robbins sat back, his square fingers absently rubbing upward on his bearded chin. "Understand, your husband suffered severe trauma, Mrs. Marshall. Forget the cuts and bruises and leg for a minute. It's the rest that's tough to get rid of: the torment of being manipulated and controlled by strangers. Seeing your family at their mercy, having them see you so vulnerable. Fortunately, there was no sexual assault on him, but the humiliation he suffered can surely be compared to rape. You see, it's all about power and control."

Lucas raped? She had come close to being raped, but Lucas? It had never once occurred to her. Had it occurred to him? She hadn't encouraged him to talk about it, thinking that the less talked about, the sooner he would recover.

"What do you suggest I do?"

He shrugged. "Give it a little while longer, I'd say. As time passes, our defense mechanisms usually kick in, pushing these kind of horrors to the background. The faces of the men, even the incident itself, will become less vivid, more a dream than real. And as that occurs, his confidence should return. Of course, if you see it isn't improving any, then you might want to seek out a therapist. Sometimes finding out that the reaction you're experiencing is not all that unusual helps a person." He looked at his watch, then closing Lucas's thin file, looked back at her. "How are the children doing?"

"Our little boy wet his bed a couple of times, expressed some questions and fears about sex, rape specifically. But both Lucas and I talked to him. Our daughter is not so quick to talk, she likes to work things out herself. In any event, we're at our summer place, and the kids love it—there's lots for them to do. Which of course makes it all that much easier to forget and move on. Also, we have a nice young man staying with us this summer. Nineteen. Simon is seeing to the upkeep of the house, things Lucas can't manage right now. He does a lot of activities with the kids, too. Actually, we're all quite fond of him."

"Good, in fact, better than good. I would think that would do a lot to ease Mr. Marshall's mind. Another man around the house, that extra little bit of security."

"Oh, yes. Definitely. He's big, too. Strong."

Dr. Robbins smiled. "And what about you?"

"Me?" Cat shrugged. "Well, if you mean does Simon's being there help me, it most as-

suredly does. In fact, at this point I don't
know what we'd do if he decided to leave.
But I'd be lying to say that I don't still get
tense, even frightened, particularly when
Lucas does. Rather than being able to provide
him a calming influence, his reaction more often influences me. And though I don't remember them much by morning, I've been
having nightmares."

He wrote out a prescription on his pad and
handed it to her. "This tranquilizer is milder
than what I prescribed for your husband. But
if you begin feeling anxious, take one. Despite
your husband's apparent philosophy, I will
assure you, it's not a blemish on your character."

"Lucas, would you consider seeing a therapist?" she asked on the way to the pharmacy,
though she knew how Lucas would despise
the idea.

"No. Why do you ask?"

"I just thought ... You've just been so on
edge lately."

"Did you discuss this with the doctor?"

"No, of course not ..." A few moments of
silence, then, "Perhaps just one or two ses-
sions, someone you can open up to, Lucas—"

"I said no! Leave it at that."

She entered the shopping plaza, pulled in

front of the pharmacy. "What are we doing here?" he asked.

"Just a few items I wanted to pick up. Do you mind?" She had never lied to Lucas before—now suddenly the lies were coming out so fast she couldn't keep track of them. She felt sick, tense. She wanted one of those tranquilizers.

"What kind of items?"

"Just stuff! For goodness' sake, Lucas. Do you really care?"

He shook his head, looked at her suspiciously, and with ample reason. It was unlike Cat to lose her cool over nothing. "No, I guess not," he said finally. "How long will you be?"

"Give me ten minutes."

Once she entered the pharmacy, he got out of the car. Though the cast had a walking bar, he felt more comfortable using one crutch to help him along. This time he hobbled to the Honda motorcycle shop across the way. Trying to put the unpleasantness with Cat out of his mind, he headed directly to a brand-new CBR 600 F2.

A one hundred horsepower engine with thermodynamic racing-style chaises and running gear. Simon—for that matter, any nineteen-year-old—would go nuts over a bike like this. Lucas might have himself at nineteen—but in those days he had been too busy getting himself through college while keeping a full-time job and watching out for his sister and mother.

The boy not only had guts, Lucas thought, he had class. He could see what was going down. It wasn't something Lucas could talk about, not even to Cat. Although these days Simon would regularly jump in to cover for him, he never made a thing of it. And he never let on that he knew Lucas was scared.

She asked for a glass of water at the pharmacy and took a pill right then and there. She hated to be that eager; like Lucas, she disliked taking drugs, particularly mood-altering drugs. But now she couldn't wait for it to begin to work. She began to think back—how long ago had it been since she last felt calm?

When she came out of the pharmacy, she spotted Lucas through the plate-glass window of the bike shop, standing back from a motorcycle, examining it. Which gave her a few minutes to run into the men's shop two doors down to pick up swimming trunks for Simon. She had noticed that morning he was still wearing Lucas's old blue and white striped trunks.

It was time he had something that fit.

Simon didn't say much when Cat gave him the two pairs of swim trunks. But later that afternoon when she was walking down the beach by herself, Simon ran after her, trying to catch up.

"Hey, Cat, wait," he called and she turned. The sun had further lightened his hair and bronzed his skin—he looked marvelously healthy. Two gulls and a sandpiper hovered nearby as he jogged toward her, reminding her of a magazine ad. "Where're you going?" he asked, falling in step with her.

She smiled, shrugged. "It's a good day for walking."

"Yeah. Well, I know Lucas went to the doctor. I don't mean to be nosey, but I was wondering—"

He stopped there—and though he wasn't going to bring up the subject, she felt it was about time she did. "Physically, he's doing fine," she said. "Emotionally, well, you can see that for yourself. It takes time to get over what he's been through."

"I wish I could do something."

"Actually, the doctor thinks you are doing something. Just being around eases the pressure on him, gives him time to work on these fears of his. I know for a fact he appreciates it." Then listening to herself and realizing how her compliments actually might be putting pressure on the boy, she added, "Sorry, Simon, I didn't mean to put it like that. I don't want to make you feel obligated. I understand that your working here is only temporary, and you're not to ever feel that you aren't free to pick up and leave when you want to."

He said nothing, just listened as he walked beside her—hands in his sweat jacket pocket, staring at the sand. And then she thought, maybe that was what he had come to tell her to begin with, and her heart sank. "You're not thinking of going . . . I mean, that's not why you wanted to talk to me, is it?"

He looked up at her. "Oh, no, nothing like that. I like it here."

She smiled. "Good." Then moving along farther, "Tell me, just what is it you like so much? From what I can gather, you don't use your bedroom. Or do you?"

"I guess not really."

"Well, if I'm not being too inquisitive, where do you sleep?"

"Outside. A few rainy nights in the cellar tool room."

"For goodness' sake, why?"

He shrugged. "Lucas told me to make myself comfortable. Hey, by the way, thanks for those swimsuits. I like them." She smiled in response and he asked, "How'd you know my size?"

She laughed. "Well, it's not all that difficult to guess those things."

"Men are easy, huh?"

Not always. Certainly Lucas wasn't easy these days. But then she wasn't thinking size.

He stopped and took her elbow, stopping her. "Look, there is a reason I wanted to talk." His blue eyes were staring into hers. "I'm glad to know my being here is helping Lucas, I really am. But sometimes I wonder . . . Look, I want to be able to help you, too."

"But you do, Simon."

He sighed. "Well, I can't help but notice how tense you get, especially with Lucas freaking out so often. I've seen you on the deck a couple of times at night. You having nightmares?" He shook his head, put up his hand before she could even reply. "Hey, forget I even asked that, okay? It's none of my business. All I really want to let you know is, I'm here. I can be as tough and mean as I need to be, I'm a decent fighter. But I don't expect I'll need to show you because I don't expect there'll be any trouble. So stop worrying, okay?" He raised his hands. "That's it. The end."

He looked embarrassed now, and she leaned forward and kissed his cheek. "Tell me something, are you this considerate and kind to everyone you meet? Or is it just the Marshall family who have become the lucky recipients?"

He shrugged, walked a little, picked up a few pebbles, and pitched a couple into the water. "I'm usually pretty much a loner. But I don't know—I guess I like you people." He flashed a pained sort of smile and asked, "Why, do I need more reason than that?"

"I guess not." As they walked on, they dropped that subject and went on to others— chatting easily about inconsequential things. Yet one thing hung in her thoughts as they talked: why on earth would anyone feel comfortable sleeping in a cellar?

Everyone else was off doing one thing or another. Lucas was feeling pretty good about the bike for Simon that the dealer promised to have fine-tuned before delivering the day after tomorrow. That's why when he saw a deliveryman at the door, he was caught off guard, thinking the bike might have come early.

But it turned out to be UPS. And the box, addressed to him, was huge. The delivery guy carried it in for him, and from there he was on his own. It took him nearly ten minutes to rip the cardboard carton open and get the motorized sand cart out. He opened the card: *Dear Lucas, sorry this took so long in coming, but it needed to be special-ordered. Designed for the discerning, the incapacitated, the plain old lazy rocky terrain traveler. Enjoy! Love, the guys and gals at the office.*

It had thick wheels, almost like a minitractor.

Haley was the first one to see it. "Wow,

who sent that?" she said, closing the sliding door.

"The people at the office."

She came over, got on it. "Does it work?"

"It's an electric motor, it ought to. Try it."

She pushed the lever, then with the steering stick, manipulated it around the furniture. It wasn't apt to win any races, but if it maneuvered as well in the sand, it wasn't bad.

"This is fun," Haley said. "Are you going to use it? Because if not, I will."

"Better watch out. Get any more lazy, I'll have to put you on vitamins." Though he was only teasing, he had noticed her lying on the beach a lot. But then again, didn't teenage girls always laze in the sun, trying to tan?

And she did seem happy, particularly when she was with Simon. In fact, in only a short time, they seemed to have developed a nice relationship. She looked up to him, and he was friendly and protective of her. He was reminded of the relationship he'd had so long ago with his own kid sister—Haley's mother.

"I am not lazy," she said, heading for the refrigerator. "It just would be fun to ride around." Then, thinking of something, she added, "Didn't they already send you a fishing rod?"

"No, that was from Jack and Linda."

"Oh." She took out a container of pineapple yogurt, pulled off the cover, and discarded it in the trash compactor. "That's right, I remember. It was flowers."

Lucas looked at her—he had forgotten all about the English garden or whatever kind of garden it was that Cat had called it. Sending both did seem like overkill, he thought.

Haley stuck a spoon in the yogurt and headed outside. "Want me to bring the cart down to the beach for you, Daddy?"

Stuck on his last thought, it wasn't until Haley said his name again that he responded. "No, it's heavy," he said, finally. "We'll let Simon do that."

As she went back to her blanket on the sand, he dialed the office, realizing it was the first time he'd called in since he'd gotten to the beach. Gearing up enthusiasm wasn't easy, but when Shirley picked up, he thought he sounded okay. "Hey there, Shirley," he began. "How're you doing? The cart's great! Thanks."

"Lucas! For goodness' sake, I thought you disowned us! Well, we're holding down the fort best we can here. What we want to know is how you are."

Lie—people expect it, in fact, count on it. "Can't complain at all," he said.

"And the family?"

"Oh, great. Great weather we're having here."

"Yes, it is." A pause, then she said, "So you do like the cart?"

"How could I not? It's great, I'll finally get down to the water. I've already gotten an offer from Haley to take it over should I decide not to use it. It must have cost big-time?"

"Oh, not so bad. You know Jack, he always knows someone to call. He got it for us at a rock-bottom price. However," she said, chuckling, "you're not supposed to know that."

"Not to worry, I already forgot it. Be sure to thank everyone for me. Listen, what's with the flowers, too?"

"What do you mean?" she asked, and he felt his heart skip. A part of him wanting to hear that answer, a part afraid. "You know," he said, following through, "the flowering plant you sent when I got out of the hospital . . ."

"Well, I don't know. Who signed the card, Lucas?"

"It simply said, 'from the guys'. Cat and I took it to mean you—" He should have known, of course. Cat should have known, too. But she wasn't about to consider anything so frightening.

"I know you're an outrageous chauvinist, Lucas. And Cat—that sweet girl has put up with you for so long, she likely has forgotten there ever was such a thing as a women's movement. But there *are* four women in this outfit—one of them being a senior engineer to boot. It would not be wise to forget."

"No, I didn't. I mean, how could I? It's just that . . . I don't know. I guess it was the only thing that seemed to make sense. You see, we hadn't really told anyone."

"Well, it wasn't us. You know the guys around here—they hardly know how to address or stamp an envelope, let alone arrange for flowers to be sent."

His mind went into a spin, rethinking all the curious episodes since the night of the attack and returning to what Shirley had just told him. The florist had been local—he remembered seeing a Clinton address on the card's envelope. First he went through the phone directory. There were only two shops—he called the first one listed and asked them to look up the records to see if his name was listed. "About a week ago it was," he told him. It wasn't listed there, but it was at the Sunset Flower Shop, which he called immediately after.

"Wasn't there a card enclosed?" the person who answered wanted to know.

"Sure, but it was one of those vague, catch-all signings that could have applied to any number of people. I really expected someone to come forward by now, at least mention it.

But no one has. So as you see, I'm in a quandary. Who do I thank?"

"Let me see what I can find out," the man said, then put him on hold. When he picked up again, he said, "I'm afraid I won't be able to be of help, Mr. Marshall. The European flower garden sent to you eight days ago was paid for in cash."

"What about the person who paid? Can you tell me something about him?"

"We're talking about more than a week ago. Considering the number of customers we deal with, that's a tall order. Besides, by the initials on the book, I wasn't the one who took the order."

"Who was?"

"Harry Landerman. He's off today, but he'll be in tomorrow. At about ten. If you want to leave your number, I can have him get back to you."

"No, that won't be necessary. I'll call him." He always called back rather than leaving a message for a stranger. He hung up and dialed the police. Lucas explained what he had found out to the chief.

"You're telling me you think it's those guys who beat you up that sent the flowers? Why the hell would they have done that?"

"I don't know. Maybe to scare me."

"If they really wanted to scare you, why not

sign it from Warren and Earl? That is what they told you their names were. Right?"

Lucas was silent while he thought about it, and he had no rational explanation to come back with. "Look," he said finally, "I'm not pretending to know why anyone did anything. I just know I need this checked through. Can I get together with a police artist to make a composite? I ought to have no trouble remembering those faces."

Cooper hissed in exasperation. "Mr. Marshall, we're only a small unit here, I thought I made that clear at the get-go. We don't have money for police artists."

"Then who does?"

"The big cities do. Not here."

"Can you give me a name of someone who does it?"

"We can't pay—"

"I understand, I'll pick up the tab."

Cooper sighed. "Okay. I'll find out and get back to you within the hour. But I've got to be honest, I think you're throwing away your money. I've heard of a lot of peculiar things in my time, but never one of those bums sending flowers to his victim."

Before Lucas hung up, he asked him not to mention any of it to Cat. He had frightened her enough with his near-hysterical responses to what usually turned out to be nothing. Always being torn up, feeling that those men weren't yet through with him. But if that were so, what was their game?

Chapter Eleven

By the time the police returned Lucas's call, the whole family had congregated around the sand cart. Simon had carried it downstairs and Cat insisted Lucas test it. He was just settling in, getting used to the steering column, when the telephone rang. He stopped what he was doing, and Cat ran upstairs to pick it up. When he heard her greet Chief Cooper, he quickly—at least as quickly as he was able these days—got out of the cart and started upstairs.

"Just a sec," she said, covering the mouthpiece. Coming toward the steps, she cried, "Wait, Lucas, don't. I'll bring it down there. Or else you can call him back."

"No, no, I'll come up," he said, already on the third step. Simon helped him the rest of the way.

He finally reached the table, and Cat handed him the phone, shaking her head. "I don't understand you, Lucas. Why wouldn't you just let me bring—"

"Because I've had enough activity for today. Now, if I could just have some privacy?"

He could see she was hurt, but she tried to cover up as best she could by beckoning to Simon as she headed down to the beach. "Come on," she said, indicating the cart, "why don't you show me how this odd-looking thing works."

The family was all out on the beach when Lucas wrote down the telephone number and address of the artist Chris Morris. His studio was about fifteen miles from Kelsy Point, and Lucas quickly called and made an appointment to see him at ten the next morning. He slipped the paper in his pocket.

Though Lucas looked for an opportunity, it was impossible to get Simon alone. If one of the kids wasn't hanging over the boy, it was Cat. So after dinner, Lucas asked Simon to help him manipulate the cart to the dock. Unfortunately, Haley jumped up, ready to tag along.

Lucas put the kibosh on that. "No, you stay here," he said. "Help your mother with the dishes."

"I did them yesterday. By myself, too," she argued. "Why don't you tell Zack—"

But Simon cut her right off. "Haley, did you hear what your father said?"

Those few unthreatening words seemed to do the trick. Apparently it was some magic in the boy's voice that neither he nor Cat had managed to develop and fine-tune themselves. Haley scowled but began to stack the dinner dishes as told.

Eager to finally get Simon's ear, Lucas was grateful. On the way down to the dock, he brought him up-to-date on the plant that he had come to find out his office staff hadn't sent.

"So you're saying that maybe it was those guys?"

"Maybe. Anything's possible."

"But why would they send flowers?"

"I haven't a clue, Simon. But whatever their purpose, I've had enough of this sitting around and waiting, always looking over my shoulder. I need to find them, and I need to do it without Cat suspecting what's up. So that's where you come in."

Dr. Robbins was right, the little yellow pills weren't that strong at all—just enough to take the edge off her tension. But it was all Cat needed. She took another before dinner, right after Lucas's implausible explanation regarding the chief's call: some kind of story about the police in Seattle reporting that they'd spotted the Bronco. However, it turned out to be a false report, which made Cat wonder why the chief would have bothered to call Lucas at all. But she didn't push further—in retrospect, she guessed perhaps she didn't really want to know.

After helping Haley clear the table and get the dishes in the dishwasher, Cat took a crossword puzzle and pencil and made herself comfortable on one of the deck loungers. Haley, who kept sneaking glances at her father and Simon down at the dock, was clearly aching to find out what all the mystery was about. But since she had no way to do that, she decided to pretend she didn't care.

"How about a game of badminton?" she asked Zack, piquing his interest.

Though Cat was also curious as to what was going on, she stayed put. Soon Lucas was riding his cart back and Simon was heading off to join the badminton game.

"I play winner," he shouted to the children, automatically taking his post beside the net as referee.

If Haley was at all annoyed with him, she forgave him immediately, a smile rushing to her lips in her confidence that she'd be the one to play Simon. Lucas looked to be in surprisingly good spirits, too. Cat put down the puzzle book and went downstairs to him.

"Sweetheart, let's take a stroll along the beach," she suggested. "This cart is really marvelous. I don't know why we didn't think to get one earlier."

"It is, isn't it? Oh, by the way, Cat, I have a little shopping to do tomorrow."

Lucas hated shopping of any kind. The thought of him going out of his way to do any was almost funny. "Oh," she said, going along, "just what did you have in mind?"

He shrugged. "Nothing too much. Magazines, paperbacks, that kind of thing."

"Oh," she said, thinking that was hardly what anyone would consider shopping. Besides, he usually trusted her to pick out his kind of books. But she didn't say so. In fact, remembering the way she had dragged him out to his doctor's appointment that morning, she was encouraged that he wanted to go anywhere.

"Sure, that's fine, Lucas," she said, thinking it might be a nice break to go out to lunch once they were through. "Any special time you had in mind?"

"Listen, Cat, I've already made arrangements. Simon is going to drive me to town tomorrow morning. In fact, that's what we were talking about earlier on the dock."

"But I don't mind taking you," she said. "You know that. Besides, I have some—"

"The thing is, Cat, I want to show him the motorcycle," he said with a slight edge to his voice. It made absolutely no sense to her, and apparently that was clear from her expression because he tried to explain further. "Well, not actually show him. I figured, we could make a stop at the Honda dealer, sort of a spur of the moment kind of thing, and look over the bikes. The CBR 600 F2, of course, included. This way I'm sure to get an honest opinion out of him."

"But I thought you were so sure he'd love the one you picked. Just this afternoon—"

"I am sure. It's just, well, I was thinking, who knows? Suppose it's one of those situations where he's had his heart set on some particular bike, and here I come along with something different? If that was the case, you know damn well he'd never let on. And I'd really like this to be a gift he won't forget."

She walked beside her husband, trying to keep with the slow pace of the cart. She didn't say anything for a few minutes. But considering the business about the bike, she supposed he was making sense. What would be the point in not getting exactly what he wanted? It's just that they'd had their heads together down at the dock so long. It all looked sort of secretive. And she finally said so.

"I don't know what you're talking about," Lucas said.

"Yes, you do. If you were simply going to ask him to drive you to town to pick up reading material, it would have taken less than a minute. Besides why the need to get him alone?"

He stopped the cart now, turned to her. "What's going on here, Cat? If I didn't know better, I'd say you were paranoid. Can't I spend a few fucking minutes alone with the boy without you wondering what's being talked about behind your back?"

She could feel tears sting her eyelids at his harsh tone, but she didn't let him see. The insane part was, he was probably right. What was she thinking of? She ought to be thrilled to the rafters that Lucas was finally beginning to forget the damn carjacking and show some enthusiasm for something else. Choosing a gift for Simon would do fine—it was a wonderful idea, one with which she totally concurred.

And here she was behaving silly and suspicious and petty and what? Jealous?

He seldom lied to Cat, but this was one of those no-choice deals that came up occasionally and presented little difficulty with respect to his conscience. What he didn't like was making her feel like shit, which he hadn't intended to do but somehow was managing just the same. But he supposed better that than the panic and scare attacks he'd been putting her through.

He didn't sleep much that night, but was

up early the next morning anyway, his mind
and body operating on nervous energy. As
soon as Winnie arrived at the house, he and
Simon were out the door. Who knew what
he'd find out today? But if either of those bastards had sent the flowers, it would mean
Lucas hadn't just imagined them being
around. And if they were around, he wanted
them caught and punished.

In any event, with Cat and Haley still sleeping, he felt more comfortable knowing Winnie
was there. Simon volunteered to use his van,
and Lucas agreed, leaving the Jeep wagon for
Cat in case she needed it. Lucas had spotted
Simon doing a quick cleaning of the van's interior the night before.

He was a funny kid, Lucas thought. In
many respects he was amazingly cocky and
confident. Yet occasionally he glimpsed the
other side, a vulnerable side. For instance, Simon was a proud kid, so he more than likely
spruced up the van just to impress Lucas.
Lucas had noticed similar things—how he'd
do tasks on his own, things Lucas hadn't even
noticed needed doing.

He had no need to try so hard, though—
Lucas had already been adequately impressed. But he did go out of his way to make
mention of how good the van interior looked
when Simon boosted him up into the passenger seat.

"Yeah, I try to keep it up," he said, making light of the comment the way he usually did with all forms of compliments. He started the van, turned it around in the dead end, then looked to Lucas for instructions. "Okay, where're we off to?"

Lucas slipped the paper with the artist's address from his pocket. "We're going to Essex," he said, "95 East to Route 153." Simon began to drive and Lucas took out his wallet and pulled out two one-hundred-dollar bills. "There's a shopping area not far from where I'm going. While I'm giving descriptions to this artist, I want you to go to some fancy store and pick up something nice for Cat."

Simon looked at Lucas, the cash, then reached for it. He slipped it in his T-shirt pocket. "Like what?"

"I don't know, you're an intelligent guy. You decide."

"Uh, what about sizes?"

"I'm not good at gauging that. I'll tell you, what I usually do is find some gal walking around the store about Cat's size, then point her out to the salesgirl. It usually works."

Chris Morris, the artist, had a clean-shaven, perfectly symmetrical head, the kind that didn't look half bad without hair. The two composites took quite a while to complete, but the results were startling. Sitting in the van on the way back to Clinton and the florist, Lucas couldn't stop staring at them.

At one point, the eyes staring back at him began to make him feel anxious. He slipped the composites back into the envelope, then stuck his head out the side window to get a big swallow of fresh air.

Simon, looking concerned, piped up. "Look, if it's going to do this to you, maybe it's not worth it."

But of course it was. Lucas was determined, and he willed the bad feelings to pass. The only response he gave was to direct Simon to the right street, then finally to the Sunset Flower Shop. Rather than call Harry Landerman in advance, he had decided to just show up. Simon came inside with him.

A curly-headed boy about seventeen, Harry was a talkative, friendly kid, quick to cooperate. Though he didn't remember who had placed the order for the plant that was sent to Kelsy Point, when Lucas took the composite of the big blond guy out, he nodded right away.

"Oh, yeah, sure, I remember him."

"You're positive?"

He smiled. "How do you forget a guy like that? I mean, he was a truck. I bet he weighed two-eighty easy."

Lucas felt as though his body had been wired—anticipation and dread pouring through his veins like electricity. So the signature on the card from "the guys" had been referring to his assailants. But why? Some kind of added trick designed to get a few more jollies while daring him to guess? Had they expected he'd guess, or were they just so arrogant and contemptuous they didn't care one way or another? He directed his chin toward the composite. "Do we have a name or address on this fellow?"

"No. I mean, I wouldn't have written it or anything, since he paid in cash. But I remember thinking he was from around here. I'm not sure why." Harry's sharp features pinched as he tried to remember. Then nodding, he said, "Okay, yeah, I asked him if he ever played high school football. I figured him being that big and all."

"And?"

"Naw. He'd been out of school a few years, but never played in any team sports. He did mention, though, that the high school he went to had the worst football record in the East. According to him, they hadn't won a homecoming game in fourteen years." Landerman grinned. "You have to admit, that is bad."

"Any idea of what school he was talking about?"

"Uh-uh. A lot of high school football teams suck—no one bothers to advertise just how much."

Simon hadn't said a word, just listened while Lucas did all the talking and questioning. So Lucas didn't notice his concerned expression until they were both outside getting back in the van. "What's wrong, Simon?" he asked.

The boy took his keys out of his pocket, jiggled them as he put them in the ignition. "Nothing," he said, shaking his head, then grimacing. "Just that you weren't kidding when you said that guy was big. I studied that picture of him while we were inside. He's got a neck the size of a frigging elephant."

As Simon backed out of the parking spot, Lucas mulled over what he'd learned about Warren or whatever his name was. Perhaps simple mean-spiritedness had inspired him to send the plant to Lucas, but the clues he'd dropped along the way just might take him and his friend down. The worst team in the East, fourteen-time loser.

From the moment Winnie got there that morning, she felt peculiar about the goings-on in the Marshall household. First Lucas had gone off so early in the kid's van, giving her no explanation as to where he was going or when he'd be back. Then she came inside to find both Cat and Haley still sound asleep. Zack seemed to be the only predictable one—he was already off to who-knows-where. The surprise from him came when at nine o'clock he came back and requested breakfast. Since when did Zack want any more than what he could easily stuff inside his pockets and save for later? She had noticed the wristwatch he'd been wearing, and the way he'd been trying to get to meals on time, but to actually come and ask for a meal? Would wonders ever cease?

He was whistling as she set the eggs and toast in front of him. She thought she'd heard him whistle the tune before. "What's the song?" she asked.

His eyes were on her, but his mind was in a totally other place. He hadn't a clue as to what she was talking about. Or maybe that she was even there. She shook her head, wagged her finger, and smiled. "Forget I even asked, champ." She went inside—and though she usually liked to finish the bedrooms first, in view of the late sleepers, she decided she'd put the bedrooms off till later.

She carried the laundry from the hamper downstairs, emptied the clothes into the washer, and started the fill cycle. She heard an odd noise behind her and swung around. But nothing was there. What did she expect to be there? She didn't ordinarily get spooked by cellars. Insects didn't bother her, and though she was quick to set traps for mice, even they didn't freak her.

No doubt her case of the heebie-jeebies was due to the Bower kid. He seemed to have taken the cellar over as though he'd staked it out as his personal territory. She had often spotted him down there, not really doing much of anything, just hanging around and watching someone who was usually not aware he was watching.

Cat finally got out of bed at ten-thirty. Though she had woken earlier, knowing Lucas was leaving, she went back to sleep. But after hearing the vacuum cleaner for about fifteen minutes, she was wide awake.

Winnie shut it off just as Cat stepped out of her bedroom. "Good morning, I didn't wake you, did I?" she asked, her face a perfect picture of innocence.

Too innocent, Cat thought. But she wasn't foolish enough to accuse her of waking her intentionally. "It's okay, I slept enough."

"Where'd Lucas go?"

Cat poured herself coffee. Then pulling up a stool and sitting at the counter, she shrugged. "Shopping."

"Shopping? Which Lucas are we talking about?"

Cat tried to explain. "Well, just books and magazines, that type of thing."

"Oh," Winnie said, still not buying it.

Cat didn't bother to add the news about the

motorcycle for Simon. Winnie would have decided they were insane to spend that kind of money on anything for Simon. Winnie was usually pretty levelheaded so it was sort of odd how she refused to acknowledge how much Cat and Lucas owed the boy.

"Where are the kids?" Cat asked, changing the subject.

"Zack ate his breakfast, then ran off again. Haley woke up a little while ago." She gestured outside. "She put on a swimsuit and went out to get more sun."

Maybe Cat would do a little jogging. Exercise was good for the spirit, they said. Whoever *they* were, of course. And though she couldn't recall having nightmares the night before, she felt uneasy and down. No particular reason, at least none she was aware of. Maybe she'd ask Haley if she wanted to come along. Surely, that girl ought to be tired of lying around, tanning herself.

They stopped at the drugstore and using their copy machine made two dozen copies of the composites before heading to the police precinct with the information.

Chief Cooper—sitting back in his chair, hands crossed over his chest—listened to all Lucas had to say. When he was finished, he sat forward and took a long look at the two pictures. He nodded thoughtfully, then dropped them on his desk.

"Well, looks like I owe you an apology. But I still don't get why they'd send you flowers."

"Maybe just to yank my chain."

"Like I said, yank it sooner by using their names on the card."

"Look, I don't know. What difference does it make? At least now we've got something to go on."

"The pictures you got here are good, I'm not saying they're not. We'll at least have faces to look for. I'll hand these out to my men right away. But as far as all this other stuff, I think you'd do better to forget about that."

"Why?"

"First off, we don't know if what the guy said was true or if he was just talking to hear himself talk. Which is by the way what most of these sleazy characters do. But any way you slice it, I simply don't have the kind of manpower necessary to let me sit a man of mine down at a desk and tell him to get in touch with every damned high school in the East to find out their football record. In the summertime no less, when the schools' sports staffs are off on vacation."

"Yeah, well, thanks for nothing," Lucas said, standing, taking his crutch, then heading toward the door. Simon was right at his heels, watching that he didn't stumble.

Once they got outside the building, Simon asked, "So what do we do now, Lucas?"

"First I'm going to make a few telephone calls, get us a couple of good solid references. Then you and me are going to go hire us a private investigator."

Chapter Twelve

Lucas called his office and Shirley gave him Stuart Pereli's phone number, the fellow who owned the guard dogs they used at the construction sites. Pereli in turn gave him two references for private detectives: one in New London, another in Bridgeport.

"I'm afraid neither one of them is really in your immediate vicinity," he said. "The thing is there's not a lot of call for us kind of fellows up your way."

Having no other criteria to go by, Lucas opted for the man nearest, Roger Davidson in New London, only a thirty-minute drive from where they were. Like Pereli, Davidson, who had operated a going investigation practice for ten years, was a former cop. Pereli suggested Lucas use his name, which he did, and the detective gave him a three o'clock appointment.

Having time to kill, Lucas and Simon stopped for lunch at a diner on the road.

While Simon ordered for them both, Lucas found a phone and called home.

The office was plain to a fault—the only decoration was a picture of four kids in a plastic frame on his desk. Davidson had pinch lines around a thin mouth and bushy eyebrows that drew in and flagged up. The man paced around the room with his hands in his pockets while Lucas told him his story: beginning at the night of the carjack and bringing him up to the present. When Lucas was finished talking, Davidson stopped pacing and looked at him.

"Okay, so what do you want me to do?"

"Follow up the clues. Find the guys."

"We're talking about tedious and time-consuming work here. Time on the phone trying to run down a high school football team that might or might not exist. If you ask me, the way to go is to follow up on the composites. I can take 'em to your local bars, clubs, hangouts, show them around to the employees, the regulars. See if I can find someone who recognizes them."

Lucas nodded. "Fine. Go both ways, then. Don't economize. I need to find them."

"I normally work on more than one case at a time—it's way more efficient for everyone involved. Don't misunderstand, if I see you require more of my time, you'll get it across the board. When necessary, I've got a couple of able-bodied guys on call who can assist. Of course, I'm going to need a retainer."

Lucas wrote out a check for two thousand dollars and handed it to him. Davidson looked at it, folded it, and slipped it into his pocket. "For what it's worth, I think these scum have lost interest in you. Taken off for parts unknown."

"Yeah, why's that?"

He shrugged. "I figure they would have been crawling up your ass by now if not."

"Yeah? That does seem to be the general consensus."

"You don't buy it?"

"No, I guess I don't."

"Before you leave, Mr. Marshall, you got a picture of your family handy?"

"Yeah, sure," Lucas said, taking out his wallet and opening it to a picture of Cat and the kids. He held it out to him and said, "What are you looking for?"

Davidson studied the picture carefully, then handed it back. "Nothing really. Just like to look over the players is all, separate the good guys from the bad guys. I've met you and Simon." Then nodding to the picture, "Now I've seen them all."

Simon didn't say much until they got within a couple of miles of Clinton. Then he glanced over at Lucas and said, "I'm hanging

219

around here for a while, Lucas. I just wanted you to know that. I mean, if it helps you any."

Yeah, it helped more than he knew, and not only because of the security factor either. Lucas had really grown to like the boy.

Winnie had left about four-thirty, after preparing a casserole that needed only to be popped in the oven. With nothing to do, Cat found herself stooped at the kitchen window, watching for Lucas and Simon, beginning to worry. According to the message Lucas had left with Winnie much earlier that afternoon, he and Simon had gotten inadvertently detained. Surely noncommittal enough. Finally when the green van pulled up, she was able to breathe easier. She rushed outdoors, getting there just as Simon was helping Lucas out of the van.

"Where've you been?"

"I called. Didn't Winnie tell you?"

"Of course. But neither of us could make heads or tails of your message. Detained how, Lucas? My gosh, you go out for an hour or two, and you're gone the entire day."

"Come on, don't get overdramatic on me," he said, trying to make light of it. He leaned over, kissed her, then nudged her to come inside with him.

But she resisted. "That's it? You're not going to tell me where you've been?"

Before Lucas could answer, Simon called back from the van. "I think you'd better give it to her now, Lucas. Unless you want to step in it so deep you'll never step out." Cat turned to Simon, as did Lucas: he was holding up a Lord and Taylor box with a red bow on top.

"Okay," Lucas said, his hand circling for Simon to bring the box in. Then with an exaggerated weariness in his voice, he complained, "I guess there's no way to surprise anyone around this house." Cat's anger by this time had been tempered, though she was well aware she was being manipulated by joint forces.

The explanation came as soon as they got into the house: according to Lucas, the main gist of the trip had been to get her a gift. Then it wasn't to buy books or magazines or show Simon the bike. But as Lucas went on to explain, "By the time I finally picked out just the right thing, it was time for lunch."

So he and Simon went to a sports bar and sat around with a few cold beers, cheeseburgers, and fries and got hooked on a Red Sox double header. Male bonding, she supposed they called it. But the gift *was* just right. In every respect. In fact, she felt embarrassed opening it with Simon standing there, watching.

But the black silk see-through shortie negligee was beautiful and sexy. Best of all, it sent a message she liked.

The night was cool and windy, and Simon excused himself right after dinner, saying he was going out for the evening. Lucas sat on the sofa, an afghan over him, reading the paper. The kids seemed a little antsy, finding themselves without Simon around to entertain them. Though they attempted a game of Monopoly, an argument ensued over the mortgage of Pennsylvania Avenue, and finally around nine-thirty Lucas sent them both to their rooms for the night.

That gave Cat just the opportunity she was waiting for. She showered and perfumed and played around with her hair, finally deciding to twist the back up, wisps falling softly at the nape of her neck and her ears. When she walked into the great room, she was wearing the negligee. Not until she came up and touched the top edge of Lucas's newspaper, lowering it, did she get his undivided attention. His stare started at her face, then inched its way down.

He reached out to touch her, but she quickly took a step back. "Oh, no, very sorry, sir. This is a showing only . . . no touching." She smiled coyly. "You remember the rules, of course?"

He ran his tongue over his lips. "Of course. Maybe you want to show me?"

"Oh, my, yes," she said, twirling twice, the short gown hem flowing and bouncing, revealing the full length of her thighs. She put the flat of her hands to the sides of her breasts, then with just the right movement and rotation drew them along her body. "Now you see, this is our very newest in bed wear. Light and airy and free and—" She stopped, her expression turning to mock concern. She went over to the sofa and stooped down. "We insist our customers be comfortable, sir. And I couldn't help but notice . . ." She drew away the afghan, unhooked the waistband on his shorts, unzipped them, then put in her hand. "Oh, yes," she sighed.

"What about the rules?" he said, his voice now hoarse.

But she didn't get to explain, because she was already in his arms and his lips were on hers, his tongue frantic and taunting. He sank back onto the sofa. His good leg up, his right leg touching the floor, he lifted her onto him, his hands caressing beneath her gown, when suddenly they heard a dull thud against the sliding glass doors.

And it was over. He jumped up, shifting her immediately to his side and twisting around toward the doors. He looked, she looked, she sighed with relief: there was nothing. No one. Still, he lifted the afghan from the floor and covered her.

"Lucas, it's windy outdoors. It must have been something blowing, hitting up against the glass. Maybe one of the kids' rubber thongs. Yes, I think that's what it was."

"Go put on a robe, Cat," he said, as though he were sending away a used toy. Okay, so he had gone limp—she didn't have to be a rocket scientist to figure that out.

"We could begin again, sweetheart. We could—" she began, but he was no longer listening or, for that matter, interested. His attention was riveted on the doors. She got up and rushed to the bedroom, took off the negligee, and flung it—it landed in a corner of the closet. Why had he gone to the trouble?

Lucas decided to forget the entire episode or at least pretend to. She guessed that meant she was supposed to do the same. By the time the truck carrying Simon's motorcycle arrived at eleven o'clock the next morning, Lucas seemed to have gotten himself together, putting on a calm, light mood she doubted he felt.

He stalled the deliveryman and called Simon in from where he was working at the dock. "What's up, Lucas?" the boy said, hurrying toward the deck.

"I've got a delivery guy out front who says he could use a little muscle."

Simon smiled, saluted, and headed off in that direction. Lucas came in, then headed toward the kitchen door. Cat and Haley hurried to follow, not wanting to miss any of the excitement. Zack was off exploring and Winnie, who had been invited to come to the door to see the goings-on, refused. She didn't miss a beat with her feather duster, apparently not even the least bit curious.

At first when Simon saw what it was, he didn't understand. After all, the kids were far too young for a motorcycle, and what would Lucas or Cat need with such a thing? Simon looked at the bike, then at Lucas, as if to say, Hey, wait, we've got a mistake here. Then he turned, looking back at the bike.

"Well, what do you think?" Lucas asked, coming up behind him, with Cat and Haley on his heels.

Simon turned to him, and the confusion in his eyes was so compelling that Lucas finally quit stalling. "It's yours," he said.

His lips parted, and he turned back to the truck, staring at the bike. Finally, ignoring the ramp, he hopped up onto the truck's bed and went over to the Honda, stooping down. He touched one thing, then another, examining.

"It's all tuned and gassed, ready to hit the road," Lucas said.

Meanwhile the delivery guy, who had stood there patiently throughout, glanced at his watch and said, "Hey, kid, what do you say we get this bike off here?"

Simon nodded. "Yeah, sure," he said, his voice more grainy than usual. Taking hold of the handlebars, he walked the bike down the ramp and parked it. Without a glance or word to anyone, he ran over to his van, and when he came back he was holding his helmet.

And before the truck had a chance to button up and pull away from the beach house, Simon—helmut snug on his head and focused on nothing but himself sitting on that Honda—gunned the motor, put it in gear, and sped away.

When Lucas turned to go back inside, Cat noticed his eyes were wet. And if she wasn't mistaken, Simon's had been, too.

The gift giving was much more emotional than Lucas had expected. Though Simon hadn't actually thanked him, at least not formally, it wasn't necessary. Anyone watching saw how overwhelmed he was at being given such a gift. Though Lucas had pretty much taken Simon's carefree life-style for granted, for the first time he wondered if perhaps the boy's life had been a lot harder than he made out.

At three-thirty that afternoon, the phone

rang. Cat answered it in the kitchen and brought the phone to the coffee table.

"For you, Lucas," she said, handing him the receiver. "Someone named Roger Davidson."

He opted for the deck phone, telling Cat he was just about to go out there anyway. "What's happening?" he asked as soon as he picked up the phone.

"Actually, plenty. Which is a lot more than I expected."

"I'm listening."

"These guys of yours. It seems they haven't taken off, at least not that far out of the area. I did some legwork this morning—I got zip. But this afternoon I was over in Mystic on a custody case I'm doing, and while I was there, I figured it wouldn't hurt to give yours a shot, too. Listen, there's a club out there, a swinging place—maybe you've heard of it, the Golden Shield?"

"No," Lucas said.

"Well, it's into heavy metal, punk, pretty popular around the county with the younger set. In any case, according to the head bartender who I showed the composites to, he thought he might of recognized the dark fellow. But it was the big blond dude who really stuck fast with him. It seems he's been in there a number of times. And wait till you hear this—best of all, he recalls the sidekick who was likely our dark, bearded fellow refer to him as Warren."

Lucas sat down, his heart racing. "When?" he began. "When did he last see him?"

"Best he could remember, several nights back. Certainly no more than a week."

Lucas let out a deep breath. "Okay, so what now?"

"What we do is stake out the club. Also I got a few buddies here on the New London force. Since we seem to have a legit first name to go along with the picture, I can try to run some things by their computer. Who knows, maybe they've been snagged on some local trouble."

"Then you think it's likely they're from around here?"

"It's hard to say on these things. They might just be hanging around temporarily. Remember, it's summertime, and it's a resort area. Again, our best bet is to continue the stakeout. See where they're staying."

Davidson made a point of saying he still believed Lucas and his family were relatively safe. Despite the flowers sent, despite the annoying telephone calls, even assuming they were responsible for other things such as the Snapple bottle on his deck: they were just things done to further agitate Lucas. More important was that neither of the two had made any attempt at personal contact. And they were talking now, what . . . close to two weeks from the time of the attack?

His family being relatively safe though wasn't hardly enough. Besides all of which, Lucas still didn't quite believe it. Nonetheless it was time to get beyond the panic—he had to view the situation rationally and calmly. Okay, so maybe everyone was right, Warren and Earl would not likely chance face-to-face contact. Certainly it would be a risky move for them to make: they had the car, what they'd come for. They'd probably sold it by now, were already enjoying the money.

But why were they still hanging around? Why were they taunting him?

He'd been sitting there only a few minutes when Cat stuck her head out on the deck. "Hey, what're you doing there? I thought you were coming back inside."

He shrugged.

"Who's Roger Davidson?" she asked.

"Business. I told Jack to forward a couple of calls to me. Take some of the pressure off him." Lying was becoming an easy, routine to fall into. "Cat, where's Simon?" he asked.

"I don't really know. He spent the last hour showing the bike to the kids. But I saw Haley lying out in the sun a while ago. So I assume that means he's off again, riding. It seems you picked—" she began, but Lucas interrupted.

"Zack?"

"Excuse me?"

"Zack. Where is he?"

"Oh, well, you know him. Out rediscovering the world."

"Still? I thought we'd gotten through to him. We've got a whole damned ocean right here at our doorstep. What's the difficulty with him exploring right here?"

"It's not the same, and you know it. Besides, you're not being fair. Zack has been marvelous about wearing his watch and getting home in time for meals."

"I see. So that's all I've got a right to expect of my kid, that he gets home for meals?"

Cat simply looked at him—one of those looks that made him want to shrivel into a corner. Deciding to end the conversation, she slammed the sliding door shut in his face. He supposed he couldn't blame her. The problem was, she didn't know what was going on. She didn't want to know, and he was simply trying to oblige her. Still, until Warren and Earl were in custody, it was going to be his way.

Winnie didn't see Simon right away, not until she'd taken out the clothes from the dryer and begun to fold them on the utility table. Startled, she dropped two clean towels. She reached to pick them up off the floor, then looked over at him: tan and good-looking, barefoot and bare-chested, leaning against the wall at the foot of the stairs. He was polishing an apple against his shorts.

"What is it with you anyway, Simon? Always sneaking around the cellar."

He bit into the apple, then smiled. "What can I say? I'm one of those cellar rats."

She went about the folding without responding at all to his sarcasm. But she could feel his eyes examining her. He was going out of his way to unnerve her with his brashness, but she was determined not to let that happen.

"Well, I really have to congratulate you, kid," she said finally. "You're good at these head games, aren't you? At least, everything seems to be going your way. So far anyway."

"Hey, want to run that by me again?"

Neither his words nor fake confusion scored any points with her—he knew exactly what she meant. Nonetheless, she spelled it out for the sake of the game. "The bike. You running rings around the Marshall family. What's your game plan, kid?"

"Haven't you heard, I don't make plans. I'm a drifter type of guy. Besides, what's it to you, Winnie?"

"Plenty. These people mean a lot to me."

"Yeah? Well, maybe they mean something to me, too. What is it, you jealous because I fit in here so well? Hey, yeah, I bet that's what the big deal is, huh?"

The kid had balls as big as soccer balls, and she wouldn't at all mind getting in some solid kicks. But that was only wishful thinking. Instead she went about her routine: lifting the folded towels, carrying them to the shower room, depositing them on the shelves in the cabinet. When she got back to the dryer, she said, "Listen, don't go speculating and over-taxing your brain on my account. If I were you, I'd hold off for when you're going to need it."

"Hey, look, lady, I'm just trying to figure you out. After all, what would I really know about someone your age? Maybe you think I want to make it with Lucas?"

"I beg your pardon?"

"Look, Winnie, you don't have to be a genius to see how much you want to fuck the guy. How long's this been going on with you? I mean, if I had to take a guess at it, I'd say you've been pining away here a good long time."

"Shut up!" she said.

But once begun, he wasn't about to show mercy. "Whoa," he said, "and competing with the Cat lady, too! Wow, what are you, some kind of masochist?"

Did it still show that much? For a long time she had suspected Cat knew, but never Lucas.

Did everybody who saw her with him know? She suddenly felt sick to her stomach, and she wanted to get out of there, away from Simon. She might have rushed out the beach-front door, but didn't think of that. Instead, with eyes lowered to avoid any more confrontation, she began past Simon.

That's when she noticed his two webbed toes. She paused, then without thinking, looked up into his face. His eyes were piercing, questioning, but she couldn't make out the question. She looked away and ran upstairs.

Chapter Thirteen

Winnie, out of the blue, looked peaked, and though she claimed she was fine, Cat insisted she go straight home to bed. So by the time Cat had prepared and got dinner on the table, they were eating quite a bit later than usual. Near the end of the meal Lucas finally broached the dreaded subject with Zack. Since Haley pretty much hung out nearby when she wasn't with Simon, Lucas didn't include her when he issued the new rule of not straying from the property.

"You mean, tonight?" Zack asked.

"I'm talking for a while. Maybe a few weeks."

Zack looked up from his plate. "Why?"

"Do I need a reason to want my son around?"

He shook his head. "But I can't."

"Why not?"

"I got lots of things to do is why. This morning Andy and I found a family of muskrats burrowed in some rocks at the Cliffs. We're going to go see them tomorrow."

"In case you didn't notice, it wasn't a request," Lucas said. "I'm sorry about it, but that's how it stands. The muskrats will just have to wait awhile."

Zack turned to his mother, his eyes pleading. But getting no response, he looked back at Lucas. "I've been home in time for meals just like you said."

"It's not that."

"Then what?"

"Nothing, Zack. You didn't do a thing. This isn't a punishment, so don't look at it that way."

His eyes went from curious to angry. "Then why?"

"Because I said so."

"What about seeing Andy?"

"Sure, fine. Have him come over here to play. And what about us spending some time together as well? Maybe we could get into a little chess?"

"You stink at chess."

"Zack!" Cat cried.

"Well, it's the truth."

"Okay, then cards. Yahtzee, whatever."

Zack looked again to his mother for some support, but now Cat avoided his eyes completely.

"Besides, as I pointed out to your mother

235

earlier, there's more than enough exploring to do right on our own property."

Zack stood up from the table, his napkin dropping to the deck floor. Lucas demanded that he sit back down, but for the first time his son outright refused. "I hate you!" he shouted at him, then turning to face his mother, "And I hate you, too!" He purposely knocked over his chair and ran off to his room.

Cat stood up, tossing her napkin onto her plate. "I won't have you—" she began.

But Lucas cut in. "Leave it alone, Cat! It's done."

She rushed to the deck stairs. Once down onto the sand, she began to run. Lucas stood up and called after her, but if she heard him call, she ignored it.

Lucas turned in time to see Simon about to go inside. "What are you doing?"

"I thought I'd see about Zack."

"You stay here," he said. He turned to Haley, who had been silent but clearly distressed at the goings-on. "You go see to your brother." She rushed away gladly. Then Lucas said to Simon, "Roger Davidson called this afternoon. Our guys have been seen a few times in Mystic, which is only about a fifteen-minute drive from here. A bartender at a club recognized them by the composites."

Simon whistled. "Wow, that was quick! Have the police picked them up yet?"

"No, not yet. We don't know where they're staying. Davidson is staking out the club in hopes that they'll show again. But meanwhile, until they're off the streets, I want the kids sticking around where you or I can keep an eye on them."

"I see your point."

Lucas turned to gaze after Cat, now off in the distance. "I can't very well tie her up, so that's where I'd like you to come in. I don't give a shit if nothing else around here gets done. But if she takes off, you take off after her. I don't want her out of your sight. Obviously if you can accompany her without arousing her suspicion, so much the better."

When Haley walked into Zack's room and shut the door behind her, she found him sitting on the bed staring at the wall, looking as angry as she'd ever seen him.

"Sorry," she said, joining him on the bed, not knowing what else to say.

"It's not your fault."

"Not Mommy's either."

"She listens to him, no matter how wrong he is. She gives him all the power."

Haley thought about what Zack had said, then thought about herself and the way she was with Simon. "Yeah, maybe. Maybe she just can't help herself."

"I don't get that."

She shrugged. "I don't either. Who knows, I don't even understand why Daddy decided to jail you. Except that he's a little nuts these days. We all know that."

Zack was silent for a while, then he said, "I wish Simon were my father, not him."

"That's so dumb, Zack. He's too young."

"Well, at least he likes me."

"So does Daddy like you."

"That's what Mommy says. But I don't think she really knows about him. She just thinks she does."

Suddenly Haley couldn't hold in her feelings any longer—she fell forward on the mattress and began to cry. Zack reached over and lightly put his hand on her head, trying to act strong so he could comfort her. That was nice of him and all and she appreciated it, but what she really needed to make her feel better was a joint. And who she really needed to comfort her was Simon.

She suspected Zack did, too. Their parents just didn't seem to be reliable anymore.

Cat hadn't had any destination in mind when she ran off, simply to get far away from Lucas. But ironically she ended up at Zack's favorite spot, the Cliffs. She climbed up a ways, then sat and looked over the area: it was low tide. She studied the huge uneven rocks, the lower sections near the water tangled with seaweed and ringed in different colors. The tide pools in the cove nearby were alive with little creatures, each of them adapting to survive along the turbulent boundary of land and sea. Everything was so very peaceful and orderly—she could see why her son liked the place.

She must have been there fifteen minutes before she heard his throat clear, and she looked up. Simon was standing about a dozen yards away.

"Mind if I come over?"

She shook her head, and he climbed up, finding a rock across from her. "You okay?"

She nodded. "Just angry," she said, taking a long, deep breath. "So angry."

He pulled some kind of rag from his pocket and held it out. "In case you need it."

"I won't. I'm okay."

Still, to convince her, he qualified it. "It's clean," he said. "I used it to shine the bike."

She smiled and took it finally. "You seemed to really like it. The bike, I mean."

"Oh, yeah. What's not to like? I just never expected to own something so great. I'm from the 'can't afford it till it's old, busted, and cheap' class."

"Then I'm doubly glad Lucas bought it.

He's quite fond of you, you know." Simon didn't say anything, just tilted his head some as though he were trying to focus in on her from another angle. "Okay," she said, "what's wrong? Something I said?"

"I just don't get you sometimes. I mean, here you are, burning mad at Lucas, and still you're out beating his drum. Talking about him like it's all okay."

"Well, it isn't all okay. And I don't mean to imply it is. But I love him."

"That's it, huh?"

"I guess."

He shook his head, picked up a few pebbles from between the rocks, and pitched them into the water.

"You ought to learn how to get things off your chest or they'll do a real number on you. You're the type who packs things inside, pretends they don't exist. And I suppose it works for a while. But one day you'll get so bloated with those bad feelings, you'll shoot off like some atomic missile."

"Yeah? How do you advise I go about getting it out? Go home and scream at Lucas?"

He shrugged, tossed out a few more pebbles. "Sure, that's one way. Or if you want, you could start off by just plain screaming. You know, do it for yourself."

"Excuse me?"

"Like this," he said, and gave off a long,

loud wail that startled her. When he finally stopped, he looked flushed and sounded out of breath. "Or if it's easier, do it with words," he said. "Shout out whatever comes to mind."

"Oh, I couldn't," she said. "What would I say?"

"That's strictly up to you." He motioned to her midsection. "It's got to come straight from the gut."

Reluctant, she looked around, but of course there wasn't a soul to be found anywhere on the beach. Still, she shook her head. "Naw, uh-uh, I couldn't."

"Yeah, well, I didn't really think so," he said, making a face. "You're not really loose enough."

She smiled. "Hey, what's this, reverse psychology?"

He clasped his hands low in front of him. "You are one real uptight lady," he said, shaking his head and not looking at her. "Tighter than I even imagined."

She took a deep breath, then began to shout: first not so loud, but then, as she really got the hang of the exercise, louder. Making and receiving echoes simultaneously.

"Damn you, Lucas!" she cried. "You pigheaded jerk! Who died and crowned you—" It was all so silly, so insane, and suddenly out of sheer embarrassment at being teased into partaking of the exercise, she began to laugh.

Then before she knew what was happening, she burst into tears.

He moved forward, putting his arms around her, drawing her to him, letting her head rest against his chest until she could stop crying. That's when she should have pulled away. But she didn't. As she enjoyed the luxury of his arms for just a little while longer, she started to become aware of things: the width of his shoulders, the tickle of his chest hairs against her cheek, the salty smell of his body . . . and his strong, cool fingers . . .

She broke free, stood up, and, without even bothering to invent a reasonable excuse, skidded down the rocks and began running, toward the house.

She had to get home to Lucas.

Two toes, webbed together. Winnie had come across such an odd phenomenon before, but though she wracked her brain, she couldn't place who or where. She stopped the car on the way home, upchucked by the roadside, and once she got in the house, just about made it to the bathroom. After a hellish few hours of emptying herself, she fell into bed, exhausted.

Despite the run of decent movies that night on HBO, Winnie was unable to get the kid with his peculiar toes and cruel taunting from her mind. Luckily she wasn't due to clean the

Marshalls' house the next day. But what about the day after? How was she going to face Simon?

"So how's the shit flying, Winnie?" Luke screeched from his cage on her dresser.

"Shut up!" she said. Already past midnight and a blanket covering his cage, yet she still couldn't get him to quiet down and get to sleep. He was still picking up her vibes: anger, frustration, confusion, and with it all that feeling—

"OO-oo, bad boy, Luke. Shut the fuck up, Luke!"

What feeling are we talking about, Winnie? The way he had talked to her, it sounded as though he had really meant to get her. And those things he said . . . Could Simon somehow know her?

That night Cat wasn't about to stop thinking about what a fool she'd made of herself, running from Simon as though he'd done or said something to frighten her. Nor could she forget it the next morning. What scared her most was her own wild, insane thoughts. For pity's sake, he was only a boy. Was she so undisciplined and needy that a nineteen-year-old boy couldn't console her without her turning it into something sexual?

Hopefully Simon would be able to pass her behavior off as simply the result of her anger at Lucas, which was surely a large part of it. When she had got back to the house, she'd tried to talk to Lucas about his hasty and unwarranted decision to ground Zack, and though he tried to allay her outrage, he kept circling back to that same feeble excuse about getting a chance to know his son better.

No, fear was still driving him, and she didn't know how long she could stand it. Or how long she could continue to allow the kids to be exposed to it. She knew how it was affecting her. So then what might it be doing to them? She thought about calling Jack, perhaps getting him down there to talk sense into Lucas. Maybe he was the right one to convince Lucas to see a therapist.

In fact, after serving the family breakfast on the deck the next morning, she went inside to call him. But according to Shirley, Jack and Linda had gone for the week to their son Gary's lakeside cottage in the White Mountains. Even as Cat heard the news, she remembered Linda mentioning it.

"Is this important, Cat?" Shirley asked. "Because if it is, I've got Gary's beeper number and—"

"No, no, don't bother them, it can wait. Please, just see that Jack calls when he gets back."

Before she returned to breakfast, she telephoned Winnie to see how she was doing, what with her looking so terrible yesterday. Though Winnie tried to convince her that the worst of the bug was over, she didn't sound good.

"I'm going to take a ride over to Winnie's later," Cat said, coming back to the deck.

"What's wrong with her?" Lucas asked.

Cat poured herself coffee, then set the pot down. "Oh, she says she's all right now. But I don't know, it seemed to me, she was barely able to talk on the phone."

"Maybe you should call a doctor instead."

"Why don't I make the judgement once I see her."

"Hey, why don't I drive you?" Simon piped up. "I've got to stop at the hardware store anyway."

She looked up at him, thinking it was an odd suggestion, then wondering if it had to do with what had happened the night before. Did he want to ask why she had run off? Or worse, had he already figured it out? But Simon's expression told her nothing. She turned to Lucas, who by his complacency apparently had found nothing odd in the offer. Nonetheless, she declined.

But about forty-five minutes later, all set to go, Cat couldn't get the Jeep's engine to do much more than sputter. Lucas, having seen her try to get started a half-dozen times with no luck, sent Simon out front to help.

"Looks like the battery," he said, after attempting with no success to start it. Finally he checked the headlights and found that they had been left on.

"I can't believe I did that," she said, though she was staring at the proof of it and knew she was the only one driving the car these days. Who else could have done it? She shook her head. "Do you think you could jump it for me?"

"Sure enough. My jumpers are shot, though," he said as he got out of the car and headed toward the rear. "So I'll need to use yours." He opened the back hatch, and that's when it dawned on Cat that they wouldn't be there: the jumper cables had been taken along with everything else in the Bronco. The plan suddenly changed on her—Simon had it already figured out: he'd drop her off at Winnie's, then while he was at the hardware anyway, he'd pick up a new pair of cables.

"It looks like I took you up on your offer after all," she said, climbing into the van, the sudden discomfort she was feeling causing her to say something dumb and obvious. Was it just being with Simon alone after last night or was it heightened by the memory of her sneaking through his glove compartment?

He just glanced at her and smiled.

No, he wasn't going to ask. She sensed a definite strain between them before she realized she'd have to bring the issue up herself and get it out of the way.

"Sorry about last night, you know, running off like that. It's just that I needed—"

"Stop, Cat, please. You don't need to explain. I completely understood."

He did? Then why not explain it to her? But naturally she didn't voice her thoughts: she just looked out the window, trying to concentrate on Winnie. She should have told her she was coming, asked her if she needed anything. *Dumb, dumb, why are you so damn dumb and helpless, Cat?* She'd have Simon stop at the supermarket anyway so she could pick up a few things.

Cat looked frazzled, Winnie thought when she opened the door and let her in. But Cat took over with a vengeance, unpacking the two grocery bags she'd brought, putting the food away on the shelves, and insisting Winnie get back to bed.

After the sounds of shuffling pots and pans in the kitchen, Cat brought Winnie in a breakfast tray of dry toast and tea. A scandal sheet and three movie magazines decorated the tray—just the kind of reading material Winnie liked. Cat fluffed her pillows, made her comfortable, then set down the tray.

"The menu isn't my best," Cat said. "But I'm hoping you'll be able to keep it down."

Never quite gotten the knack for receiving kindness graciously, Winnie did what she normally did to hide her awkwardness: protested a lot and bawled out the giver for going to the trouble. But Cat really didn't pay much attention, and Winnie nibbled away at the toast. It tasted good on her empty stomach.

She yakked on about the miserable night she'd had: she was just about convinced that it was a stomach virus, the timing of it coincidental with her run-in with Simon. Then as she began to eat the other piece of toast, she said, "You're not looking so great yourself."

"I guess I've had better nights. Lucas tosses and turns constantly. Bangs me with his cast. I've got bruises to prove it. Winnie, I've got to get him to see someone."

Winnie stopped chewing and stared at Cat. "He's an emotional wreck. Though he hasn't actually come right out and said so, he expects those awful men to come back. He jumps at the least provocation, frightens me and the children out of our wits. And trying to talk reason doesn't—"

But Winnie had turned her attention away, and Cat followed the direction of her gaze. Simon was standing in her doorway, bold and smiling, with a bouquet of yellow gladioli wrapped in green tissue paper. Winnie's least favorite flower, as it happened.

A *coincidence.*

"The kitchen door was open," Simon explained. "So I just came right in."

"How thoughtful, Simon," Cat said, referring to the flowers. Turning to Winnie, she said, "The battery on the Jeep died this morning. Would you believe between the two of us, we couldn't come up with a pair of working cables? Anyway, Simon was on his way to the hardware store, so he was nice enough to give me a lift."

Winnie thought about the way Simon always leered at Cat. So why not invent a few choice occasions for them to be alone? A wild accusation, maybe. Still, Cat couldn't have looked more uneasy had she heard Winnie actually say it.

Cat got up, and way too cheerful to sound natural, she said, "Look, why don't I get a vase for those flowers?" She hurried off to the kitchen, leaving Simon and Winnie alone to exchange sour looks. The toast that seemed to have agreed fine with Winnie's digestive system only moments earlier suddenly felt like lead.

"Well, aren't you going to say something to your guest, Winnie?" Simon said.

"Yeah, sure. What're you doing here?"

"Just trying to apologize. I thought maybe it was my toes got you sick yesterday."

Was he waiting for some kind of answer to that? Was he right, *did* his toes freak her? Why should they? "I'm going to figure it out, you know," Winnie said.

"Pardon me?"

"Who you are, Simon, and what you're doing here." The words had come out of her mouth, all right—there was no other loose mouth around to pin it on. But she wasn't at all sure what she meant by them.

Chapter Fourteen

"That was thoughtful of you," Cat said to Simon once they had finally left Winnie's and climbed back into the van. "I mean, to bring her those flowers."

He shrugged. "Not a big deal."

Neither of them spoke much on the ten-minute ride home. A few times she sensed him looking at her, but maybe that was just her imagination. She had taken a Valium at Winnie's house—she carried them in her handbag, no need for Lucas to know. Now she was waiting patiently for the pill to take effect.

At home, her mood didn't pick up much. Haley was asleep on the beach, and according to Lucas, who was out on the deck, Zack had been holed up in his room the entire morning. She went upstairs to try to talk to him, but for the first time she could remember, her son turned away from her, refusing to talk.

"Stop worrying about it," Lucas said when she told him. "He'll get over it."

Finally she went to put on a swimsuit and noticed Lucas's gun box in the bedroom had been moved from the closet shelf to the top of his chest of drawers. Oh, fine . . . That much handier, that much easier to get his hands on it. She took another Valium from the vial in her handbag, then went to the kitchen to get water.

"Want to go out on the boat?" She jumped—Simon was standing there, and likely had seen her take the pill. "Look at you, you're a wreck. Come on, it'll do you good."

She hadn't even had time to recuperate from the surprise of him watching her, much less consider the question, when Lucas came in and asked, "What's that, Simon?"

Simon directed his proposal now to Lucas. "I was just asking Cat to come on the boat. I couldn't help but see how uptight she was this morning. I figured getting out on the sea for a couple hours would do her good."

"I think so, too."

"Hello!" she shouted, raising her hands. "Here I am—Catherine Marshall! I move and talk, and can do both at the same time! So please, dammit, stop talking around me as though I weren't here!" She rushed off to the bedroom and fell on the bed. Lucas came right in after her, but she turned away.

"I'm sorry about that," he said. "I didn't mean it to sound like I was talking for you." When she didn't respond, he said, "Something happen at Winnie's?"

"No nothing. I just don't want to go on the boat. And I don't want you bothering me."

She could feel the mattress in back of her sink as he sat down. "I bother you?"

She sighed. "I'm just tense."

"I know," he said, putting a hand on her shoulder. "I worry about you."

She didn't say anything, and he went on. "Look, you do whatever makes you happy, but I'm with Simon on this. How many times through the years have you made it a point to tell me how peaceful you find it to get out on the ocean? Yet since we've gotten here, you haven't been on the boat once."

She could feel her insides start to relax, finally the pills beginning to work. She rolled over and looked up at him. "Why can't you take me, Lucas?" She felt silly and childish even suggesting it, but he took her hand in both of his.

"You know I can't, Cat. If an emergency arises, I'd be good for nothing. You want me having to swim with a cast dragging both of us down?" She shook her head, smiled. "Look, Simon's not the type of kid to invade your space, Cat. In fact, I'll tell him not to initiate any conversation. That is, unless you want him to."

Before she knew what was happening, she was on the boat, heading out to sea with Simon. She noticed in a corner the picnic basket—someone had even thought to put together a lunch.

Lucas didn't even hear Haley come upon him until she was standing practically in front of him, at which time he jumped, scaring her. Her hand went to her chest.

"Sorry, honey," he said, immediately feeling guilty, something he felt on a regular basis these days. "It wasn't intentional."

She gestured toward the dock. "Where's the boat?"

"Simon went out."

"Alone?"

"No. With your mother."

"What?"

It was only a word, but her tone and expression annoyed him immediately. Clearly she was disapproving. "Look, Haley, what's the problem here? The boat belongs to me, not you. And I like to think it's for the pleasure of this family. Which includes all of us, not just you exclusively."

"I wanted to go!"

"So? You'll go another time. Right now your mother is the one who needed a little

R and R, and Simon offered. The bottom line is, it'll do her good."

"Who cares? What about me? What's going to do me good? Staying here with you?"

He raised his hand, and she jumped back. It was all he could do to keep from whacking her. "Get the hell up to your bedroom and stay there!" he said.

It was a routine kind of thing these days: whenever Haley would feel especially bad, she'd go to see Simon, and he'd likely give her pot, maybe even talk to her to make her feel better. He'd always ration the smoke though so she wouldn't end up doing too much: he worried about stuff like that.

Twice he had decided she was too blah, so he gave her some little pink pills. They woke her up so much, she even felt like asking one of her friends from home to visit. But when she thought about the prospect once the effect of the pills had worn away, she couldn't believe she had even considered it.

It was complicated with Simon—so complicated, she wasn't even sure how it had gotten that way. Simon was not only handsome and smart and interesting, he was complex; more so than anyone she'd ever met. And he kept her on her toes, never knowing from one minute to the next what to expect.

When he wanted something, he wanted it

right then and there. Not that he asked her to do anything real bad: mostly it was easy-to-do things—clean some mess he'd made or fix him something to eat or tell him more about the family or insist she keep her head underwater until he gave her permission to come up for air.

He even watched the way she behaved with her mom and dad. For instance, if he had seen the way she had just mouthed off at her father, Simon would have been upset. And the last thing she wanted to do was make Simon upset.

He didn't hit her or anything—Simon said he didn't believe in violence, he believed in more effective punishment. And his punishment was so simple it was maddening: he'd take himself away from her. He'd barely look at her, but when he did, his eyes would go through her as though she were invisible. When he had no choice but to talk to her, his voice would sound flat. And then he'd go off and be happy and charming and wonderful to everyone else, making her feel as though she'd died. The door opened, and she looked up to see Zack come in.

"Don't you believe in knocking?" she asked.

"I saw the boat's gone. Simon is, too," he said, taking himself a seat on her bed without even being asked. "I thought for sure you'd be off with him."

"So you came up here to snoop?"

"No," Zack said. "I heard you in here."

"Well, now that you know I'm here, leave."

But he went on, "So why aren't you with him?"

"None of your business," she said. Even if she knew why, she wouldn't tell him. Simon was big on privacy: he wouldn't let Haley talk to anyone about what they talked about or did together. Though he didn't exactly spell out his reasons for this, she could understand how he felt. After all, they were old enough to deal with their own relationship without other people butting in. And it implied that what was between her and Simon was special.

But there *was* one huge issue that if she could have talked to her mother about it, she would have. If she could figure it out, her relationship with Simon would become that much more special. She knew Simon thought she was beautiful, he'd told her that the day in the boat. So how did she go about getting him to kiss her?

She must have said something out loud, because Zack said, "What'd you say?"

"Nothing. I didn't say anything."

He pulled his Game Boy from his back pocket, turned it on, and began to stack up critters on Yoshi. She groaned, wishing he'd leave. She didn't want anybody's company but Simon's.

One of the first things Winnie did when they'd left was to take the gladioli from the vase on her nightstand where Cat had put it and dump them in the kitchen trash. Then she came back to bed and turned off the television. She even put the movie magazines Cat had brought in the drawer so as not to tempt her.

Then she picked up a pen and pad of paper—she would go about this methodically. She would make a list of any man she'd ever had the slightest thing to do with. She rolled the bottom corner of the pages between her fingers, thinking it might require a lot of paper. But this time she was really determined.

Maybe it was listening to Cat complain like that—it wasn't at all like her to complain: more than two weeks since the attack and to listen to Cat tell it, Lucas was no better off than he was to begin with. And looking at the rings under Cat's eyes these days, neither was she. The relationship between those two was as bad as Winnie had ever seen it. And then with this kid coming out of nowhere ... Well, who was to say he wasn't aggravating an already bad situation?

On the top sheet of paper, she wrote out: *Who is Simon?* There was a slew of questions in her head. Why in the world was he so eager to be a part of the Marshall household? What was so fascinating for a kid Simon's age? A good paycheck? Not worth it to a kid who claimed to be the happy renegade traveler. And another thing, how could he have possibly known of Winnie's dislike of gladioli? Maybe it was just the way he looked at her when handing her the flowers, she didn't know for sure . . . But she could tell he knew.

How had Simon guessed how she felt about Lucas? She'd thought about that one a whole lot, more than she liked to. And she came to the conclusion that while Lucas or Cat might suspect her, a stranger never would. Winnie was hardly the sweet, lay-your-feelings-on-the-line type of lady. In fact, if anyone would have heard the way she talked to Lucas, they more than likely would have concluded she could barely put up with him.

True to Lucas's promise, Simon didn't initiate any conversation. In fact, the best she could judge, he hadn't so much as looked at her. While he sat back steering the boat, Cat sat on the bow, her head up, eyes half closed—knees to her chest, arms wrapped around her legs, the wind and hot sun spilling over her face. The pills she had taken earlier were going full steam, and in her lovely state of calm, she took off her sweatshirt, tossed it aside, and lay down on her stomach.

It wasn't until she was partially dozing that she realized the boat had stopped—it was rocking slightly, and there were hands at her back. She felt the cool fingers touching, untying the strings, then gently tugging the halter top from beneath her. She could have stopped him, of course, but she didn't make a move.

His hands were now on her hips—he had hooked his fingers inside the bikini bottoms, then his fingers along with the suit slid down her hips, her thighs, her legs . . .

Now his hands were massaging her. She wouldn't dare open her eyes. If she did, the hands would surely go away. Then when she thought she'd burst from wanting him, he turned her over onto her back.

Then suddenly the hands drew back, leaving nothing on her but his eyes. A game? She waited, seconds seeming like forever, but still nothing. She took a deep breath, then finally opened her eyes: an ache set in her belly: so big, so handsome, so eager . . .

But with a cool harness on his eagerness . . . "Ask me first," he said.

The day before the chief of police had been unreachable, so when Lucas called to tell him about Warren and Earl being spotted in Mystic, he underlined with the dispatcher the importance of Chief Cooper getting back to him as soon as possible. Nonetheless by two-thirty, when he still hadn't called, Lucas tried again. This time he was there, and he got on the phone immediately.

"You don't answer your messages, Chief?"

"I do occasionally have other things on my blotter. I tried twice, but I got no answer."

"Impossible. I've been home all day."

"I tell you I tried—"

"Okay, forget it. The reason I called . . ." he began, and went through the entire story, about hiring a PI, about what he was doing. Though there was an edge of annoyance in Cooper's voice at learning he'd been replaced, he sounded genuinely pleased when Lucas filled him in on the progress.

He said he would get some copies of those composites to the Mystic police so they could be on the alert.

"Any more phone calls?"

"None lately," Lucas admitted. So assuming they had been calling, did that mean their interest was passing? Nothing could have made him happier than to believe that. But now with them in such close proximity, his anxiety was mixing with excitement. He wanted no less than their asses on a platter.

The odd thing was, just doing something was helping him through the feelings. Not that he was claiming he wasn't scared shit of those sick bastards, but if it was the cat-mouse game, who was chasing who? Now, at least, he too was on the offensive.

After talking to Cooper, he set up a game of chess in the hope of urging Zack to take him on, maybe even teach his old man something about the strategy. But Zack turned him down cold. Now he sat there alone, trying to remember how the pieces moved.

She asked, and asked, and asked again. Their lovemaking was passionate, untamed, at moments almost savage. They went on for nearly two hours, and when they were finished, she went right off to sleep. Because she was satisfied, because she was exhausted, because she couldn't bear to think of what she'd done.

When Simon came over and offered her lunch later, she shook her head and closed her eyes again. But she was awake and aware, and she had nowhere to let her mind go but to think about it. All the wonderful release and satisfaction she'd felt only a short while ago suddenly seemed insignificant compared to the lie she'd now be forced to live with. She sat up finally and, without turning toward Simon, put on her swimsuit, her sweatshirt.

"I think maybe we'd better head on back," she called to him, without really looking.

He put down his fishing rod and came over to her, smiling. "Hey, what's wrong?"

"Nothing." Then she sighed deeply. "Everything. I shouldn't have, Simon."

"It made you feel good. What's so bad about letting yourself feel good?"

"Please, Simon," she said, "I don't really want to talk about it now. Okay?" And she didn't. But the ramifications of what she'd done were growing right before her eyes. What about Simon now? He couldn't possibly stay with them after this. Could he? Damn, what an awful mess she had made.

Though Cat managed to busy herself preparing dinner when she got home, the actual meal was far more difficult. Lucas attempted to elicit conversation from the children, but struck out soundly, and though Cat tried to carry her end of the conversation, she felt self-conscious and uncomfortable. Finally Simon engaged Lucas in sports talk, and together they covered the silence.

Though for some reason she expected Simon might decide to go out after dinner, as he sometimes did, when Lucas suggested they all play Monopoly, Simon leapt at his suggestion. But he was the only one, and Lucas tried again.

"Come on, guys. What's the matter, afraid

the old man might whip you in the real estate market?"

Still no takers—that is, until Simon spoke up. "Come on, stop wasting time here, let's get going. We're playing." He held up the pieces to Zack. "Okay, what's your pleasure, *kemosabe?*" Then turning, "Hey, you with us there, Haley?"

Zack's body language loosened, relenting, Haley, too. They called out their choice of pieces, came to the table, and pulled out chairs to sit. Simon appointed Zack the banker and put Haley in charge of properties.

Lucas looked at Cat. "What about you, babe?"

She shook her head, stunned at the miraculous turnaround Simon had effected. Hadn't Lucas noticed? If he had, he wasn't paying attention. "I'll sit out," she said.

She sat there watching as the play began: the children—now smiling and into the game—Lucas, then Simon. She shivered suddenly, and lifting her arms, hugged them at her chest. Simon immediately picked up on the movement, unhitched the sweat jacket tied around his waist, and tossed it cavalierly over her shoulders. "Cold?" Lucas said, seeing what Simon had done.

Now she was feeling sick to her stomach, too. She stood, slipped the sweat jacket off her shoulders, and handed it back to Simon. "Thanks," she said. "I'll get my own."

As she headed to her bedroom, she heard Simon say to Lucas, "She looks a little funny, don't you think? I hope she hasn't gone and picked up Winnie's bug." Cat couldn't believe how cool the kid was.

Not stopping once, Winnie had filled four pages and gotten really nowhere, except to wonder how she'd ever managed to get to know so many men. The bird, who after yesterday's all-nighter had slept all day, was up again yapping and yakking. Great, just what Winnie needed now: a talkative, rude bird who didn't know his days from his nights.

When she decided to break finally for dinner, though, the knot seemed to untangle. She was on her way to the kitchen when she'd noticed one yellow gladioli on the floor—she must have dropped it there earlier. She picked it up. But when she spotted the second flower lying at the kitchen threshold, she realized all this time she'd been asking herself the wrong question.

The question was, why didn't she like gladioli? And then it began to come to her: the raspy voice that she'd noticed right from the start . . . the webbed toes, a way about him . . . She rushed to the kitchen telephone, and with clumsy fingers dialed Lucas's number. But it rang and rang and rang with no answer.

Cat was more agitated than before, if that was possible. Though she'd taken a chair near Lucas to watch the Monopoly game unfold, she kept jumping up every few minutes.

"Come sit down, will you?" Lucas said, seeing her go from the refrigerator to a cabinet and back to the refrigerator without taking a thing from any.

"I'm getting a drink," she said, deciding it at that moment. "Anyone want a root beer?"

Orders all around came in, and as she was pouring the sodas into glasses, she glanced over at the telephone. "What's happened here?" she said.

Lucas looked up. Simon got off his chair and went over to see. "Looks like someone must have hit the ringer accidentally. Turned it off." He pushed it back.

Lucas immediately remembered the police chief's claim that he'd called the house twice. But they had four phones in all. So what about the other ringers? Lucas was about to ask Simon to check the upstairs phone while he checked the ones in the bedroom and on the porch when the boy raised his hand. Starting toward the bedroom, he said, "Relax, let me go see, Lucas." Within a few minutes he had checked them all and was on his way back to the game, carrying two sodas. He set one in front of Lucas. "No problem, A-OK."

It was nearly ten when Winnie returned to the bedroom, heading to the dresser to get out clean clothes. So Cat and Lucas and the kids had apparently gone out for the evening. Maybe to a movie or bowling. Who knows? Maybe they took a ride to the public beach. But she had already decided that if they weren't back by the time she arrived there, she'd wait. Lucas had to be told about this. And that's exactly what she was thinking when the lights went out.

"Holy Christ, girl. Will ya get the god-damned lights on?" Luke screeched.

Shit, a fuse must have blown. Did she want to bother with that now? No, she'd do it later, she decided as she heard the first noise on the cellar stairs.

She listened.

She could feel her heart stop for a moment, then began a drumroll as she heard another footstep. Then another. Loud, unhurried—brazen. Coming to get her.

"Who's there?" she called out, thinking while she said it, there ought to be a TV show named 'Stupid Things People Say.' Wasn't that something like 'Stupid Human Tricks' on David Letterman? Winnie could picture the audiences roaring at the clumsy-tongued contestants. Why did it seem as though her thoughts had been dipped in machine oil, slipping and sliding all over the place? As loose as a fucking goose. And her body was stone.

Luke started mimicking her, shouting, "Who's there? Who's there?" Forcing herself, she pushed out her arms, trying to find the telephone in the darkness. But she only managed to hit it, sending it falling to the floor. She knelt down to get it, but her fingers were numb and useless. Besides, it was too late: the footsteps were in her bedroom.

"Simon, is that you?" she asked, clasping her hands in front of her. She had never gotten on her knees in prayer before. Hell, she never even prayed before. But this time was the one exception: this time she knew she was about to die.

"Heigh-ho, Winnie," the deep voice crooned.

She felt a sharp pain at her throat, then something warm gush out and spill over her chest. It was her blood. Her body began to slip away ... She felt warm, tired, the pain suddenly and miraculously gone. And somewhere way out in the distance was Luke singing to her ...

"Heigh-ho, the deereo, the farmer in the dell."

Chapter Fifteen

Maybe it was her mind-set at that point—so angry at herself for allowing such a thing to happen with Simon. But nonetheless, she was suddenly seeing Simon in another light. Last night for the first time she had stepped back from the various interactions and watched. And was stunned to discover what had taken place right before her eyes. Simon had not only woven himself into their hearts and household, he was, though perhaps not consciously, trying to take Lucas's place.

Certainly the children were responding to him as though he were the head of this household. They were solicitous of him, almost submissive. Something, despite Lucas's firmness, they weren't with him. Then, of course, there was her—the ultimate disloyalty to Lucas was surely hers. Thinking about it for a few moments, she wondered if perhaps Simon had planned their having sex all along. Or was she simply trying to lighten her own guilty conscience?

It was insane—why would he purposely set out to hurt Lucas? For goodness' sake, he saved his life. And hadn't she herself noticed how hard he tried to please Lucas? No, the only thing clear to Cat was Simon would have to go.

And she would have to be the one to tell him. As far as their getting along without him, they had no other choice. Maybe Lucas would rather cut the summer vacation short, go back to Massachusetts—maybe that was preferable. Then she could look into family therapy. Lucas might be hard-pressed to refuse therapy if he felt his presence was necessary for Cat and the children.

And it was . . .

So when she began to get concerned about Winnie, she asked Simon to drive her to the house, figuring it would be an opportunity for them to talk alone. Though she hadn't really expected Winnie to show up that morning, she had expected a call. When Winnie failed to call, Cat naturally tried her. When there was no answer, Cat assumed she was in the shower and tried several times after.

Finally by eleven o'clock Cat was imagining that perhaps Winnie was feeling too poorly even to get to a phone. The last thing Lucas said to Cat before she left with Simon was,

"Tell her to see a doctor. If she's too damn cheap, have them bill us."

Though Cat might have found an easier way to say it, she couldn't think of one. So she plunged right in and said, "Simon, I think it might be better if you left."

She could feel the van swerve a little off course. "It's not that you haven't been a wonderful help and a good friend," she went on. "But I think Lucas and myself and the children . . . Well, we need to work on being a family again."

"This is all about yesterday, isn't it? About what happened with us in the boat."

"Partially, but not totally. The fact is, we've relied on you way too much. We've let you become too wrapped up in our problems. So much so that it's not good for any of us." She hated the sound of her own words—sweet and polite and face-saving. What she really wanted to say was she'd just had a peek at what was going on. And though she didn't quite understand what he was after, he frightened her.

"I see," he said. "So you're ready to go it alone?"

"Well, we'll have to. Won't we?"

"Lucas, too?"

"I haven't said anything about this to Lucas yet. What I hoped was that you'd approach him about this yourself. Tell him you're ready to move on."

Silence, just a nod of the head, as though he were mulling it over and interpreting what she was really saying and piling up a list of pros and cons on the issue.

"Simon, I don't mean to be unappreciative. We—Lucas and I and the children—have so much to thank you for. But this just isn't working. In fact, the Marshall family as a whole isn't working. None of the parts seem to be functioning the way they ought to be. So I've got to try to pull it back together."

"Sure, I get it," he said, his voice a little subdued and unnatural, but if he didn't buy what she was saying, he wasn't letting on. And she realized then that she'd never seen Simon angry or impolite. That only made her feel twice as ashamed to be doing this to so nice a young man. But Cat was convinced— though however difficult at the moment—his leaving would be better all the way around. By the time Simon pulled his van in Winnie's driveway behind her car, the moment of guilt was past.

Cat unhitched her seat belt. "Well, it looks like she's home," she said, gesturing with a nod to the car.

"Yeah. Want me to come in?"

"If she's ill, she might feel more comfortable if I went in alone," she said, thinking of

Winnie's dislike of the boy. "So if you don't mind, Simon?"

"No, go ahead," he said.

Cat stepped down from the van and looked at him. "Thank you," she said.

"For what?"

"For being understanding. For agreeing to do it this way."

"But I didn't."

"You were listening, you seemed to con-cur—"

"I listened, that's it. Lucas hired me; when he fires me, then I'll think about leaving."

She stood there a moment, staring at him, stunned. Yes, she had been prepared for bruised feelings, even anger, but she hadn't been prepared for this. He was effectively tell-ing her she'd have to get Lucas to fire him. And of course to do that, she'd have to tell him what had happened between them.

She turned, rushed to Winnie's back door, and rang the bell. She waited, fidgeting, her head feeling as though it were about to split. Why was he doing this to them? And where in the hell was Winnie? She rang again, then banged with her fist on the door. After several minutes Simon got out of the van and came up to her.

"You think she's sleeping?"

She didn't want to look at him, let alone

273

talk to him, but she hadn't much choice. "No, not really," she said.

"Is there another way inside?"

"The front door, of course, but I'm sure it's locked. Winnie's a believer in locked doors."

Simon began to go around the house, looking at windows. He stopped at the bathroom window, which was open. He jumped and grabbed onto the ledge. Freeing one of his hands, he manipulated the screen, tearing it some to get it up. Finally, using both hands, he shimmied upward and through the window. Within moments he was opening the back door for her.

The parrot was screeching away, singing of all things, "The Farmer in the Dell." "Winnie?" Cat called out, feeling something dark and frightening as she started toward Winnie's bedroom. Simon followed her and she was suddenly glad despite what had just transpired to have him along. Because when she saw Winnie lying in all that blood, her hands in prayer, her neck slit from one side to the other, she passed out.

Cat later learned that Simon had notified the police, then Lucas—in that order. Lucas found a doctor willing to make a home visit, and when Cat finally woke from all the medication he'd given her, it was already evening. She could remember only vaguely being driven home by Simon, being carried into the bedroom, then seeing Lucas standing over her, looking concerned, then not much else. Now she heard voices coming from the great room.

Simon was the first to see Cat come out of the bedroom. He gestured to Lucas, who was talking to Chief Cooper while one of the officers stood off to the side. Silence fell all around as Lucas got up from the sofa and went to her.

"How're you feeling, babe?"

She nodded as he hugged her. "What happened, Lucas?"

"Simon brought you home, but you were so out of it . . ."

"I mean Winnie," she said. She directed her question to the chief. "What happened? Why?"

"It looks like a robbery. Her purse was taken, and the drawers were gone through. According to her cousin Audrey, who I got over there to look at things, there were two silver dishes missing, a television, a gold charm bracelet, maybe a few pieces of costume jewelry as well. She couldn't be sure. And some cash. The cousin didn't know an exact amount, just that she usually kept about seventy-five dollars socked away in her top dresser drawer."

"So okay, someone broke in and robbed her. But why would anyone kill her?"

"Cat, I want you to go back to bed," Lucas said.

But she held her ground. "No, Lucas, don't you understand . . . I need to know!"

"Well," the chief said, "we figure she was asleep—according to the county coroner, the murder took place somewhere between eight and midnight. I understand she was getting over some kind of virus." Cat nodded, and he went on. "She must have heard a noise coming from the cellar. We've got the point of entrance nailed down to a window facing her backyard.

"She likely tried to turn on the lamp when she woke, but if so, it was a wasted effort—the intruder had already pulled the main switch on the fuse box. So she went for the telephone in the dark, knocked it right off the bedside table, got down on the floor, trying to get it, then—"

The horror of seeing Winnie lying there came rushing back, and this time when Lucas tried to lead her back to bed, she let him. As she climbed into bed, she asked, "What about the funeral, Lucas?"

"I spoke to Audrey. She's arranging it for the day after tomorrow. Badet's funeral home on North Main. Apparently Winnie had adequate savings to cover it."

"Flowers, Lucas. I want her to have lots of flowers."

"Okay. We'll see to it tomorrow."

"Dear God, Winnie is dead," she said, still not able to really grasp something so horrible. Then her thoughts went to Haley and Zack. "The children, have they been told?"

"While I was dealing with getting a doctor here, Simon took them out on the beach and broke the news to them. They were naturally upset, but he seemed to have handled it well. They both went upstairs to their rooms early. Simon checked on them for me at about nine, and they were asleep. Thank goodness for Simon."

Thank goodness for Simon. She was so sick of those words, and to make it worse, how could she argue with them? But what had happened in the car earlier came back to mind. She sighed, wiped away the thought, knowing she could do nothing about Simon at this moment. First they somehow had to get through Winnie's funeral.

Lucas handed her a pill with water.

"What's this?"

"The doctor prescribed it—Elavil, an anti-depressant and sedative. Take it."

She did, and in the few minutes before she fell asleep, she had an overwhelming urge to pile the kids and Lucas into the Jeep, lock the doors, and drive out of there as fast as she could.

Lucas was trying to hold his tongue for Cat's sake. She was frightened enough without him adding his implausible suspicions and fears to the boiling pot. But he couldn't buy Chief Cooper's theory of a robbery gone sour either.

The very fact that the crime had been early in the evening bothered him. He would guess that most people—aside from those who have to be up at dawn for a specific purpose—weren't in the habit of going to bed before eleven-thirty, twelve. Certainly a burglar would choose a later hour. What kind of thief chose to rob a house where people are home and possibly still awake? Once Cat had finally gone back to bed, Lucas verbalized his feelings for Chief Cooper.

"It makes no difference how early it was," the chief said. "According to the position of all the light switches, the house was pitch-dark. Which is reason enough for the thieves to conclude that anyone there would be sleeping."

"Okay, so she's wide awake when the thief gets to the bedroom. But she can't see him in the dark. So why doesn't he just run, get the hell out of there? Why kill her?"

"People panic, they do things they don't

plan to do. Very few thieves would win awards for their well-planned missions or for their high IQ scores. Look, Mr. Marshall, I know you've known Winnie Rawson for a long time and were fond of her, but why don't you let us handle this? It's what we're trained for."

The chief and his officer left and Simon headed out. "Where're you going to be?" Lucas asked, for the first time questioning Simon's plans. And for the first time consciously wishing he'd not go out.

"On the beach, Lucas. But not far. If you need me, holler."

Lucas stayed out on the sofa for a while, thinking. He hadn't brought up the possibility of a connection between Winnie's murder and the carjacking because Cooper would surely have considered him paranoid. And maybe he was. To assume a connection, he'd then have to devise a motive. What would it be? Winnie, for all the years he'd known her, had been nothing more than a housekeeper. If someone really wanted to get Lucas, why not go for his family?

Just on that thought, the phone rang. He got over to it and picked it up fast so as not to wake Cat. But all he got was a click in his ear. Was this intended to be some kind of message?

The receiver still in his hand, he called

Roger Davidson, but got only the answering machine. He left his name and number, then went to both doors, looked out, rechecked the locks. Finally he headed to his bedroom, his mind racing. He took the gun box off the top of his dresser and set it on the nightstand.

As he got into bed beside Cat, he could see light coming in from the bathroom. Cat always left the bathroom lights on. Upstairs, too. In case anyone woke at night. He supposed most people did that. But apparently not their Winnie. According to the chief, all the switches had been found in the off position.

Rolling over, he noticed a fresh black and blue mark on the back of Cat's neck. Careful not to wake her, he touched his lips to it. How did that get there? he wondered.

For the first time Simon had given Haley pot to smoke alone in her bedroom. But it was just one joint, and he made her cross her heart and hope to die that she'd blow the smoke out the window, then flush any sign of it down the toilet.

Even he had seen how much she needed it. Simon had come to Haley's bedroom at nine o'clock to check on her and found her staring up at the ceiling, not able to get the pictures Simon had described to them out of her mind:

Winnie's throat slashed, lying in a pool of blood with her hands together, praying. . . .

"We're all going to die soon, anyway," she told Simon.

"Get off of it, will you?"

"No, I know it's true. You'll see. Me and my family."

"What about me?" he asked.

She looked at him as though she were using some secret guide in her head to appraise him, then shrugged. "I don't know. I can't be sure about you."

"You know, Haley, I don't have the time or patience to deal with any more of this morbid crap. Don't you think I have enough to do handling your mom and dad and Zack?"

He wasn't lying, he was telling it like it was. Nothing seemed to happen anymore in the household without Simon having a part in it. Pretty soon they'd be lining up at the cellar door to consult with him. What an interesting idea: King Simon choosing the dirty, musty old tool room as his headquarters to hold court. She guessed she did sound more than a little demented these days.

"Just give me a joint," she said. "Please, Simon. Please."

He did.

The one thing she didn't want was to die scared. Like poor Winnie.

* * *

Simon had already come in from his run, and with Zack's help made breakfast. While the family was eating, Davidson's return call came and Lucas went inside to take it. He reported zero progress on the stakeout and the same with respect to the New London and Mystic police departments—he had checked with both. Lucas proceeded to tell him about Winnie's murder, and when he got to the part of the light switches being off, Davidson didn't find it particularly peculiar.

"You say she was sick, right? Chances are she'd fallen asleep before it got dark."

Though he supposed it did make sense, none of it really made sense. Why Winnie? Why now? Dammit, why not choose a more impressive house, a place that looked like it might produce some serious valuables? "How many homicides do you think Clinton has seen in, say, the last ten years?" Lucas asked him.

"Two, three," Davidson said, clearly guessing.

"Even better," Lucas said. "Clinton hasn't seen a murder in eleven years."

There was a long pause. "So what're you saying?"

"I'm saying, you have a town with minimum crime. No murders. Then suddenly my family and I get abducted, come within inches of getting killed. Then not two weeks later, out of the blue, my housekeeper gets murdered. Supposedly it's the result of robbery ... or set up nicely to look like one."

"Go on."

"Maybe it's connected."

"Why go after your housekeeper?"

"I don't know. I've asked myself that same question. We've known each other for years—the kids, Cat, myself, all cared a lot about her. But no one—at least, no one who didn't know us personally—would have known that. It's not as if we had some kind of social thing going. Aside from a couple of telephone calls through the winter, usually to do with getting the beach house opened, Christmas or birthday gifts sent back and forth, we had no other contact."

"So what're you saying, there is or isn't a connection?"

"I'm saying there is, but it's remote. Certainly enough so to make me wonder. If someone was out there with his sights on me, he'd have to believe getting Winnie was a way to send me a message. Maybe a way to warn me my family was next."

"It sounds a bit farfetched to me. People don't plan and execute murders just to send a message to a third party they hardly even know. Someone who's going to go that far out on a limb is one of two things: Mafia connected or someone who believes you wronged him bad. Now I asked you when we first met—"

"And I told you then," Lucas said, "if I did something like that, I sure in hell don't know about it. I'm not claiming to have lived a pristine existence—far from it, I've made my share of screwups. But I've never embezzled or swindled or cheated anyone out of anything, and I never intentionally hurt another human being. Now, I'm sorry, but that's the best I can give you."

A sigh from the other end of the line. "Okay. So what is it you want me to do?"

"Stake out my house. I feel they're heading here next."

"Okay, it's your money, it's your call. I'll find someone to cover the club for another couple of days. I'm not willing to give up on that yet. Meanwhile, let's concentrate on night surveillance. No one's about to prance into your house in broad daylight. The element of surprise, coming in while people are asleep, is what they'd need. Particularly considering three adults including the boy are in your household."

"And Simon's rarely away from the house during the day. Though he might go out at night, he's usually back fairly early. And unless it's bad weather—at which point, he sleeps in—he normally sacks out right on the beach."

Davidson chuckled, and Lucas could almost hear him shaking his head. Thinking likely what he himself had thought: how nice to be so young and unhampered. Davidson took down the makes and descriptions of both Lucas's car and Simon's van. "Don't worry," he said. "No vehicle other than those will get within fifty yards of your property. At least not without me on their ass first."

Lucas would gladly ditch the heavy-duty suspense, pack up his family, and get the hell back to Massachusetts if he knew for certain the nightmare would end there. But the question was, would it? Though he never had seen any purpose in mentioning it to Cat, the bottom line was, Warren and Earl had their home address, too. Not that they couldn't have gotten it a half-dozen ways from Sunday anyhow, but one of the things left in the stolen Bronco was the leather briefcase Cat had given him: his name and address were inscribed in the inside pocket.

Zack and Haley succumbed to Simon's gentle but firm browbeating to get them to eat breakfast, but Cat didn't. After Simon's second time urging her to drink her juice, and Cat holding back the desire to scream, she took her coffee mug and went into the house, where Lucas was hanging up the phone at the kitchen counter.

"You okay?" he asked.

"I don't know," she said, sinking onto an arm of the sofa. "What's okay? It still makes absolutely no sense. Lucas, do you think maybe we ought to close up the beach house and go back to Greenfield after the funeral?"

"Why?"

She shook her head. "I don't know, it's just a foreboding I have. I felt it when I was going into Winnie's bedroom, and I feel it still. Suppose something more happens. What is it they're always saying, things happen in threes?"

"Since when are you superstitious?"

She shrugged. She wanted to talk to him about Simon, but what was she going to say? Instead she changed her thoughts to the funeral. "Did you call about the flowers?"

He nodded. "Six dozen, mixed. I told them to make up two nice arrangements and have it delivered in the morning to the funeral home. The funeral's at eleven."

"What about a wake?"

"No. There'll be an open casket I guess."

Murders, wakes, open caskets, funerals, flowers, Winnie gone forever and ever—it was all so awful. The fear was like an anchor dragging on her mind, getting heavier and harder to shake with each moment.

Chapter Sixteen

Cat was determined to keep busy, and after taking another one of those pills to settle her nerves, she lugged the dirty laundry downstairs and ran into Simon, who was doing his laundry. As she stood there waiting for him to transfer the wet clothes into the dryer, freeing the washer for her, she had the peculiar feeling she was actually the guest here. She began to run a series of approaches through her mind, trying to come up with one that might convince him to leave quietly.

"Is it money you want, Simon?" she asked finally.

He ignored her. Instead he plucked one of the short-sleeved shirts from his pile and held it up for her to see.

"So what do you say to this, Cat? Will it be fancy enough for the funeral?"

She shook her head. "I don't understand . . ."

"I really liked Winnie, she had spunk. You don't mind me going, do you?"

Winnie hadn't liked him, of course. But Simon might not have known that. In any event, who was she to decide if he should go to the funeral? She shook her head. "No, of course not. I'm sure the shirt will be fine."

He took the basket of clothes from her hands and set it down next to his. "You leave this. I'll take care of it." He began to sort her clothes, then glanced up. "Why don't you go lie out in the sun? You're not looking so good."

"Why are you doing this?"

Suddenly he looked up at her, his stare almost stinging, and though she thought for a tense moment she was finally about to see a show of his temper, she was wrong. His supposed indignation was delivered with a chilling calm.

"You know, I just don't get you at all, Cat," he began. "What is it you want from me anyway? I'm out here busting my butt for you and Lucas and the kids, trying to get you past all this stuff. What did I do that was so wrong, huh? We had sex. So if you didn't want it, why did you beg for more?"

It was the first night of Roger Davidson's stakeout at the beach house. Between his fifteen years on the city's payroll, then ten years by himself, he knew enough to do his home-work. First he checked out the Jeep wagon and green van out front, making sure he wouldn't confuse either of them with other vehicles that might come around. Then he examined the property, both front and back.

From the perspective of a stakeout, a dead end was a good setup: the property came to a point. There was quite a distance between this one and the abutting beach-front houses. Also in terms of real estate, it was dynamite property, worth some pretty decent change.

He could see why Lucas Marshall didn't bat an eye at footing the bill for his investigating services. Or for the additional services of his man, Benny, who Davidson had assigned to-night to watch the Golden Shield in Mystic.

Lucas Marshall seemed to have it all. Two good-looking kids, a young, beautiful wife—at least from the picture he'd seen. And of course, this house. Shit, most fellows he knew or dealt with were more in line with his own circumstances: a little punchy from the fallout of a nasty divorce, kids growing up and into their own lives, no longer giving a rat's hairy heiny if they talked to him or not. And between that and the ex bitching for more dough every time he called, fighting to keep up any semblance of communication between himself and the kids seemed hardly worth the effort.

He looked out at the beach front—the deck lights were on, and he spotted the kid, Simon, not far from the dock. He was spread on a blanket on the sand, smoking a butt. The kid didn't spot him, and that was the way he liked it. Finally Davidson went back to the street side and selected a sight behind a dune to watch from, close enough to the property that he could see what was going on. He lit up a cigarette himself and sank down onto a wide rock. From how he viewed the case, the night promised to be long and uneventful.

Yeah, Lucas Marshall had just about everything. Except, of course, peace of mind.

At Lucas's request—and though Cat didn't particularly like it, she was in no mood to argue the issue—Simon was the one who drove the wagon the next day to the funeral. Cat sat in the backseat with the kids. Lucas seemed preoccupied, his eyes scrutinizing the streets as though he were expecting to spot someone he knew. No one else seemed to notice, and Cat didn't mention it.

Besides the Marshall family, thirty-two people came to the funeral. Cat counted, one of the senseless things she sometimes did to stop herself from thinking. Though the children chose not to go past the open casket, Cat couldn't so easily avoid it. Lucas took Cat's arm and led her over to say good-bye to Winnie.

Simon followed.

Cat had heard whispering comments on how good Winnie looked: her face heavy with makeup, her hair tightly curled, wearing a high-necked pastel pink, full-skirted silk dress—none of which Winnie would be caught alive in. Cat made the decision right then that when the time came, she'd be cremated.

After the ceremony, after the burial, when they were on their way back to the car, Audrey pulled Cat aside. "I want to thank you for everything," she said, tears falling on full cheeks. "She loved you . . . all of you. Not just—" She stopped.

Not just Lucas was what Audrey meant. "I know," Cat said, her eyes saying she needn't finish. Cat had been aware of Winnie's feelings for Lucas from the very start, though she never let on. Maybe it was just one of those things women were quicker to pick up on. She was fairly certain Lucas never suspected.

Although Cat considered firing Winnie when she first noticed, to do so she would have needed to tell Lucas what Winnie obviously didn't want him knowing. So suddenly, without volunteering for the job, she became a keeper of Winnie's secret. And then it didn't take long, of course, before she had begun to like Winnie. Respect her. And most important, she supposed, trust her.

"And those flowers," Audrey was now saying, "they are absolutely magnificent, and of course not one gladioli." Cat smiled, mystified—and it showed, because Audrey went on to say, "Well, you must have given the florist specific instructions, how else would he have known not to use them? I can't remember seeing a funeral arrangement without at least some gladioli."

"Yes, I see what you mean," Cat said, though she still wasn't sure she did. She leaned over and kissed Audrey's cheek. Then busy trying to unscramble the last thirty seconds of conversation, she hurried back to the car, climbing in the backseat again with the children. She put one arm protectively around Haley, the other around Zack. Neither of them looked up—they just sat there stiff and silent.

Gladioli. Winnie apparently hadn't liked them. Lucas must have known. And Simon, of course, wouldn't know . . . How would he know? Besides, if he had, why would he have picked them of all flowers to bring her the other day?

By the time they got home, it was close to dinnertime. Simon and the kids headed with a blanket to the sand. As Lucas settled on the sofa with the newspaper, Cat said, "Audrey thanked us for the flowers. She thought they were beautiful. She made particular mention of the gladioli." She had gotten his attention—he looked up at her. "Just that there weren't any in the arrangement."

"No, there weren't. I told them not to include any. Winnie didn't like them."

"Why not?"

His features pinched a little as he considered the question, then smoothed. "I don't really remember. I just recall her doing a lot of bitching to me about them. You know me, I wouldn't know one flower from the next. But I guess the name somehow stuck with me. Why the inquisition?"

"Just that it struck me odd. The other day when Simon dropped me off to visit with Winnie, he came back carrying a bouquet of gladioli for her. Don't you think that's odd?"

"Why, because he made a wrong choice?"

She shrugged, stood up, looked at the time—six thirty. "I don't know. I guess it wasn't so odd." And it wasn't—at least not from Lucas's perspective. Cat's perspective of Simon, though, was getting to be quite different. And it seemed there wasn't much he did lately that didn't ultimately arouse her suspicion. She went to the refrigerator and looked inside, though not in any mood to think of food.

What're we having for dinner? she wondered, and as she did, she thought of Winnie, who must have asked that same question of her hundreds of times. The realization that Winnie wouldn't be back now came spinning toward her like a top. She sank down on the stool and began to sob. Lucas came over and took her in his arms.

"Oh, Lucas, what's going to happen?" she murmured, and with that, her thoughts lumped in everything that had gone sour since they left Greenfield.

"It's going to be okay, Cat. Soon." Taking a napkin and wiping away her tears with it, he said, "Look, why don't you forget about cooking tonight? Let's order in. What about pizza, huh? Have Simon go pick up a couple of pies."

She stopped when she was about a quarter of the way down to the blanket and called, but her voice couldn't be heard above the rock music blaring out of Haley's radio. Haley did spot her, though, and lowered the volume.

"Simon," Cat called. "Please come here."

Simon stood up right away, brushed off his jeans, then came trotting through the sand, not stopping until he reached her. "Something wrong, Cat?"

"Actually, yes," she said, although she really hadn't intended to go into it. "Tell me, why did you bring Winnie gladioli when you knew she didn't like them?"

His hands went to his chest, and he smiled. "Whoa, wait, what is this?"

"You did know, didn't you?"

"How would I? She never said. Besides, if that was the case, why would I bring them?"

"I don't know. I just wish I did. The only thing I'm certain of is you need to leave here." He began to talk, but she raised her hand. "No, I understand you won't go unless Lucas asks you. Well, he will ... as soon as I tell him."

Though this decision seemed to come on the spur of the moment, it didn't really. Yesterday, and again today—despite her grief about Winnie, the issue of Simon hadn't really left her mind. And though she hadn't thought she'd reached a firm decision on what to do about it, as she spoke to him now she realized she had.

She wasn't sure exactly why, but she was scared of Simon. And though she was also terrified of telling Lucas what had happened on the boat, she couldn't allow Simon to sit back and blackmail her. At the expense of her family's well-being.

"Aren't you being a little foolish?"

"Maybe," she admitted. "Probably."

He took a long, deep breath, looked down at the sand, then looked up, everywhere but at her. Finally when he did face her, he said, "So when're you planning this confession?"

"Tonight. Once the kids are in bed. So if you're thinking of doing the right thing, let me know before."

With her ultimatum finally out and digested, a smile returned to his lips, and when she said they were ordering out pizzas for dinner, he even volunteered to pick them up. She was amazed at his restraint—if he was feeling any anger or pain, he had it neatly tucked away where no one could see.

Suddenly she was reminded of a conversation between them only a few days back: he had told her how rough and mean he could be if the occasion called for it. His statement hadn't seemed particularly ominous then. Yet it did now.

No one seemed to have much of an appetite. In fact, one whole pizza was left untouched, which Cat refrigerated. Zack and Haley and Simon played a few card games, and when Simon abruptly stood up and said he was heading out for a couple of hours, Cat's one last hope of him suddenly changing his mind was gone. The kids unhappily marched upstairs to their rooms. So thanks to Simon, it was barely nine o'clock when Cat found herself alone with Lucas.

After some forty-five minutes of wrestling

with herself, rehearsing in her mind what she would say or how to say it, all between trying to come up with some ingenious alternative which would get Simon out without her having to say any of it, she finally gave up. She went over and turned off the television, which got Lucas's immediate attention. She took the chair across from him.

"We need to talk," she said.

He put down a magazine. "Go on, talk."

"I've been noticing things lately with the kids."

"Cat, it's been a hard few weeks. For everyone."

"No, wait, listen. It's more than that. This has to do with Simon." Lucas waited for more and she said, "I feel he's gotten too close to the children."

His eyebrows drew together. "I don't understand. What does that mean?"

"I've noticed the way he is with them, as if he's trying to sit in for you. And the children are practically mesmerized. They look up to him, they obey him."

"Obey him how?"

She shrugged. "I don't know. If he tells them to go to bed, eat, whatever it is."

She knew it was all sounding so petty, so his teasing response was no surprise. "Well, what do you think we ought to do to the bastard?" he said. "What about a good tar and feathering?"

"This isn't a joke."

"Well, forgive me, but it sounds like one. If Simon is sitting in for me, as you put it, maybe I ought to consider giving him a raise. In case you haven't been paying attention, I've not been in much physical or emotional shape these days to do the job justice. And if the kids like and trust Simon, so what? Why shouldn't they? I like and trust him, too. And I was under the impression you did as well."

"I'm not so sure any longer."

"Why not?"

"Because I don't think he's what he pretends to be."

Lucas stood up, lifting his crutch, then went toward the refrigerator and took out a beer. "Okay, now we seem to be moving ahead. Maybe you can embellish on that."

"Don't talk down to me."

"Is that what I'm doing? Okay, well again, you'll have to forgive me. But you come in here casting stones at a boy that's done so damn much for this family. So I simply ask you to give me something concrete! Is that really asking too much?"

"Okay. I think he's manipulative, Lucas. Controlling."

"Give me an example."

"You just don't want to let him go, do you? Under any circumstances. Nothing I say—"

Now he walked closer to the sofa where she was sitting. "Goddammit, Cat, just give me one lousy example! Did he do something he shouldn't have? Did he say something he shouldn't have? Something disrespectful or maybe off color to you or Haley? Did he try to hit on—"

It was likely the look on Cat's face when he'd said it that made him stop there. He put down the beer can and came over to her.

"Haley?" he said, disbelief on his face. "He tried something with Haley?"

She shook her head, tears beginning down her cheeks. She wiped them away with her palms. "Not Haley," she said.

His eyes burned into her. "What are you saying, Cat? Are you saying, he did something to you?"

She stood up, reached up, and stroked his cheek. "No, no, it wasn't like that," she said, and for one insane moment she wished she could explain the whole thing away that easily. "It was just something that happened. The other day on the boat."

"Just something that *happened*?"

A mix of incredulity and pain distorted his face, and she wanted to run from him so she wouldn't have to look at what she'd done. Her voice broke. "Forgive me, Lucas."

He yanked her hand from his face as though it might infect him. Disgusted, he said, "This wasn't about Simon and the children at all, Cat, was it? It was about you!" He turned from her, went to the fireplace, lifted his crutch, and with a cry of rage smashed it against the brick, splitting it. He let the pieces fall into the hearth. She ached to go to him, but knew he would never let her near him. He gripped the mantel, then bowing his head, rested it against the brick.

"Why are you telling me this?"

She swallowed hard, tasting tears. "Because he won't leave. Not unless you ask him."

He didn't believe her about the rest of her accusations, and she couldn't blame him. It was all so subtle, she couldn't be sure herself that she wasn't letting her experience with Simon slant her against him. Despondent, she got up and headed toward the deck. Just as she went to open the door, it slid aside.

Simon was standing there.

Hearing the door, Lucas turned.

"It looks like I interrupted," Simon said. Did he know Cat had told him? Lucas studied the boy's eyes, decided he did. "Hey, maybe I should come back—"

"No," Lucas said. "Stay."

He pulled his checkbook from his back pocket, then reached over and grabbed a pen from the coffee table. With fumbling fingers he wrote a check, tore it loose, went up to Simon, and held it out. "Consider us even. Now pick up your things and get out."

"But hey, wait," Simon said, holding his hands up as though he had something to explain.

Dammit, didn't he understand? He'd crossed the line, betrayed his trust, there was nothing left to say or hear. The thought of him and Cat together made Lucas sick. And it made him just as sick to think what a fool he'd been to care about him. But Winnie had him pegged from the start—he should have listened. He grabbed Simon's sweatshirt around his collar and smashed him up against the wall.

"Don't you get it? It's too late. There's nothing you can say now that'll make a difference."

"Lucas, please—" Cat cried.

Simon pushed himself free and Lucas stepped back to let him. Cat stood watching, her eyes wide and scared and expectant as though she thought Simon would go berserk.

But he didn't—he headed farther into the house. Lucas at first assumed he was going upstairs to retrieve his things, but was surprised to see him stop at the kitchen. Simon opened the refrigerator as though nothing had happened. He calmly reached inside, took out the leftover box of pizza and a six-pack of beer.

"What do you think you're doing?" Lucas demanded to know, heading toward him. Was this a ploy designed to get even, to raise his blood pressure? Because if so, it was working.

Simon set everything on the counter, then with almost feverish excitement said, "Hey, Lucas, that's what I was trying to tell you. Until you got all unstrung like that. How do you expect me to leave now? I brought us back company!"

With that, he took a step toward the cellar door and swung it open. Lucas stopped in his tracks, suddenly knowing who he was about to see. Everything that followed became the background for a horror show: Cat's terrified screams, the kids rushing out of their bedrooms to see what was going on. And Simon in a loud roar of pleasure, "Come, say hello to my buddies!"

First Earl. Then Warren: long, greasy yellow hair, he stooped to clear the doorway, then raised a thick arm in a salute directed at Lucas. "Heigh-ho, folks!"

Chapter Seventeen

And though at the last moment it had dawned on Lucas who would be coming through the door, his mind was still unable to assimilate it. So he was only able to stare at them as they walked around the house gaping and grinning and giving one another congratulatory nods. Lucas tried to grasp the meaning of it all. Had it all been some kind of elaborate setup? And if so, why him?

The anger he'd felt earlier immediately overridden, he instinctively reached out a protective arm toward Cat and brought her beside him. Stunned, catatonic, she could only gape. Simon looked upstairs, and with a hand beckoned to the children.

"Come on, guys. Get down here and say hello to my buddies. They're good people, it's just a matter of getting to know them."

"Stay upstairs," Lucas said to the kids.

Simon looked at Lucas, then back at the children. "Now, make your decision quick.

You either listen to your dad and give yourself a hard time, or you listen to me. I think you're both savvy enough to know which way you ought to go here."

Haley took Zack's hand, but he pulled back and his eyes went to his father. He was looking for reassurance, which Lucas had none to give. The fact was, at this point, he was better off going along with what Simon asked. So when Simon said "Come on, *kemosabe*," Lucas nodded, and Zack followed with Haley.

"Relax, guys. These aren't exactly the steps to hell, you know," Simon said, in an attempt to make light of their terror. Warren and Earl were standing beside Simon, grinning stupidly at his attempt at humor. "This is me, your old buddy, Simon," he went on. "Remember? There's nothing to be afraid of."

When they got downstairs, Simon went on. "See what I'm saying? No one is going to hurt you. Just so long as you keep tight with Simon." He gestured to the pizza and beer sitting on the counter. "Now, be good guys and set the table for Warren and Earl."

Still in shock, but going through the motions, the kids set out pizza, napkins, plates, and beer mugs. Lucas stood by helpless, feeling humiliated and furious and a whole mix of other useless emotions. What was he to do, demand they leave? No, it had gone beyond that. Way beyond. And he hadn't a clue as to how or why it had happened.

If he could somehow get to the gun, he thought. Or do something to attract Davidson's attention. Because their biggest hope now had to be the detective, who at this moment was outdoors watching the house. The fact that they'd gotten past him was understandable—Lucas in his stupidity had introduced Simon as one of the good guys.

Simon looked at Lucas. "I don't want to mess up your thought pattern or anything—I can see you're really trying to figure a way out of this—but I don't want you getting stuck on something not important. So in case it ranks high in your plan," he said, looking in the direction of the bedroom, "let me clue you in now. Your revolver's not loaded. I took the ammunition out days ago. I think Cat was right about that. You could have hurt someone fooling around with a weapon."

Lucas ached to pounce on the boy, to wrap his fingers around his neck and squeeze until the arrogance vanished, but it clearly wasn't an option. Instead he took a deep breath to repress his anger, then in the most passive tone he could come up with, asked, "What is this about, Simon? Maybe if we could talk. If you could tell me—"

"There's really not much to tell. I like it here, I want to stay, and so do my friends. So let's just relax and enjoy this vacation, not make a big issue over this. Lucky for us, we've still got the better part of the summer yet to go." With that possibility tossed out and left hanging, Cat's entire body began to tremble.

"Please, Simon, let me get something for her," he said.

Had he asked it right, groveled sufficiently? Apparently yes, because Simon turned to Earl, the dark, bearded one about to bring a slice of pizza to his mouth, and gestured to the bedroom. "There's a bottle of pills on the night table. Elavil. Get it." Earl left the pizza on his plate and hurried off to get the pills. Simon looked at Lucas. "See, Lucas, everything's cool. There's nothing to worry about."

He was clearly in charge. The ringleader. Lucas had been dreading and anticipating the other two showing up while all the time Simon, the kingpin, was right there in his face. His thoughts circled around, catching on bits and pieces: the crank calls, the cars parked at night outside the house, the Bronco in the shopping plaza, the Snapple, the runner, the raccoon loose in the cellar, something hitting the sliders. . . . All set up to scare him. To make Simon a hero.

He studied their faces, thinking that maybe if he looked long enough, he would register some flicker of recognition. A disgruntled em-

ployee, someone he fired or never hired?
Someone he'd done business with? But he
drew blanks, still convinced that the night of
the carjacking was the first time he'd seen
them. So why such a convoluted scam to be
played out on a stranger? What could Simon
possibly want from him that he hadn't been
ready to give?

Lucas had insisted she take two pills. Although the drug didn't perform miracles, it
put a working distance between Cat and the
fear, enough to allow her muscles to unlock
and her mind to function, albeit not to full capacity. Which caused every unanswered question to circle above and around her, the ends
always slipping by before she could reach out
and pluck them.

She watched calmly as Simon took their car
keys away—hers from her purse; Lucas took
his key ring from his pants pocket and
handed it over to him.

Was she responsible for spurring this on by
insisting Simon leave? If she hadn't forced the
issue, would he have been satisfied to go
along like before? Leave at the end of the
summer, no one the wiser, and his mission ac-
complished?

But what was the mission?

Time must have passed because before she
knew it she could barely keep her eyes open,

and Lucas—obviously with permission of the gestapo—was leading her to bed. The little slimy one with the beard reached his hand out and cupped her rear as she passed by, but Lucas didn't notice. And she tried to pretend it didn't happen.

The big one—the yellow pig—was standing at the bedroom doorway: grinning, watching, supervising, eavesdropping. It was hard to tell which. Lucas helped her into bed—she didn't know why he was putting her to bed so early.

"What about the kids?" she asked.

"They'll be okay, Cat," he said. "I'll be there." She wondered how that would help, how anything now would help them. But she didn't say that to Lucas. She let him unfold the cover at the bottom of the bed, knowing she wasn't really cold, knowing she was afraid to sleep. If she slept, what assurance did she have that Lucas and the kids would be there when she woke?

Lucas must have sensed that because he leaned over and whispered in her ear, "It's important you go to sleep now, Cat. I'm going to figure a way out of this. You've got to believe that."

She nodded agreeably. He was only trying to make her feel better, and though she didn't believe a word he was saying, she had to pretend. Lucky she was so good at this.

"Hey, man, what're you saying to her?" the pig asked, coming in toward them, reminding Cat how frightened she'd been of him last time. She supposed she was frightened now, too, but it was more something she knew than felt, her body being too numbed to feel with that kind of urgency. Lucas pulled the cotton quilt over her, and the pig, who was now next to the bed, reached out to pull it away.

"Hey, fucker, what about her clothes?" he said.

Why didn't he like the clothes she's wearing? Or maybe he didn't like her wearing clothes at all? Lucas clearly didn't like him trying to uncover her, and he let him know by pushing his hand away. That must have been just the excuse Warren was looking for. The pig went for Lucas, his big sweaty body suddenly pushing him back toward the wall.

Lucas swung, only grazing his jaw, and the pig grabbed his arm, pinning it in back of him. He folded his other beefy arm around Lucas's neck and squeezed. Though fear began to seep through the cracks of the medication, Cat didn't scream. The noise of the fight, however, brought Simon to the doorway to break it up. Once again, coming to save the day. Thank goodness for Simon. She wanted to laugh, cry, scream, but no emotion was close enough to actually touch.

Angry, sulking, Warren walked away. Simon came in and yanked the telephone wires from the wall. Uh-oh, no way to call a friend today, she thought, recalling some silly advertising jingle.

"Don't worry about this," Simon said, putting a comforting hand on Lucas's shoulder. "Warren didn't mean any harm by it. He's not used to living in a normal house with normal people. It's just going to take some getting used to, everyone learning the rules, that sort of thing. But we'll get it together."

He gestured for Lucas to follow him from the room before he went on: "Who knows, maybe tomorrow she'll want to put on that little peek-a-boo number I picked up for her the other day. You know, Lucas, I don't want you to think I forced her into anything on the boat. Or would do anything like that to your lady. I mean, I played it by the book. If you don't believe me, ask her."

The door closed behind them, the lights went out.

Quick to rescue Lucas from Warren, so he could lead him to the slaughter himself. Simon was using all the weapons she and Lucas had so foolishly given him. He was the one who chose the black negligee, not Lucas. So the blue ribbon was hers after all: she hadn't misinterpreted the message, just who it was from.

* * *

310

Lucas was relieved to have Cat temporarily safe and out of the picture. He was scared to imagine what would have occurred if Simon hadn't stepped in and stopped Warren. But to Lucas's surprise—and as much as he hated to even think the word gratitude, it was there—he had, after all, stopped him. Clearly not much went down among the three of them without Simon's okay. But what about the next time? Because if they couldn't escape this trap soon, there would surely be a next time. Would Simon stop it then, or would he be the one demanding the liberties?

Lucas had to be a quick study on those rules Simon mentioned, assuming he could figure out what they were. But for now he would be grateful just to get the kids safely in bed. And by the haggard look of their faces, if given the chance to go to their rooms, they would have grabbed it. But Simon had his own agenda.

"Want to play a game?" he asked everyone.

"Sure," Earl said, taking from his pocket a bag that contained some white powder substance. Though Lucas had never actually seen any, he had to assume it was cocaine.

"You want to get my buddy a mirror?" Simon said to Zack. The boy looked at him as though he hadn't heard right. "Hey, *kemosabe*, you know what a mirror is?"

"Yeah, sure . . ."

311

"Okay. Please get one."

As Zack came back from the bathroom with a hand mirror and gave it to Earl, Lucas tried to appeal to him. "You know, Simon, it's getting a little late. The kids have been through a lot. I thought maybe you could let them go upstairs."

"Did he ask you to think, motherfucker?" Warren said.

"I was talking to Simon."

"Sorry about that, Lucas, but I'm going to have to turn you down. Maybe later," Simon said, not looking at him. Warren gloated as though Lucas's loss to Simon was a plus for him. Earl poured a bit of the powder onto the mirror, then slipping a razor from his shirt pocket, he used it to cut lines.

"Any straws?" Earl asked Simon.

"Be my guest," Simon said, taking a crisp bill out of his pocket and flying it over. Earl rolled the bill, put one tip to the coke, the other to his nose, and snorted.

Simon looked at Haley. "Want to try some?"

"Dammit, no!" Lucas shouted, hoping Simon would realize the danger in giving that kind of shit to a kid. But on this point he clearly didn't agree.

Simon raised his finger to Lucas. "Hey, come on, don't do that. You're going to confuse her, give her mixed messages. I'm in charge here, not you. So don't go trying to mess up her head." Turning his attention back to Haley, he asked again. But she shook her head.

"It's good stuff. You know I wouldn't—"

But before he finished the sentence, Haley put her hands to her mouth, jumped up, and raced to the bathroom.

"Let me go to her," Lucas said.

"You're the asshole got her sick," Earl said.

It was Simon who finally went in when she was done vomiting and brought her back to the great room; his arm was around her, she was leaning against him. He sat her down at the dining-room table and announced, "We're going to play a game. Warren, go get the Risk." Simon pointed at the game cabinet, and though Warren looked annoyed at being selected gofer, he obeyed the order.

Simon took a line of coke up his nose, and when Warren came back with the Risk, he took two. And the game started—all but Lucas were playing. Though the kids remained subdued, Simon and his friends became progressively louder, howling as they bombarded countries across the game board. During one of Simon's turns Lucas—being as unobtrusive as he knew how—stood up and headed to the kitchen.

"Where're you going?" Simon said without even looking up.

"Just getting something to eat."

"Sure, no problem with that, Lucas. But next time, ask. Okay? Just so I can keep track."

"Got some cookies?" Warren said.

"I'll see if we have any," Lucas said, and he opened the kitchen drawer where they kept candles and flashlights. He took out the flashlight. With one of the cabinet doors open, hiding him from those at the dining-room table, he flashed the beam of light out the kitchen window. On and off—fragments of the Morse code he only partially remembered from when he was a kid. Maybe not accurate, but the flickering should be enough to cause Davidson to wonder.

"What the fuck is taking so long?" Warren said after about thirty seconds of signaling. Quickly switching off the flashlight, Lucas set it far back on the top cabinet shelf. He took a package of Oreos out and brought them to the table.

On this second night of the stakeout at Kelsy Point, Roger Davidson started the shift at about eight o'clock, before it had gotten dark. He had seen Simon leave in his van at eight-thirty, and during the time he was away, Davidson went over to the beach side and looked around. The deck was lit, so was the dock.

He was just being cautious, Davidson

didn't think those guys would come by foot or, for that matter, by boat. No, the kind of stupid slime that got their kicks from carjacking and beating up people were the kind who operated on whim. Nothing too fancy or well thought out. Not exactly creative themselves, they would stick to what they knew: motor vehicles, a quick and easy getaway.

Less than ninety minutes later, Simon had come back. That meant he was not big on night life, which Davidson found to be a little surprising, considering he was such a good-looking kid. The kind of guy girls would fall all over their own feet to get at. Stepping from behind a sand dune, Davidson could make out Simon as he got out of the van, then headed to the darkness of the beach.

That's why at eleven-thirty when Davidson saw the flashes of light on the van, he didn't really know what to make of it. They seemed to be coming from the kitchen window, yet no one had come by, much less try to stop. And the kid was on the beach, likely watching over things from that end. Still, it did seem like some kind of signal, something he ought to check out.

He was careful going over, not wanting to attract attention. He looked, listened, first around the street side, then on the beach. Though he didn't see Simon, everything looked fine—no people in sight, no boats but the ones that belonged there. Finally he went and got a rock he could lift, set it under the kitchen window. With it, he was just tall enough to peek inside through the see-through curtain.

He could see Simon shaking dice, and the girl he recognized from the picture. He couldn't really see the rest of the players, but he guessed they were Lucas, maybe the wife and the son. The family was playing some board game. So no one had flashed a signal at all, just one of the kids fooling with a flashlight. Likely the little boy.

His insides, which had constricted some as they did often in tense moments, now relaxed. He got down from the rock, returned it from where he'd gotten it, then went to the house, climbed the stairs to the kitchen entrance, and knocked.

He'd alert Lucas Marshall. One problem he didn't need was a kid spooking him while he was trying to take care of business.

Out of everyone, Simon proved to have the quickest reflexes. He had barely heard the knock on the kitchen door before he'd slid his knife from beneath his pants leg. Holding it against Haley's throat, he pulled her up and out of the chair.

"You see this, Lucas," he said quietly, the

tip of the knife dimpling her skin. "I don't want to hurt her, so don't make me. Okay?" Haley stood there stiffly, swallowing hard, a flat little moan coming from deep within her throat. Zack looked on with fearful eyes that moved from his sister to his father to Simon.

Lucas nodded. Yes, he understood only too well. Simon gestured to his friends, who were already up and ready to act: Earl with a gun, Warren with the same black-handled knife Lucas remembered he had that first night. Any boisterous outbursts from their drug high were seemingly put on hold while they waited—eyes bright with anticipation and excitement—to receive their leader's next command.

"Why don't I answer—" Lucas began, but Simon shut him up quickly, ordering him to back up toward the other end of the room, out of sight. Why in the world would Davidson come marching up to the door anyway? Lucas wondered. Whatever happened to sneaking up in back of your enemy and catching him by surprise? Or had Lucas just been reading too many spy novels?

Entrusting Haley's captivity to Earl, Simon handed her over. "Keep the gun at her head," he said, "but don't mess a hair on it unless I give the say so. You got it straight?" Earl nodded and led Haley over to the sliders leading to the deck. Glancing over at Warren, Simon said, "We'll handle this, my man. Right? I let him in, you stand back there and be ready." Simon pointed behind the highboy, where Warren would be out of view to anyone walking in.

Lucas could still hear Haley's moaning, and he looked over at Earl holding her. Earl's eyes met his—wild, challenging, daring him to do or say something. Lucas remembered those same eyes from last time. Despite Simon's firm warning to him, how little would it take for him to fire that gun?

Lucas heard Simon greet Davidson, and he felt a tickling sensation as the hairs on the back of his neck began to rise. A sense of doom seemed to come into the house along with the soft night air. He wanted to shout, to warn Davidson against what was about to come down, but of course he wouldn't. And Simon was confident he wouldn't.

Davidson asked to see Lucas.

"Sure, come on in. We were playing a game. Hey, maybe you want to join us?" Simon said.

"I'm afraid not. Listen, I didn't mean to interrupt," he said. Abruptly his voice dropped and Lucas heard the footsteps in the kitchen come to a halt. "Look," Davidson said, "I think I'm going to wait right here. Do me a favor, go tell Lucas I want to see him."

"Sure, whatever you want. You're not interrupting, though. We really could use another player. Maybe Lucas can convince you—" At that moment, Warren, unable to control his eagerness, lunged out from his hiding place. Practically lifting the detective off the floor, he dragged him from the kitchen to the great room.

Davidson began to swing at Warren, but his wild punches only served to further excite Warren who flicked them away as though they'd come from a child. With the zeal of a madman, he wrestled Davidson to the floor, knocking the ceramic planter holding the flower garden he'd sent Lucas off the table. It crashed to the floor. Warren, then anchored like a two-ton barge on Davidson's chest, squeezed the man's head between his two hands, lifted it, and smashed it against the bare floor. The second blow made him lose consciousness.

Lucas, appalled by the brutality and re-lieved that it was over, took a deep breath. At least the man was still alive. But the thought was premature. With no warning, Warren, grinning like a chimpanzee, took Davidson's head and with a sharp, forceful motion twisted it. Lucas could hear a bone crack.

He gasped. Bitter acid rose from his stom-ach to his throat, but he somehow managed to swallow it. He looked at the kids—both had their eyes shut, refusing to see. If Lucas had been scared before, he was now chilled to the bone. Though he'd done a two-year stint in the service, he had been stationed in the States, never actually seeing action. And while he'd participated in a number of fistfights in his youth, he'd never seen a person murdered.

Not until now.

"Did I tell you to kill him, asshole?" Simon shouted at Warren.

"Well, you didn't say not to."

"What do I have to do, draw you a fucking diagram? Rehearse it with you?"

Had Simon rehearsed Warren and Earl for that night in the woods at Chatfield Hollow? He guessed so. Because if not, he and Cat and the kids would likely be dead, too. But Simon, for reasons which Lucas was not yet privy to, wanted them alive—at least, for now. Why? So he could pretend to rescue them?

The carjacking had been planned from the beginning. Simon had known he was coming along—he had picked him and his family specifically. A shudder crept along Lucas's shoulders as his thoughts detoured to Winnie. He had no idea why they would have murdered her, only that they did. Simon had been at the beach house that night, which meant Warren and Earl did the actual killing.

That was the same night Cat had discovered the ringer on the kitchen telephone had been turned off. An accident? Lucas remembered how quickly Simon had gotten up and rushed around the house checking on the other telephones. Why? To make sure Lucas wouldn't get up and do it himself. Because if he had, he might have discovered that all of them had been turned off.

He looked over at Simon and, his voice shaking, gestured to his daughter. "Tell him to let Haley go. Please."

"Take the gun off her and bring her back to the table," Simon said. Then he brought his attention back to Warren and the dead man he hadn't counted on.

"Well, where do you want me to put him?" Warren asked, his excitement ended abruptly by Simon's scolding.

Simon stooped over, searched Davidson's body for a gun. When he didn't find one, he took his key from his ring and handed it to Warren. "Take him down to the tool room for now. Lock him in with Rex." He turned to Zack and said, "Hey, *kemosabe*, what do you say? Want to meet old Rex?"

Lucas had no idea who Rex was, and if Zack did, he seemed too overwhelmed by the shock of what had just happened to care one way or another. What did surprise Lucas was the key. There had never been a lock on the tool room before. So much had been going on and he hadn't been aware of any of it.

"Don't worry, Zack, he doesn't like the taste

of humans." Simon looked at Warren. "Take the kid. It'll give him something to do." Simon pointed at the dirt and pebbles and broken glass on the carpet. "Then get back here and clean this mess."

He ordered Earl to disconnect all the phones. The cellular phone from the deck would be assigned to whoever did guard duty to wear on his belt.

As Zack followed Warren to the cellar, Simon went over to Haley and put an arm around her. "Look, I'm going to help you. Okay?" She looked at him, nodded. "Now, you listen to what I tell you, and you're going to be okay." He took the cocaine off the table and cut her a line. Rolling another bill, he put it to her nose. "Now sniff in. It's easy, easier than the pot. And it's better—wait, you'll see."

Powerless to stop her, Lucas stood there and watched his thirteen-year-old daughter snort up a line of coke. All that kept going through his mind was, *Where have I been?* Simon had been playing head games with his kids, giving Haley marijuana and who knows what else? And Zack, what about Zack?

All those times Haley had been sleeping on the beach. Were her eyes bloodshot, too? What about her behavior? All the fucking things any parent knew to look for, but he'd been oblivious.

So, Lucas, here you all are, captives of maniacs, freaks of nature, trapped in a bizarre scheme that is surely as close to hell as you've ever imagined being. Your private investigator is dead, no longer even a possibility to help you get your family unstuck from this nightmare. So what now?

Chapter Eighteen

You don't die from being scared. Zack learned that momentous lesson in the first thirty minutes of Warren and Earl being there. And the proof was, he'd never been so scared in his whole life, but he was still walking and talking and breathing as he followed Warren to the cellar to see Simon's bull snake. The one Simon lied about, the one he'd told Zack he'd killed before he left home.

Everything in the boy's life had again suddenly flipped upside down with no warning. Simon wasn't who he said he was, who Zack thought he was. He was someone else, someone Zack didn't know. Someone bad who didn't seem hardly upset enough that his friend just snapped a guy's neck.

Simon was good at pretending; he sure had him fooled. He was still pretending to be his friend when he really wasn't. Zack could see only one honest-to-God constant in all this scariness: Simon was still running things.

Warren slung the dead man's body over his shoulder and carried it downstairs. When he got to the tool room, he took out the key Simon had given him, and for the first time Zack noticed the lock Simon must have put on. Warren unlocked the door and pushed it open. Hesitating at the threshold, he looked around, as though he wasn't so sure he wanted to go inside.

"I thought Simon said Rex won't hurt," Zack said.

"Yeah, well, according to Simon he only eats rats. I just don't like them slimy things around me."

Snakes weren't slimy at all, but Zack didn't bother saying so. Zack heard the sharp hiss before he spotted the huge bull snake wrapped around Daddy's saw horse, looking at them.

"Sonofabitch," Warren said, flinching.

The snake was pale brown with rows of reddish-brown squares over the back and sides.

Warren took a cautious step in, and on the shelf next to the door was a cage filled with rats. Zack had seen that cage a couple of weeks earlier in Simon's van, but then it was empty. Warren cracked open the wire door, then his bottom lip curling distastefully, he pulled out a rat by its tail and tossed it to Rex. It landed on the cement with a thud and a squeal, then scrambled off with Rex slithering after it.

Meanwhile, Warren dumped the body of the man on the floor and backed up to the door. "Okay, kid," he said, "I think you've seen enough, let's go." Zack stared hard at the monster man, thinking how weird it was that only a few minutes ago he had murdered a man with no trouble. Now he was squirming and sweating and his face was turning red. Because of a harmless snake.

It took a few moments for the dark memories of the night before to rush in, and Cat's eyes opened to the sun splashing in the window—jarring her, mocking the evil that was happening right now in her house. She turned and sat up—Lucas wasn't in bed with her. She got out of bed, rushed to the door, and opened it.

Lucas had been asleep on the sofa, but the door opening woke him instantly, and he sat up. Earl, who had been standing outside on the deck, reached inside his shirt to a holster, but seeing it was her, left the gun in place. Cat rushed to Lucas, "Where are the children?" she asked.

"Upstairs. Locked in their bedrooms." Lucas glanced over at Earl, then said quietly, "They've been rotating, someone's always awake, keeping watch."

"What are we going to do?"

"I don't know yet, babe. Give me a little time to figure out what the rules are, how it's going to operate. Then—" He stopped, put his hand to her face, and took a deep, uneven breath. "I'm going to need your help with this, Cat."

That meant, of course, she'd have to keep a clear head—no more of those pills. She put her arms around him, leaning her head against his chest. Earl came up behind her and roughly brushed his fingers against her neck. She jumped, jerking her head and dislodging his hand. Lucas pulled her back and glared at Earl.

"I'm hungry," the thug said, nodding toward the kitchen. "Go make breakfast."

She got up and went quickly to the kitchen, not giving him another chance to touch her. A big breakfast would be needed. There was a big guest list, big appetites: keep them well fed and they won't be as mean, she thought, wondering if there was any truth to that. Or did that just apply to animals?

She took out two dozen eggs and a box of pancake mix. While she prepared the food, Earl stood there, looking her over casually. Warren came downstairs from the spare bedroom wearing too-tight jeans and a T-shirt that rode up, showing white flabby flesh pinched at his waistband and oozing over. At that moment Simon came up from the cellar, his hair wet from the shower. He sent Warren to wake the kids.

"Then take a shower," he called up after him. "You smell like a pig."

Cat's sentiments exactly. Wasn't it nice, they could concur on something?

Yes, a clear mind—no drugs. Besides, shouldn't it all be easier from here on? Surely she couldn't be frightened more than she already was. Yet there she was, whipping up a mighty breakfast as if everything in her world were sane.

She thought of Winnie for a moment and wondered if they'd been the ones to murder her, and realizing, of course, that they had. But the idea was so monstrous and unthinkable she couldn't really contemplate it for long. She glanced over at Lucas, who was on the sofa listening, watching, taking mental notes. She took a deep shuddering breath to stop the nervous tears that were threatening at any moment to escape. Salt in the blueberry pancakes? No, it wouldn't do.

So she would survive without pills or fits of panic. Somehow she had to.

Lucas was viewing Simon with a sharply attentive eye. He had to get inside the boy's head, see what he was really about. Of course, if someone had asked him yesterday if he knew Simon Bower, he would have said yes. And he had, of course—at least with respect to those parts he had allowed Lucas to see. But his life, his family, was now dependent on getting to know all of him.

Simon was intelligent, manipulative, convincing, charming, certainly a leader. He was competitive, a game player. He was clean and orderly. Lucas had seen that in his work habits, his personal habits. Even the inside of his van was spit-and-shine, everything stacked on shelves that he had likely constructed himself.

Like Lucas. Or at least like him until he had got married and his neurotic bachelor ways were necessarily watered down by Cat's more spontaneous lifestyle. So after breakfast, when Simon called out the duty roster, Lucas's only surprise was that he had not been included. Perhaps special privileges for the aged and infirm.

Cat was in charge of cooking, Haley and Earl were elected to clean, which, judging by Earl's grumbling, did not sit well with him: Haley was to do the upstairs, Earl, the main floor. Zack was assigned to feed Rex, and while Simon was off shopping for groceries, Warren would be left in charge to stand guard.

"Who's this Rex?" Lucas asked Zack as he stood up to go to work.

"Hey, Lucas, if you have a question, I want

you to feel free to ask me direct," Simon said, as though he wanted to be helpful. "Rex is my pet snake."

"Is it dangerous?"

"If you don't bother it, it won't bother you."

That was the best he was going to get, he guessed. Simon handed the single key to Zack, and he headed downstairs with it. "So what about me?" Lucas asked.

"Volunteering for work, huh? See how this kind of cooperative life can begin to grow on you?" Lucas didn't respond, and Simon added, "I don't mean the part about Davidson getting killed or anything. That wasn't really in the plan. From what I could tell, he wasn't a half-bad guy. But accidents sometimes happen, particularly to people in that kind of dangerous business. I mean, the bottom line is, even if he didn't get killed, what were we going to do with him?"

"I don't know. What do you plan to do with us?"

"Stop worrying so much, Lucas. You're in one piece so far, aren't you?"

"So what you're saying is we're safe here?"

"Sure you are. Not that something unexpected couldn't happen. I mean, read the papers, Lucas, no one is totally safe these days. But I'm still here, working for you, trying my best to keep things as normal as possible.

Look around, other than a couple of hungry house guests, what's so different?"

Lucas looked at him, trying to decide what kind of head game he was playing. "In other words, if we try to leave here, you or your monkeys won't attempt to stop—"

"You know that's not what I mean," Simon said. "I *want* you guys here."

"Why? What do you need us for? You've got the beach, the cabin cruiser, the house."

"And I suppose you'd just walk away from it all. Is that what you're saying?"

The prospect was surely inviting, he'd certainly be willing to sacrifice anything to get his family out of there. But once they were on safe ground, he'd head straight for the police, and, of course, Simon wasn't dumb enough to think otherwise. Fortunately, there was no need to pretend otherwise: the conversation broke when Cat came onto the deck, holding a beach towel in front of herself, trying to hide the scant bikini she was wearing. "Warren picked it out, he insisted I wear it," she said to Lucas.

He looked at Simon. "So what about this? One minute you tell me not to worry, then we have to contend with this," he said, gesturing to Cat. "Do you really think these guys are going to be able to keep their hands off Cat and Haley while you're shopping? Why don't you let Warren do it and you stay here?"

"If you were so good at running things, Lucas, maybe you'd still be running things. Maybe your family wouldn't be in the position they're in now. Look, so you won't get in a sweat over this, I want you to know, these guys do what I tell them." To prove his statement, after sending Cat to the beach, he called Warren out to the deck. He was wearing the same short white T-shirt and Simon stepped up to him, his hands going for one of his sleeves.

But the bigger man yanked his arm away. "What the fuck do you think—"

"Relax a minute and shut up," Simon said, grabbing his arm and pushing the right short sleeve up to expose his shoulder. Warren stood there, his eyes avoiding them as Simon twisted his arm enough so Lucas could see.

On Warren's shoulder were five letters that had been thinly carved into his skin: SIMON.

Lucas was still at a loss for words as he stood alone on the deck listening to Simon going over the rules with his buddies inside: no drugs allowed while on duty; no one was to be physically harmed without provocation. "Provocation means someone deliberately causing trouble, like trying to get away," Simon added to ensure their understanding. "And though I have no problem with you browsing, keep your hands off the merchandise."

"I don't like this," Earl whined. "It's not like you said it would be."

A pause, then, "What is it you don't like?"

"You said we'd have fun with the ladies. I didn't come here just to look."

"No, I guess not," Simon said. "You came because I asked, and you'll stay for the same reason. But you're losing trust, my man, you shouldn't do that. All good things come to those who wait. Ever hear that said?" When there was no response from Earl, he went on, "Look, what's your rush? Being here a while, I got to know them a little ... I figure I owe them some extra time."

"How much?"

"I don't know, a few days maybe. Meanwhile, what's so bad? Listen, I said you'd have your fun with the ladies, and you will. Before we get rid of them."

Lucas heard the kitchen door bang, the van start up and take off down the road, and while he listened to these sounds, Simon's final words echoed through his brain. A few seconds later Warren came onto the deck, mumbling to himself while he lit up a cigarette without a filter. Agitated, he leaned over the railing, his weight bowing the rails. His stare settled in on Cat, and he licked his lips.

Lucas looked up and down the private

beaches, for the first time hating their seclusion. He had to come up with a viable escape plan, and he had to do it quick. Before Simon decided whatever debt he thought he owed them was paid . . . or his leadership was challenged internally. If Simon's structure began to shake, there'd be a lot of fallout, and there was no telling who would be killed then.

Zack found it strange that Simon still trusted him—he really shouldn't, Zack thought. But he'd given him the key and sent him down to the cellar alone. Now that he'd fed the bull snake, even gone over and petted Rex, he walked around the tool room. Looking, but not sure exactly what he was looking for.

Finally he picked up a short screwdriver, felt the tip with his finger and wondered if it was sharp enough to stick into someone's flesh. He didn't know. Besides, even if it was that sharp, he wasn't sure he'd have the guts to do a thing like that. He had never been able to hurt an animal, not even a fish, so he didn't suppose a human would be any easier. But he put it in his back pocket anyway, hidden under his untucked T-shirt.

Twice he'd passed the dead man's body lying on the floor. He had stopped to look at it, examine it, wondering if the dead man knew someone who might be out right now looking for him. Then finding an old tarp that had been used for painting on one of the shelves, he unfolded it and tossed it over the body.

Finally he left the tool room, locking the door behind him and putting the key in his pocket. Then he went over to the door leading to the beach. Looking out, he could see his mother lying on a beach towel. Up above, standing on the deck, was the monster man watching her.

He wanted to fuck her.

Zack hated him, he hated Earl, too—he wished he could stick the screwdriver into their hearts and kill them. He looked even farther over onto the deck, and saw his dad, just sitting there. When was he going to do something?

"Hey, kid, what're you doing down there?" a voice called to him from the kitchen doorway. Zack jumped and headed upstairs. Earl was waiting for him.

Haley usually hated to clean, but now she didn't mind. If nothing else it was keeping her busy enough so she wouldn't have to look at or be near Simon's repulsive friends. Or Simon. She even went to the trouble to change the sheets and pillowcases on hers and Zack's beds. Her brother had peed again. Wasn't Simon supposed to have performed some magic to make him stop?

She guessed not. Simon was just some sort of apparition, something she had made up in her head. And though in some ways he made it seem like he was still her friend, how could she possibly trust him now? Last night before she fell asleep, she heard Simon warn his friends not to go in her or Zack's bedrooms.

So he was still kind of looking out for them, wasn't he? But if that was so, why had he brought Warren and Earl to the beach house? Why had he had Dad beaten up that night? The more she thought about all the terrible things Simon had done, the more she decided Daddy had gotten the worst of it.

She was still thinking of that when she walked into the spare bedroom where Earl and Warren had taken turns sleeping the night before. Really it was Simon's bedroom, but she had never seen him sleep there. Still on top of the dresser, though, was his green duffel bag, the same one he put there the day he arrived.

Haley went to the door and peeked downstairs—Earl was vacuuming the carpets. She shut the door quietly, went back and took the duffel bag off the dresser, and brought it to the bed. She unzipped it and looked in: a red-print scarf, the kind Simon sometimes wore around his head, a pack of breath mints, three fresh rolls of Kodak film, and a camera. She lifted the camera out, wondering if Simon had used it since he'd been there. That's when she spotted the sealed manila envelope.

She took it out and stared at it, dying to know what it contained. What would he do if she did open it and he noticed? He'd want to know who'd unsealed it, of course, and then what kind of punishment ... But likely he hadn't even looked at the duffel bag since he'd left it. So why would he look now?

Before she could change her mind, she ripped open the seal, then took a deep breath. Oh, boy, she had actually done it, she could be in serious trouble now. She peeked inside the envelope: photographs, just like she had thought. A stack of them. She reached in, took them out ...

Daddy? But when?

He hated to have pictures taken of himself. She wondered how Simon had gotten him to pose when she and Mommy nearly had to bribe—Looking closer at a picture of him in the bathroom shaving, though, Daddy didn't really look like he was posing. No, more likely Simon had caught him off guard.

She flipped to the next picture. Again, him—this time working the gizmo on the TV. She began to go through the other pictures— Daddy on the deck, on a lounger, reading a newspaper, opening the door—his hands were up protesting that time—looking for food in the refrigerator, cutting a watermelon, on the boat, eating a hot dog, under the shower, fast asleep in bed . . .

The boat? But he wasn't—She looked back to the picture of him in the boat, and that's when it dawned on her that in none of the pictures was her father wearing a leg cast. She began to examine all of them more closely: Daddy looked thinner, younger.

But that didn't make any sense at all. If Daddy had known Simon before that night at Chatfield Hollow, wouldn't he have said so? Despite the strangeness of it all, Haley's first inclination was to put the pictures back in the envelope so no one else would violate Simon's privacy. Then suddenly she realized how she could really get him. She would show those pictures to her folks.

Cat had been lying on the sand for more than an hour. Though she wasn't facing his direction, she could feel Warren's presence back on the deck, his eyes following her every movement. Determined to be aware of what was happening around her, she had forgone the pills. Of course she was frightened, yet peculiarly not with the same intensity as earlier. It was as though her brain in response to her fear had released some panic control chemical of its own.

Lying there, she tried to remember everything that had happened since the start of the whole ordeal, no matter how inconsequential it seemed. If she could see all the puzzle pieces in front of her, she might discover something to help them out of this.

Her thoughts kept returning to Winnie's murder. Though Cat was now certain Simon and his friends were responsible for her death, she couldn't figure out why. Was it simply Winnie not liking Simon and vice versa? Not a rational motive for murder, assuming any murder was rational. But suppose Winnie had somehow become an obstacle in their scheme? Suppose Winnie had discovered Simon's involvement in this . . .

The idea was tossed aside as her daughter unexpectedly dropped onto her knees beside her in the sand. She was wearing a sweat suit with her belted purse. Cat began to sit up, but Haley shook her head. "Wait, don't do that. I'll lie next to you. That way he won't see," she said, referring of course to Warren. Cat scrunched over, making enough room for Haley on the towel.

"They didn't object to you coming out?" Cat said.

She shook her head. "Warren made me open my purse and show him what I kept inside before he let me leave, though," she said, her voice starting to break. "Mom, he made me open the zipper compartment, too. You know, where I keep my pads." Haley had begun her period only a few months ago, and ever since had kept a mini-pad in her purse for emergencies. Without further warning, tears began to course down her cheeks. Cat put her arm around her daughter, bringing her face close and kissing her, but the sobbing went on.

Although Haley was surely sensitive about the issue, Cat doubted it was causing the tears. She was substituting the issues, protecting herself from her real fears. How amazing it was that her adopted daughter was so much like her.

"It's going to be okay, honey," she said, using Lucas's words, and knowing if they had any chance, they'd have to believe it. "We're going to get out of this."

"I loved him so much, Mommy," she said, automatically referring to Simon. "I trusted him. And I thought he felt the same about me. But all that time he was laughing at me."

"We all trusted him. We all liked him—even your father, who I've never known to be gullible. Simon is quite a convincing young man. We can't blame ourselves for that."

Haley wiped her eyes and looked up at Cat. "Mom, I found some pictures I think you should see." Taken aback, Cat just looked at her. "Pictures of Daddy," she said.

After looking up and around, she reached into one of the side pockets of her sweatpants and withdrew a stack of photographs, held together by an elastic band.

Still unsure why Haley was being so secretive, Cat discreetly took the pictures from her daughter and removed the elastic. As she began to look through the photographs of Lucas, she narrowed her eyes in puzzlement. She'd never seen any of them before. They clearly had been taken when Lucas was younger, before she had even met him. And, that one: that was taken before the beach house kitchen was revamped. Startled, she looked at Haley. "Where did you find these?"

"Sealed in an envelope in Simon's duffel bag. Upstairs in the spare bedroom."

Cat sucked in a breath. "Oh, yes, this must be it." She had no idea how this piece fit, only that it did. The pictures had everything to do with Simon's being here. Since he would have been far too young to take them himself, he'd have to have gotten them from a third party. Someone he knew, someone Lucas knew.

And Winnie, who'd been around the beach house nearly as long as Lucas, must have figured out who that person was.

Chapter Nineteen

When Simon returned, loaded down with bags of food, the house went from grim silence to maniacal activity. Like a campground, a steak and sausage barbecue was planned for lunch, and Simon and the kids helped Cat set it up. A roster of activities were scheduled for the afternoon: swimming, volleyball, table tennis, sailing, fishing, motorcycling.

All these things Simon had done before, but now in addition to Haley and Zack, who he included in the activities, Warren or Earl would join in, too. Soon they started chugging beer, firing up joints—Haley bowing out this time. Now there seemed to be a frenzy and passion in every move Simon made.

By late afternoon Lucas began to see patterns. For instance, every four hours guard duty changed. One of the three stepped back from the fun and, sporting a pistol in a shoulder holster and the cellular phone on his belt, watched rather than joined the activities. Being the responsible one, the guard did no drugs while on duty. He remained either in the house or out on the deck with Lucas, who was limited to those areas. Though Cat was under scrutiny, too, she was given a lot more leeway, able to go down to the water, join the activities, or go to her room.

Simon made it clear that if by chance a person should approach the house or property, Lucas would be in immediate jeopardy, which discouraged Cat or the children from even considering alerting anyone of their ordeal. The night before Simon had said he wanted Lucas to sleep on the sofa, where the man on patrol could keep his eye on him. Lucas had no reason to believe tonight would be any different.

As a result, Lucas decided, Cat and the kids might well have the opportunity to get out from under the siege, if circumstances were just right, if no one expected it. If he could somehow engage the guard.

Lucas began to consider the internal workings of the group. Rather than dread the moment when Simon and Warren and Earl would ultimately butt heads, what if he were instrumental in determining when it would occur? He could prepare Cat and the kids, get them ready to take advantage of the moment, and pounce on it. More important, he had to convince them to escape without him.

Warren was the pressure cooker, of course, his nozzle was within centimeters of blowing. If Lucas were to play with someone's mind, he would be the one.

Benny Cusack was a thirty-five-year man, a retired night-watchman from Pratt & Whitney. He'd retired seven years ago on a pension that looked good only on paper. Since then, to sweeten the finances, he'd been working occasionally for Roger Davidson. Stakeouts mostly, finding out where people were holing up, hiding from bill collectors, from wives going after alimony and child support payments. The work was easy, just a matter of being on your toes. Recognizing a person from a picture, then following him home and reporting the findings to Davidson.

The policy was for Benny to call in his report at nine o'clock the morning after a job, and find out if Davidson wanted him to continue with it. If his boss wasn't in—which sometimes happened—Benny left a message on the answering machine. But never did he remember him not returning his call by noon.

Already close to five, Benny called again, got the machine again, and left another message. He hadn't a clue as to what Davidson wanted: should he stake out the club again or not? So far he hadn't had any luck, maybe it was a bad bet. Maybe the client didn't want to put up more money on it. Still and all . . .

Some people were reliable and you came to expect reliability. Others were as unpredictable as the weather forecast—something wise people knew not to count on. Davidson was one of those people you could count on, just about set your watch by. The kind you worried about when this kind of shit occurred.

If he could have, Benny would have called someone, inquired if everything was okay. But who? No secretary, no wife, and as far as Benny knew, not even a girlfriend. The guy lived alone in the two back rooms of his office.

Since all the horror and fear had entered their lives, Cat had been out of tune with Lucas. But apparently that part of their marriage was once again operating: Cat had been convinced since that afternoon that Lucas wanted to talk to her alone. And certainly she needed to talk to him about those pictures.

She had taken the photographs inside by hiding them in her beach towel and finally when she went to her bedroom to change, she put them in her nightstand drawer. But since then they hadn't had a minute alone. Simon was now on guard duty, so when the cellular phone on his belt rang, he unhooked it and handed it to her. Then he took his gun out and went over to Lucas.

"Okay, Cat," he began, "whoever it is, get rid of them. But don't be rude, I don't want them getting suspicious. No weepy voice, okay? I want to make it clear, there are no second chances."

With that, he put the muzzle of the gun to Lucas's head. She took a deep breath and when she finally turned the phone on and greeted the caller on the fifth ring, her voice quavered only slightly.

"Cat, that you?"

"Yes," she said brightly. Too brightly.

"I was beginning to think you people were out."

"Oh, no, we're in. You know us stay-at-homers. So what can I do for you, Jack?"

"I thought it was the other way around." When she didn't answer, he said, "I got a message here from Shirley. It says to call you as soon as I get back from the mountains."

"Oh, gosh, yes. Would you believe it slipped my mind? What's the matter with me? I'm afraid my memory is beginning to go downhill lately." She chuckled, thinking it sounded unnatural. She looked at Simon, who didn't bat an eye, so she guessed it was acceptable. "So how's Gary, how's his family?"

"Oh, great, the kids are all doing swell. Sandi, the youngest, is going into high school next year. A real math whiz—her school counselor recommends that she be put in an accelerated class. But enough of me bragging about the grandkids, that's not why I called. So what is it you called about, Cat?"

"Oh, it's nothing really."

"What does that mean? It was worth a call, it must have been something."

"Oh, the same old thing. Just that I was concerned about Lucas. He seemed awfully down for a while—"

"Listen, I was thinking. Linda and I, in fact, were discussing it on the way home from New Hampshire. I've noticed myself that Lucas doesn't seem right. So we thought maybe it'd be a good idea to come out there, spend a couple of days"

The idea for a moment sounded like a godsend, someone coming to the rescue! Until Cat thought of the ramifications, Jack and Linda walking into the middle of all this, unsuspecting and vulnerable . . .

"No, wait, before you go ahead and make plans," she said. "I mean, not that we wouldn't love to see you. But . . . well, just the other day Lucas started to snap out of his depression. The leg cast is about to come off— the appointment's in about a week, so that's helping his spirits. And . . . well, since things have been so distant, I kind of counted on these next couple of weeks . . . It's been so long—"

"Jesus, what an idiot I am! Sure, I get it, of course, you kids want to be alone," he teased. "Hey, what do you think, I need you to draw me a diagram?"

She chuckled again, this time easier. "I'll be sure to tell Lucas you called him a kid. He's apt to kiss you."

At that, Jack laughed. But when he said he was about to put Linda on, she backed out of it. "We're right in the middle of a tense Scrabble match, and it's my turn," she said. "Lucas and the kids are looking at me with their daggers honed. Will you tell Linda I'll call her soon? And tell her I love her. You, too, Jack."

She turned off the phone and laid it on the coffee table. When she stepped away, her eyes were wet. But she'd done good, she could tell that by the way Lucas was looking at her. And Simon took the gun muzzle from his head.

That night, Simon sent the kids to bed early and announced that the guys were going to play poker. "Lucas, that's your game, right?" Lucas nodded, and Simon said, "Hey, guys, we're in for a real treat. Lucas used to be one of those big-time players." Again he looked at Lucas and grinned. "Right?" Though Lucas felt a setup coming on, he was left no choice but to agree.

"That's what I like—winners," Simon said. He glanced at Warren, who was just coming down from locking the kids in. "Get the cards, and poker chips." To Earl, who was on guard duty, he gestured toward the kitchen. "Take out some poker food. You can play, but no booze or coke."

Cat stood up. "I'm tired. So if you don't mind," she said, directing her request to Simon, "I'm going to go to my room."

Simon nodded. "Sure enough, pretty lady, you do whatever makes you happy. If you're in the mood—now, I'm not pushing you, just suggesting, but you could put on that nice negligee. Maybe model it for us during a break." He looked at the guys for affirmation. "Wouldn't that be nice, guys?"

She ignored his taunting, knowing it was primarily meant to provide a jolly for his buddies. They obliged him by smirking, chuckling, and giving her indecent looks. But she tried to ignore all that, to approach her next request of Simon in just the right voice.

"Simon, I was wondering, could I talk to Lucas? It would be just a matter of—"

"Sorry," he said, cutting her right off, "your guy's about to compete." Taking the cards from Warren, he began to shuffle. "What's your game, Lucas?"

Cat could see Lucas's disappointment at being denied time with her, but Simon forged ahead, and she left it alone, heading toward the bedroom. As she did, she felt a hand on her bottom, and she spun to see Earl's smirking face look up at her.

Sneaky, slimy, and disgusting. She jerked as though a bug had lighted on her, displacing his hand. No one else was aware it had happened. She hurried into the bedroom and closed the door, feeling dirty and relieved to be out of reach.

"Okay, name it, Lucas," she heard Simon say. "What's your passion, my man?"

Five-card stud, Lucas told him, and Earl complained, saying it was boring.

"Earl's kind of game is one-eyed jacks and black ladies wild," Warren said.

"Well, relax, my friends. This game is Lucas's, he calls the shots." Simon began dealing.

Unable to keep his mind on the game, within two hours Lucas had lost his chips and Earl was down to a few. The remainder were pretty evenly distributed between Simon and Warren. So when the next pot was taken by Simon, Lucas pushed back his chair.

Warren reached out and grabbed his wrist, stopping him. "Hey there, man. Now where in the fuck do you think you're going off to?"

"My money's gone," Lucas said.

"Well, there are other things beside money worth playing for." Not subtle, he nodded his head toward the bedroom, indicating he meant Cat. "Get my drift?"

Lucas didn't answer—instead he looked toward Simon. Though he didn't know exactly what reaction he expected, Simon in his own peculiar way had been insulating the Marshalls against his accomplices' more immediate threats. What he saw in Simon's face now, however, made his stomach knot.

"The man makes a legitimate offer, he's got money left, you don't. So he's willing to accept his payment in other things," Simon said. "Hell, what could be nicer?"

Lucas swallowed over a swell in his throat. Was the extra time Simon felt he owed them drawing to a close? "You implied yesterday, no one would get hurt," he said.

Simon smiled. "Get a grip, Lucas, last I noticed, fucking doesn't hurt one iota. The lady herself told me how good it felt. You want me to get her up now and ask her?"

Lucas had an overwhelming urge to smash that smile off his face. But even if he was crazy enough to take a shot, what would it solve? Certainly not a thing with respect to Cat. Instead, Lucas tried to appeal to Simon's selective sense of justice. And in the process, he said something that nearly choked him.

"Well, Simon, maybe that's because she chose to give it to you," he said. "You didn't take it without asking."

"No, I didn't, did I?" Simon said, thoughtful as though he were considering Lucas's argument. "But, Lucas, we are talking right now about getting it fair and square. No one's suggesting Warren ought to just take what isn't his. Hey, that's called rape last time I checked. And that's off-limits."

Limits. It was impossible to know what Simon's limits were, Lucas was seeing that more and more. He thought back to that night at Chatfield Hollow when Earl had been just about to force Cat down on him. Just where did that fall in Simon's scale of right and wrong? Would he have jumped in to stop it if Lucas hadn't?

"Of course, if Warren wins her," Simon went on, "then she's his to use. At least temporarily. Right?"

"She's not mine to lose, though, is she?" Lucas came back.

"Yeah, true. But I was just trying to be a good guy, letting you act on her behalf. Sort of like an executor of a last will and testament. I mean, I figure you know more about poker than she. So this way it gives her a better shot."

Lucas couldn't believe he was even having this conversation. Finally he said, firmly, "Forget it. I have no intention of making that kind of bet. Money, goods, property, you name it. But not that." He began to push away from the table when Simon stood up, walked to the bedroom door, and put his hand over the knob. "What are you doing?" he asked, though he already knew.

"If you won't play for her, then she'll have to play. And if she refuses, she reneges, which in effect is the same as losing. I'm trying to be decent here, Lucas, make sure everyone has a good time. But if you and Cat are going to refuse to join the activities, why should I put myself out?"

Simon, having baited Lucas fully, paused a moment, giving him time. They were all watching Lucas now, waiting. Earl with his dark eyes glowing, and Warren grinning like a village idiot. The knot in Lucas's stomach was now so tight, it felt like it was tearing into his stomach. Finally, he picked up the cards and looked across the table.

"Okay, Warren, you've got yourself a game. It's just you and me. Right?"

"Hey, what about me?" Earl piped up, suddenly deciding he'd been left out.

But Simon put that complaint to rest. "Keep a lid on it," he said. "It's Lucas's call."

Warren wrung his big, chunky hands and looked at Lucas. "Yes, my man. Just you and me. You know acey-deucey?"

Lucas did—a game with a simple concept that he used to play years ago. You anted up a set amount, then were dealt two cards—both of which were face-up. When the dealer got to you, you either passed or bid: the bid being that the third card the dealer would turn up for you would fall between—but not match—the original two cards. The amount of the bid could go from one cent to the entire pot. You either added to or subtracted from the pot depending on the amount of your bid, depending if you won or lost. After each player took a turn, new cards were dealt.

Lucas nodded. "We each start with five hundred in chips; we ante ten apiece, the pot beginning at twenty bucks. When the pot's gone or a player is bankrupted—whichever comes first—the game is over. The one with the most money in his till wins. The only stipulation being the game must go around at least twice first. Is that agreed upon?"

Warren took a toothpick, stuck it next to his decayed tooth, then leaned his chair back and howled. "A deal, old man. Shit," he said, "I can smell pussy right from here." He leaned forward and said to Lucas, "I'm already so hard, I could drill a hole in a brick. Want to take a feel?" He and Earl began to roar.

Simon was flying too high to waste his time laughing. He took the cards from Lucas and announced he'd be dealer. "I've got to say, this is exciting business. How about it, Lucas? Here you've been letting yourself get out of shape, maybe a little dull. Likely the only thing hardening on you these days are your arteries. And to make it sadder, I bet you were a wild man when you were young."

Lucas's only thought was, What will I do if I lose? Dozens of answers came rushing at him—not one of them logical or possible. So the bottom line was, he'd have to take his best shot at them, and let them beat him up until he lost consciousness. At that point he wouldn't have to know or see what was happening to Cat.

But he wasn't there yet. Though Lucas hadn't gambled seriously in years, he remembered the key rule of poker: the guy who is scared to lose, loses. He simply had to be confident.

Easier said than done.

But everything counted on it. So he forced his mind to put Cat aside, to think of this game in terms of cash value only.

And waited for the cards to come. His first cards were a nine and a queen. A ten and a jack would be the only winning cards—he passed. Warren got a three and an eight—a poor bet, only four cards would make him a winner. But he took a shot on the entire twenty. He drew a jack and had to match the pot.

The pot now held forty dollars.

Benny finally decided not to go on the stakeout without Davidson's okay. At about nine o'clock that night, he put in a call to the New London police. He felt a little foolish doing it, but he'd remembered that Davidson knew a lot of the cops on the force. So what would it hurt to let them know he was concerned? For that matter, maybe Davidson had met with an accident, in which case they might know about it.

A lieutenant named Lester Hutchins took the call, and Benny laid it out, trying not to make it sound like a major deal, which would label him a flake right off.

"Any idea what case he was on?" Hutchins asked after he took down his name and number.

"Yeah, sure. He had me doing a stakeout on it, too. The client's name is Marshall. Davidson was looking for two guys who'd beaten up this Marshall fellow a few weeks back. The client lived over at the point in Clinton. Don't know the first name."

"Look, what I'm going to do is put a note on the bulletin board here," Hutchins said. "See if one of the fellows on the day shift has any information. If not, I'll see that the

Clinton police are called. Maybe they know something we don't."

Fifteen minutes had gone by, a long time for one game. But Lucas had seen it occur before. Guys tended to bet on anything when the stakes were peanuts, but once the pot grew big, they made the error of letting the money amount be the betting guide, not the cards.

Another factor entered his calculations as well: the ability to remember cards. Like blackjack, the deck was not reshuffled until it was fully played out. So if a player had good mathematical recall, he was able to make a knowledgeable guess as to what cards were left in the deck.

Lucas had always been good at this part— and good at waiting, too. He simply had to wait until the right combination presented itself, and then he'd go for it. So far he hadn't seen his chance. The pot was now up past seven hundred dollars—most of it having been put in by Warren. Still, if he won it, he'd surpass Lucas.

Warren was dealt a two and a ten—a fairly good hand, seven cards could win it for him. But from Lucas's computations, the deck was way overdue for a picture card. Any of which would lose the pot for him—and bankrupt him. Lucas felt his heart begin to hammer.

Yes, go ahead, bet it all, you bastard.

Warren looked at the cards, at the money in the center, taking a rough accounting of what he had left on the table. The beads of sweat that had hung firm to his forehead now began to slide down his face.

"Go for it," Earl said. "It's a good bet."

Lucas shrugged, as though to question Earl's assessment. As he intended, Warren picked up on it. "What's the matter, fuck-off, you don't think it's a good bet?"

"Did you hear me say anything?"

"No, you didn't have to. What do you think I am, some kind of schmuck? You think I don't know you're trying to make me doubt it? My buddy's right, it is a good bet."

Lucas looked at Warren's depleted money pile and shook his head. "Hey, each to his own style of playing," he said. "You like it, then by all means bet it."

Warren took a rag from his pocket and wiped the sweat from his face. "Okay, uh, maybe . . . I'm going to bet . . . but I don't know if I should go for it all. Maybe—"

The way Warren was hemming and hawing, he'd likely bet but it didn't look like he had the guts to bet it all. At least until Simon did a chicken cackle.

"Okay, time's a-ticking. What do you want to ride on it, chicken little, a sawbuck?"

It was Simon's put down that cinched it. Warren, unable to stomach the idea that Simon might think he was a gutless wonder, squeezed the rag in his fist and licked his beefy lips. "Okay. I bet the fucking pot!"

As in slow motion, Lucas watched Simon as he began to pull the top card. An eerie silence descended on the room, as though Lucas's eardrums had been pressurized. Simon snapped the card onto the table.

"A king of spades! You're over!" Simon shouted, looking at Warren. "Looks like you lose."

Warren, unable to take his wrath out on Simon, turned instead on Earl, shouting and cursing at him while Earl backed off. Simon nodded to Lucas. "A good game," he said, putting his hand out to shake. But Lucas stood up, went into the kitchen, and turned on the cold water faucet. He held his head under the water for a few seconds.

Finally he yanked the kitchen towel off the rack and dried his hair and face. He felt as though a two-ton truck had just backed off his chest.

Just at that moment Cat began to scream. Lucas started toward the bedroom, but Warren, done intimidating Earl, stepped in front of Lucas, blocking his path.

Chapter Twenty

An hour and a half had passed since Cat excused herself to go to her bedroom. She hadn't actually slept, but now she was pretending to have had a nightmare. So when Simon came rushing in, she sat up, looked right through him, and went on screaming. Her fear came easily, and once she got into the screaming, the only difficult part was to stop.

Unable to quiet her, Simon left, and a few moments later Lucas was let in. Even beyond her act, his presence calmed her down. To be alone with him, his strong arms around her, momentarily obliterated all the horror around them. After last night's admission to Lucas, she wasn't so sure those arms would ever be around her again. But last night already seemed light-years away.

"Lucas, you're all wet," she said, feeling his hair against her face. "What happened?" But he shook his head as though it were nothing for her to be concerned about; relieved, she

360

dropped it. "I needed to talk to you," she said.

"Me, too," he said, his lips burying through her hair, kissing her. Finally he pulled away and looked at her. "We don't have much time to talk, Cat," he said softly. "Maybe only a few minutes before Simon is at the door wanting me out of here. So I need you to pay attention to what I'm going to say."

She sighed, nodded. "I'm listening."

"Babe, if we want to get out of here, we're going to have to do it ourselves. And we're going to have to do it before—" He stopped as though he'd taken the wrong track, then backed up. "Cat, if I've ever needed you to be strong—"

She put her hands to his lips, stopping him. "What do you want me to do?"

"I have no hard, fast plan—it's going to have to play by ear. What I'm going to try to do is use what I know about them to manipulate the situation. Provide an opportunity where they're too preoccupied to notice what's going on. And when the opportunity comes, I want you and the kids ready to get out of here."

"Provide it how?"

"Mainly by working on Warren. Hopefully tonight while he's on duty and the others are asleep, then again tomorrow. He's the weak link here, Cat, the one who's about to lose it either way. I'm just going to hurry up the process some. And hopefully when he blows, it will be Simon he goes for, not us."

"I still don't understand what—"

"Just go along with whatever I come up with, assuming, of course, you can make it appear natural. I'm leaning toward this all coming together by tomorrow night, once it starts to get dark. And though Warren won't be on duty at the time I have in mind, I'm going to do my best to change that. If I can execute this right, I ought to piss off Warren sufficiently to bring the house down."

"Okay, so you're saying there'll be some kind of blowup between them?" He nodded his head, and she said, "But I don't get it. How are we supposed to get away?"

"How does the Jeep sound?"

"Did you forget, Simon took our keys?"

He opened his wallet, and as he took the spare Jeep key out, she remembered when he'd put it there. Now he slipped it into her nightstand drawer. "Tomorrow morning when you get up, put this on you and keep it on you."

His idea seemed so unplanned, so vague, and incredibly chancy. "Don't you think Simon will notice if we all get up and march away? Even if he's got his hands full with Warren?"

"Simple plans are always the best. Watch

for my signal. When I give it to you, just take the kids and run. Let me worry about whether Simon notices."

"But you'll be—"

Before he shook his head, she realized what he was about to say. He wasn't going with them. "No," she said, shaking her head. "I won't go without you."

He grasped her upper arms firmly, his fingers digging hard into her flesh. "Listen to me, Cat, you have to. If I'm right in their faces, then they won't bother looking for you or the kids. Please, babe, trust me. You can do this."

"But what about you?"

"I'll be okay—at least until someone gets back here to bail me out. That's where I'm counting on you. Be sure those cops don't make any pit stops on the way."

His meager attempt at humor fell flat. "But, suppose I can't—" she started, but then ended abruptly as the door flew open. Simon was standing there.

"What's going on here, Lucas? I said a few minutes with your lady, and you agreed."

Lucas turned. "You're right, you did. But she was pretty shook. One more minute, Simon?"

Simon looked at them, his watch, then sighing, shook his head. "Okay, you've got it. One minute. You're on the clock." He stepped back and closed the door.

Now they had no time at all to talk. She pulled open the nightstand drawer, took out the batch of photographs, and held it out to Lucas. "Look at these when you're alone," she said. "Haley found them upstairs in Simon's knapsack."

His eyebrows drew together. "But what?" he began.

"Thirty seconds," Simon called out.

"Just take them," she said, starting to panic at the thought that Simon would open the door again and this time not close it.

Seeing her agitation, Lucas took the photographs and shoved them in his shorts side pocket, making sure his T-shirt covered the bulge. He leaned over and kissed her. "It's almost over," he said, the slight break in his voice at odds with his otherwise measured tone. "Hey, babe, have I mentioned how much I love you?"

Oh, yes, Lucas, many, many times . . . She watched him leave—the single most important person in her life. She swallowed hard, tears starting to stream down her cheeks. What if she and the kids did make it, but she couldn't get to the police in enough time? What would Simon and his friends do to Lucas?

* * *

When Lucas left the room, he went to the sofa, sat down, and watched the party in front of him go on. Simon and Earl were snorting coke. Warren, who had just started his guard rotation, thus not allowed to do drugs, was pacifying himself with food. His gun in his shoulder holster, he sat at the dining-room table, a salami in one hand, a half loaf of French bread smeared with butter in the other. Grease covered his lips and collected in peaks at the corners of his mouth. Lucas, repulsed by the sight of him, wished he would choke.

Finally, Lucas stood up and headed to the bathroom. Warren reached toward his gun. "Where're you going, old man?"

"To take a shit. Is that okay?"

Warren, apparently the poker loss already stored away in his mindless head, dallied with him. "Sure. Be sure to call me in to watch you wipe your ass."

Locked alone in the bathroom, Lucas took out the photographs from his pocket and began to look through them. Of him. And apparently taken many years ago. How had Simon come across them? Unless, of course, he took them from Cat's albums.

He swallowed hard—no, Cat would have said if she'd seen the pictures before. Not until he got to the fifth picture—the look of surprise, his hands up as if to block the camera lens—did he finally realize what he was actually looking at . . .

He'd had a bad bout of pneumonia that winter—about two years after he'd bought the beach property. That would be about twenty-two years ago. Though he was pretty much over the pneumonia and back on his feet by late spring, he hadn't quite gotten his strength back. On doctor's orders he'd decided to take a few weeks off, recuperate, and get back in shape at the beach house.

He'd really been sticking to the program: no partying, gambling, women, whatever. Just the beach, lots of sunshine and fun. Good food, jogging every morning and night, boating, fishing, reading, sports on TV, plenty of rest.

So when he answered the kitchen door one afternoon and found a good-looking blonde standing there holding a camera, he was caught off guard. He knew he hadn't invited anyone. But before he could even ask what she'd wanted, the camera flash went off in his eyes. And he raised his hands in protest.

"What the hell—" he began.

"Oh, no, no. Don't be upset. I just needed to get a snapshot to go with the house." She slid past him, walked through the kitchen, into the great room. Lucas could picture her now as he'd seen her then: great tits, great ass. She was wearing high heels, a black and white striped dress. "Oh, my, yes, it's perfect," she gushed. "Just like I knew it would be." Her voice was deep for a woman, kind of scratchy.

Like Simon's. Was there a resemblance? Lucas compared the two faces in his head and decided there was. And then he remembered she'd had webbed toes.

Lucas was now beginning to feel warm. Since there was no window, he reached out and switched on the fan. Then he lowered himself onto the toilet seat. He turned one of the snapshots in his hand, looking to read the date printed on the side. Yes, he was right in his calculations—he had known her twenty-two years ago. Relieved to have that reaffirmed, his mind went back to that day.

She had begun taking more pictures and more pictures, and Lucas, getting more than mildly pissed, went to lift the camera out of her hands. But she ducked away.

"Look, why don't you tell me what this is about?"

She smiled at him, shrugging off his annoyance. "So when I list the house—"

"Want to tell me what the hell you're talking about? If you're a real estate broker, you'd better go hunt up a better prospect. I have no intention of selling."

"But I could get you major bucks for this." She backed up, began to snap pictures of him, too. "Oh, I love it—surprise, indignation, anger. Your expressions are magical."

"Look, would you stop it?" he said. "I'm going to take the fucking camera and smash it!"

She lowered the camera finally and shrugged. "You can't blame a girl for trying, can you?"

He knew women well enough to recognize the body language, sort of a kittenish quality. She was definitely flirting with him. But he ignored it, asking instead, "Is this how you usually get your listings? Bust right into people's houses."

"You'd be surprised what works." She looked toward the sliding doors again, at the ocean. "It is a fantastic property, though. I know I've been a nuisance." She waited for his denial. When it didn't come, she said, "Mind if I take a swim out there?"

"It's a public watering hole," he said, thinking it odd that she'd be wearing a swimsuit under her clothes. The lady was apparently well prepared.

She headed toward the sliders, opened them, and turned. "I'll just leave my things on your deck, then pick them up before I go. That is, if you don't mind." He shook his head, and she added, "Don't worry, I won't disturb you again."

Closing the sliders after her, she went to

one of the deck loungers and set down her camera. Standing with her back to him, she took off her shoes, set them down next to the camera. Then finally she lifted her dress, pulled it over her head.

She was wearing nothing beneath . . .

A short-lived celibacy, he remembered thinking as he opened the doors to the deck. She didn't attempt to turn until she heard him come up in back of her, and then when she did try, he held her firm, not letting her. "You lied," he whispered in her ear.

"Oh?"

"I'm disturbed." He then lifted her partway onto the table and entered her from the back.

"What are you doing, shitting bricks?" Warren shouted from outside the bathroom door, jolting him out of his thoughts. Lucas quickly slid the pictures back into his pocket, but the memories kept coming.

He had fucked her—on the deck, in the kitchen, then again in bed before he finally asked her name. Pamela Bowerman. She pronounced it with a long O. She wasn't a real estate broker at all. She was from out west, had come east for vacation. Apparently she'd spotted Lucas in the Ocean Haven Diner having breakfast, the place where Winnie used to waitress. And she followed him back to the house.

She stayed there for nine days—great sex.

But she was nuts. Really certifiable. The picture taking went on and on—he couldn't take a leak without her jumping in with a camera to get it for posterity. She was so insecure, she'd hang up the telephone on his business calls. And the goddamned flowers . . . Yes, the gladiolis, all over the house. Even on his dinner plate.

It was hell getting rid of her. She broke into the beach house twice after, and he'd warned her, one more time and he'd swear out a police complaint. And the calls were unrelenting. He finally had to get an unlisted number. About a month later, she began to call his office in Massachusetts—he had left orders not to put her through.

Just when he thought he'd seen the last of her, she showed up at the beach house again. He was only there for the weekend and, not anticipating it was her, answered the door. That was the same night she told him she was pregnant.

The door now burst open, and Simon was standing there. "Hey, want to tell me what the hell you're doing?"

Fortunately, Simon didn't require an answer to his question. Lucas quietly followed him from the bathroom to the great room and sat on the sofa, his head still spinning. He had given Pamela money for an abortion. She had wanted to marry him, but he refused. Dammit, he didn't trust her. He wasn't even sure she was telling the truth about the pregnancy, let alone about it being his kid. Besides, the idea of marriage to her was beyond ridiculous—there was no way he was going to compound one mistake with another . . .

But the crucial element was, all this had happened twenty-two years ago. Simon was only nineteen—Lucas was certain he remembered him saying so that first day he came to the beach house. So why pick out Lucas? Maybe Simon had it all mixed up. Was it possible he thought Lucas was his father?

"Simon," he said finally, the name coming out before he even knew he was going to say it. Simon, who had been listening to a CD, seeming a little buzzed from the drugs, looked up when he said his name. "Can I talk to you?" he asked.

"Sure, Lucas. Go ahead, talk."

"No. Alone. Can we be alone?"

Simon looked around, then with his thumb toward the sliders, he motioned the guys out.

"Shit, it's cold out there tonight," Warren complained.

"Don't let it bother you. With a gut that size, you're not apt to freeze."

Though Earl chuckled, Warren didn't find Simon humorous. Still he handed Simon the gun and followed Earl out to the deck. Then

Simon went and turned off the CD. "Okay, what's on your mind?"

"You remind me of someone," Lucas said, not knowing what other way to begin.

"Hey, maybe I'm your fantasy girl."

"I used to know a woman—"

"Wow, isn't that something—"

"Are you going to let me talk or not?"

"Hey, sure, I'm sorry," he said, actually looking sorry. "Go on and talk."

Lucas finally took the plunge and said, "The lady's name was Pamela Bowerman. She was your mother, wasn't she?"

Simon's eyes widened. His legs, which had been carelessly draped over the side of the chair, now lifted back to the floor. He sat forward and asked, "You remember her?"

Not fond memories certainly, and until tonight he hadn't thought of her in years. But of course he remembered her. How could he not? He nodded his head. "What happened to her?"

"She made one of those dramatic and unforgettable exits. When I was six months old she slit her wrists. She died. I guess she didn't much like my looks."

The cavalier way Simon said it only served to heighten the effect. Lucas felt a shock pedal down his neck, feeling suddenly as though he'd somehow had a hand in her death. But that was insane: he had hardly known Pamela

Bowerman, her suicide hadn't occurred until three years after their brief affair. And obviously she'd had other involvements since theirs. "I'm sorry," Lucas said finally.

"I guess you don't miss what you never had."

More trite stuff people say to try to deal with their feelings. So he didn't contradict him. "What year did you say that was?" Lucas asked.

"I didn't. But if you're asking because you're wondering if you're my old man, you can relax. I thought I told you I was nineteen when we first met?"

"You did, but ... Well, it's surely no coincidence you're here." When Simon didn't respond, Lucas said, "I remember you mentioning your aunt brought you up. What about your father?"

Simon shrugged. "What about him?"

"Where is he?"

"He took off on her. I never got to know him."

The kid had been gypped twice. But sadly, Lucas could relate to any guy taking off on Pamela. "Well, then, why me, Simon? Why all this elaborate plot?"

"You were her main man. The one she loved."

"No, I think you're mistaken. The truth is, I didn't even know her long."

"I've got pictures of you. Lots of pictures. Even movies. Want to see them?"

Lucas shook his head. Now that Simon said it, he recalled the home movies ... Shit, he even remembered her setting up a movie camera to operate while they were having sex. Did Simon have that, too? "Simon, ever think of trying to find your father? With enough money, it might not be so hard to do."

"Forget it. I have no burning need to meet him. You were the one she cared about."

Trying to talk him out of it seemed useless. So Lucas gave up and went on from there. "Even assuming that were true, which is unlikely since she obviously later had a relationship with your father, what is it you want from me?"

He shrugged. "I don't know, maybe just to feel close to her. She loved you, but not me—at least not enough to stay alive. So who better to get near to get a feel for her?"

"This is insane."

"Tell me something about her." Now he crossed his arms at his chest and stared at Lucas, waiting.

Lucas cleared his throat. What do you tell a kid about a mother he'd never known, one who was a mental case? And still try to keep to some truth. "When I knew her, she was vibrant," he said. "She seemed to have life by the tail."

"Good-looking?" Simon asked, smiling. As he did, he looked like the slightly shy boy who had come to the beach house three weeks earlier, the boy Lucas liked. But now he had to remind himself that this boy was a killer.

Lucas nodded. "You must have seen pictures. Beautiful. Classic looks. Blond. You look like her. You even sound like her. She had a unique voice."

"But you didn't notice any of that before?"

"It's been a long time, Simon."

"Did you love her?"

Damn. Not so easy to come up with an acceptable truth for that. "I admired her, Simon," Lucas hedged. "Your mother didn't seem afraid of anything. Not like other people—no inhibitions, no fears. She went after what she wanted full speed. You almost had to laugh. Not at her, of course. But she had a lot of guts. No matter what, no one could take that from her."

"You didn't love her?"

"It was only a short relationship, Simon. Less than two weeks."

"But did you love her?"

Clearly the boy wanted affirmation, but Lucas couldn't stretch the truth that far. So when he didn't answer, Simon withdrew the question by flip-flopping to a new subject. "Winnie was the one who screwed it up between you," he said. "She really hated my mother."

Simon's mention of Winnie now in this new light made Lucas cringe. Was that why he'd had his goons kill her, because he thought Winnie had somehow scuttled Lucas's relationship with his mother? "What makes you say that?" he asked. "Aside from maybe seeing her once or twice when she came to clean, I doubt they even knew one another."

"No, you've got it wrong, Lucas. When my mother tried to reach you, Winnie gave her a lot of flak. When my mother confronted Winnie one night outside her diner, she ran off at the mouth about you not wanting to see her. About how she'd better stay out of your face. Of course, Winnie was in love with you herself, so she had her own agenda."

Winnie had been trying to run interference for him. Maybe he hadn't come right out and asked her to, but as he recalled the scenario, he would have taken any help offered. But Winnie in love with Lucas? More likely Pamela had assessed the situation wrong. In any event, Simon hadn't got that misconception from the pictures. So who had filled his head with this garbage?

"You're mother died when you were just a baby, Simon. So how do you know so much about the time she spent here?"

"It started with my aunt. Oh, she loved to

torture me with stories about my mother. She was nuttier than a fruitcake."

The aunt must have been a replica of the sister, Lucas decided. If that was true, Simon had been cheated once again. Apparently catching some of what was going through Lucas's head and not wanting any part of his sympathy, Simon put the kibosh to it.

"Don't waste your tears. When I was sixteen, my aunt tossed me out on the street, and it was for the best. I left with the clothes on my back, Rex, and two boxes that belonged to my mother. In it were her diaries, snapshots, videotapes. All about you, Lucas."

Lucas was quiet for a few minutes. Where to go from here? How to convince him to give up this obsession about him and his mother? Finally he stood up. "Maybe I can help you."

"How?"

"I don't know. Get you a good lawyer. You're young yet, juries take those things into consideration." As Lucas began to speak, he started toward Simon.

Simon pulled his gun, pointed it at him. "You're not a bad guy, Lucas. I don't know if you've noticed, but I've been trying to go easy on you because of it." A curtain seemed to draw over his eyes now, making his expression seem faraway. "Still when the time comes, you're going to have to die. All of you."

Chapter Twenty-one

So the kid had seen all the pictures, the movies, read some diaries. Not knowing what his mother was like, that her viewpoint wasn't apt to be based on reality, he had come up with all the wrong conclusions. She had been more likely torn up over the guy who fathered her child then dumped her.

Though Simon wasn't saying it, he must have concluded that Lucas was responsible for his mother's suicide. What other reason would he have had for going to all that trouble to get him? For torturing his family? And when Lucas had tried to get him to admit it so they could perhaps have a new starting point, Simon had cut him off.

He went to the deck, called in his two partners, gave over the gun and phone to Warren, and rushed downstairs to the dust and discomfort of the tool room. To be in the company of a bull snake and a corpse. What kind of torture would a kid—any kid—have had to be put through to opt for that?

Earl took a handful of cookies upstairs with him, leaving Lucas alone with Warren.

Lucas suddenly felt exhausted: he was tired of trying to make sense out of what didn't make sense. He wished he could sleep for a week or get drunk, anything to stop him from thinking about it. But he had to keep thinking. He had to clear his mind of anything that might interfere with getting Cat and Haley and Zack safely out.

Still when the time comes, you're going to have to die. All of you.

He'd have to remember those words lest he be struck with misplaced sympathy, get the idea that Simon wasn't dangerous.

Warren, wearing a sleeveless T-shirt, got a can of 7UP and a bag of Doritos. Carrying them back to the dining area, he planted himself at the table to feed. It was one of those humid nights, and Warren's face and arms were slick with sweat. "I bet a cold beer would taste good about now," Lucas said.

"Hey?" Warren said, tilting his head a little as though he hadn't caught it.

"A beer, I said. It would taste good."

"Well, we don't all get what we want, ass wipe. So if you're thirsty, take water."

"No, I guess we don't. Apparently that applies to you, too."

He looked up. "What's that supposed to mean?"

Lucas shrugged. "Nothing too deep. Just that a big guy like you, well, it seems to me, you ought to be able to have a beer whenever the hell you please."

"Well, I can. Just that when I'm on duty—"

Lucas nodded knowingly. "Yeah, sure," he said, "I know the feeling. Rules. We're pretty much bombarded with them these days. There are people out there always coming up with more rules for other people to obey. They must get off on it, huh?"

Warren looked as though he were considering Lucas's observation carefully. Then he responded, "Well, I guess that's just the good ol' fucking American way."

"Hey, you're right, Warren. There's the rulers and there's the losers. Me, I'm in the loser column these days. Of course, a big guy like you ought to have it made."

"Yeah, I guess I do. I pretty much call my own shots." Though he said it and Lucas dutifully nodded, Lucas could spot the uncertain edge in his voice.

"You must have known Simon forever, huh?"

"What's it to you?"

Lucas shrugged. "Nothing really, just making small talk. You guys seem tight."

"Yeah, well, looks may be deceiving. Me and Earl, we're the ones tight, we grew up together. We only just met Simon about three, four months back."

"Really? Then I don't get it. I mean, it seems to me it's Simon's party. Not yours. What's your stake in all this?"

Warren guzzled some of his soda, then looked up, smiling. "Me and Earl got a cut from selling the Bronco."

"I bet it pulled in pretty good money. What made you pick out my car?"

Warren ran the back of his hand over his mouth, wiping away wet crumbs. "That's the one Simon told us he wanted, so that's the one we did. It meant nothing to us either way. I mean, who gives a flying fuck which car?"

Lucas nodded. He was likely telling the truth. To a simpleton like Warren, who or what he went after or what he had to do in the process made little difference. It had to do with getting his kicks and getting his money. Simple stuff. "So how about now?" Lucas asked.

"What do you mean?"

"I mean, you did a job, and by selling the car, you got reimbursed for your trouble. That makes sense. But what do you get for what you're doing now?"

His arm, holding the soda can, waved through the air. "We get to stay at this here place. Which isn't half bad." Lucas shook his head and sighed. "What's with the sound effects?" Warren asked.

Lucas continued to bait him. "Nothing. Hey, it's not really that important."

Warren came over to him, grabbed him by the shirt, and lifted him to his feet. "Well, I say it's important. Now, what's on your mind, motherfucker?"

"Okay, take it easy, no need to get mad. I was just thinking that this place must be a hell of a lot more than 'not bad.' I mean, it must be one fucking place to convince an aggressive guy like yourself to let a young guy like Simon lead you around by the nose."

He didn't bring up how Simon had branded his shoulder, there was no need to. When Lucas saw his oversize features tighten, he knew he had touched a button too many. Warren moved his hands to Lucas's collar, nearly lifting him off the floor, then put his mouth up to his, blowing foul breath in his face.

Warren took out his knife and brought it down to Lucas's crotch, the blade tearing through his short pants, the cool tip reaching bare skin. Lucas froze. "You've got balls, don't you, mister? So big and ripe and juicy that I might want to slice them up and fry 'em with butter for breakfast." Lucas didn't move so much as to blink, afraid that if he did, Warren would make good on the threat. "Now, I don't want to hear your mouth again tonight! You hear?"

Lucas nodded gingerly, and Warren shoved him down to the sofa. The force of the impact stunned him, causing a deep throbbing to begin in his bad leg. That put an abrupt end to their conversation.

Much later, he saw Warren go to the refrigerator and take out a cold beer for himself. One of Simon's rules broken: progress.

"Want to go for a walk?"

It was seven a.m. and Zack, barefoot with rolled jeans, was sitting on the dock where Earl could watch him from the deck. He had been fooling around with his Game Boy, but he looked up now to see Simon coming toward him. He was barefoot, too, wearing a sweat suit. Zack shook his head.

"I was thinking of going to the Cliffs."

Zack didn't answer.

"Come on, *kemosabe*. What good is it to be mad? It's not going to change anything. This way, at least you'll get to go to the Cliffs. It's been a while since you've been, huh? Hey, wasn't there some family of muskrats you wanted to check on?" Simon took two bananas from his pockets, and held one out to Zack.

Zack hesitated, then put his Game Boy in his pocket and took the banana. As Simon began to walk away along the wet sand, Zack hurried to catch up. They walked for a good ten minutes before Zack broke the silence between them.

"Hey, why're you doing this to us, Simon?"

He shrugged, picked up a few pebbles, and pitched them. "You have to do what you have to do."

"You were my best friend. I never said so maybe, but that's what I thought."

Simon looked at him, then ruffled his hair the way he sometimes did. "So, tell you what, I'll still be your best friend."

Zack shook his head. It wasn't that simple, even though Simon wanted to pretend it was. "Uh-uh, I can't. You're a killer. I could never be friends with a killer."

"Oh. Well, hey, that's how it goes," Simon said as though that was that and so what? To change the subject he looked off to the Cliffs ahead. "Want to have a race to the yellow rock?" Zack didn't really, so when Simon started running, he just followed along walking, arriving at the rock long after Simon.

He didn't go up and sit next to Simon either. Instead he headed for that family of muskrats.

After taking a shower, Cat dropped the car key inside her bra, then dressed in jeans and a T-shirt. Lucas didn't look good, but when she came out and asked him if he was feeling unwell, he said no. She wanted to have a word with the kids—Haley was sleeping late, and she couldn't seem to catch Zack alone. Finally at about eleven, she spotted him sitting in the sand, not far from the deck.

Earl was on watch, Simon had gone for a ride on his bike, and Warren was down near the dock smoking a joint. She went over to Zack. "What's up?" she said, sitting next to him.

He kept his eyes lowered. "I went to the Cliffs before. Simon took me."

"Yes, I saw. Listen, I need to talk—"

"When's Daddy going to do something?"

"We're going to do something, Zack. All of us. That's what I wanted to talk about."

Zack's interest was piqued. He looked at her, and she essentially told him all she knew. "I don't get it, though," he said. "Why can't Daddy come, too?"

She explained it as Lucas had explained it to her. She reassured Zack that Lucas would be safe—the police would get to him quickly and get him out of there. But she thought of how he looked just that morning: how dark the circles beneath his eyes were, as though he hadn't slept at all last night. And he was limping, much worse than before, as though he were in pain. Zack didn't buy any of Cat's reassurances, and she didn't suppose she did either.

Just as Cat was getting up to leave, she felt a hand on her chest, and fell back on the sand. When she looked up, Warren was standing over her.

It all happened so fast: Lucas heard Cat scream, and when he looked up Warren was all over her, tearing at her blouse. Zack started shouting, and trying to pull Warren off her. Lucas started down the deck with Earl after him, shouting that he was going to shoot.

But he didn't. Lucas reached them and, using all his strength, managed to pull him off her. Bellowing, Warren turned on him. He grabbed him around the neck, tightening his hands until he began to choke. Though he was aware of Cat screaming, it was finally Earl who got Warren's hands off him.

"Simon's going to be fucking mad!"

But Warren's rage wasn't satisfied. "Give me the gun," he said, holding his hand out to Earl.

"What are you doing?"

"I'm going to earn me a medal. This guy

here tried to run away. You saw him leave the deck, I saw it, too. So we had no choice but to shoot. Maybe a bullet in the leg would be a nice touch. That way if he lives, he'll stay put."

Earl looked unsure, but he gave Warren the gun. Cat reached out and began to pull at Warren's pants legs, sobbing. "Please, oh, please, let him go back!"

Brutally he kicked her off him. Then he faced Lucas toward the street. "Go on, start walking."

Zack had thought of the bull snake right away because he knew without Simon there to control Warren, no one could. No one missed Zack when he dashed off from the clamor, and as he returned, dragging the nine-foot Rex with him, no one noticed until he came up behind Warren and shouted, "Watch out!"

Warren looked down, but by that time Zack had let go of the snake and it was coming toward him. He dropped the gun and fell to the sand, with Rex landing on him. Though Lucas lunged for the gun, he couldn't get there fast enough.

Earl snatched it up and stood back. "Okay," he said, nervous now. "Everyone just stay where they are!"

Warren was lying on the ground, his teeth

chattering and his eyes fixed on the snake slithering across his bare stomach. "Get it off," he pleaded softly.

"Uh-uh, I ain't fucking touching it," Earl said. "Just get up."

"I can't move, I got a cramp."

The group stood frozen for what seemed like forever, until Simon came back and got things under control. He sent Lucas and Cat to the house, then after chewing out Warren, he wrapped Rex around his neck and headed with Zack for the cellar.

At first Haley thought it was a coincidence when she came out of the bathroom to find Daddy heading in there himself. But then she thought maybe it wasn't a coincidence at all. He came up close to her: he had a red mark around his neck. She wondered how he'd gotten it there, but decided not to ask.

"Listen to me, I don't have much time," he said.

Warren was on guard duty, Haley knew. Suppose he saw them talking?

"You and your mother and brother are going to get out of here. Tonight."

Had Daddy totally lost it? Didn't he know who he was dealing with here?

"You only need to know a couple of things, so go along with me. If your mother or I suggest something, be agreeable, maybe even enthusiastic. Be natural, use your influence."

Now she knew for certain he had lost it. Influence with who, Simon? But she nodded anyway and swallowed over the sudden dryness in her throat. Sneaking out those pictures from Simon's duffel bag was one thing. He might never miss them. But to just get up right in front of Simon and run away?

What if he caught them? And of course he *would* catch them. He knew a lot about people—the way to read them and the way to work them. That's probably why he always knew when she really needed a joint. Probably why he could scare a big mean ape like Warren into doing all his dirty work. What made Daddy think that any of them was a match for Simon?

Lucas could still feel Warren's strong hands squeezing his neck. If not for Zack's quick thinking, buying him those few extra minutes, well, who knew?

Now it was midmorning. Warren had been on guard duty for an hour, saying nothing, smoking one cigarette after another. Maybe angry, maybe embarrassed, or maybe trying to get rid of the image of the snake crawling on his stomach. Cat was sitting on the deck, staring at the same clue in a crossword puzzle book now for ten minutes, not yet past what had happened earlier.

Not quite sure how to make amends with Warren, Lucas finally decided to just jump in, hoping the time elapsed had soothed his ego some. "Hey, what is it, Warren?" he began. "Is it my imagination or are you always the unlucky guy who pulls guard duty?"

Warren walked over to the sliders, looked out at the beach. Simon and Earl and Haley had smoked pot. Now Simon and Earl were clowning, running around, whipping each other with soaking wet towels. Warren didn't answer.

"Of course, Simon's smart, he keeps a low profile."

Warren looked at him. "What do you mean?"

"Just that he wouldn't want to stand out. Do anything considered illegal."

"I don't get you."

"Simon knows enough to keep his hands clean, that's all. I mean, he kept himself mighty sweet-smelling as far as that whole carjacking went. After the way he played out his hand: helping me, calling the ambulance, the police."

When Warren said nothing, Lucas took it as an invitation to go on. "Well, I'm hardly a lawyer, but I'd say it'd be one hell of a job to prove he was even involved in it. Then, of course, there's my housekeeper's murder. Though I believe he played a big part in it, the fact is, he's got an airtight alibi. Unlike you, he was sitting right here with me and my family that night. Playing a board game."

Lucas could almost see the information slowly process through Warren's brain, making him anxious and unsure. Finally, he took a shot at Lucas's logic. "I'd say just him being in this house is illegal enough," Warren said.

"Sure, well, that might have been so if he'd forced his way in. But he's too smart for that. He got me to practically beg him to stay here. So yeah, maybe he's guilty of a misdemeanor, at least as far as anyone can prove. Not exactly equal to your crimes."

Warren didn't deny it, didn't admit it—in fact, he didn't say anything. Just looked again to the beach. His teeth gnawed at his lower lip, his forehead was creased. He was thinking about what Lucas was saying, getting a clearer picture. And wasn't happy with it.

"Listen, Warren, maybe I shouldn't have gone on about this. The last thing I need here is more trouble. I'm not ashamed to admit it, the guy scares me, too."

At that point Warren rushed over to him and dragged him to his feet, causing a sharp pain through his right leg. Using his palm, he whacked him. Lucas's hands went to his nose, which was bleeding. He took out a handkerchief from his pants pocket and held it to stop the blood while Warren stood over him.

"Look, I want you to shut the fuck up!" he said. "Maybe you're crapping your pants over him, but I'm not."

There was no more talk after that—not until Lucas overheard him with Earl later. Though Lucas couldn't make out exactly what he was saying, the subject had to be Simon. By Earl's gestures, he seemed to be trying to appease Warren. After a few tense moments he did, which was all right with Lucas. He had planted the seed of doubt, of discontent.

At lunch, Simon noticed the blood encrusted around Lucas's nose and questioned Warren about it. But when Warren lied, saying it just started on its own accord, Lucas went along with his story, even embellishing on it, saying he'd had a history of nosebleeds.

Tattling to Simon would serve no purpose. Besides, he didn't want the conversation proceeding Warren's fit of anger to be raised. Apparently Warren felt similarly. Which meant he hadn't totally dismissed it.

At four o'clock Lester Hutchins began his shift at the New London police headquarters. He headed first to the bulletin board to see if any notations had been scribbled on the bottom of the inquiry about Roger Davidson. There weren't—still, he turned to the dispatcher sitting beside the board at the main desk.

"Any messages, Lenny?"

Lenny nodded, handing him a small stack. "None about Davidson though."

Hutchins went to his desk and, as promised, dialed the police in Clinton. An officer named Rudy answered and told him Chief Cooper wouldn't be on duty until that evening. The lieutenant briefly explained the situation to him, asking that Cooper get back to him if he knew anything about the missing detective. Maybe he could even take a few minutes to contact the Marshalls, see if they could help. Either way, he'd sure appreciate it.

Finally Hutchins put down the phone and started to go through his messages.

During lunch, Lucas had mentioned the round robin table tennis tournaments they had played in the past. Last year, after twelve intense games, Cat had taken over the official crown from Lucas: a red beanie with a twirly bird and the words "Ping-Pong Champ" written in white across the front.

He brought up the topic again near the finish of dinner, at which time Cat—still unnerved by the Warren incident that morning—picked up on it. Taunting lightly, she noted what a pity it was that not one of them had the guts to suggest a follow-up competition.

Haley agreed that they were due for another tournament; Zack took up the challenge with even more enthusiasm. Cat then looked at Lucas for affirmation: had she picked up on it right or had he something entirely different in mind? His eyes told her she was exactly on the mark as he made his own excuse. "Sorry, guys," he said, looking at the kids. "Much as I'd like the chance to take back the crown from your mother, she's too good a player to oppose in my condition."

He was counting on Simon not to pass up the match, and he wasn't disappointed. "Well, hey, look," Simon said, "why don't I go for it instead?" When no one objected, he said, "We can start after dinner."

Everyone thought it was a good idea—that is, except for Warren, who grumbled that he never had seen much point in bouncing a little ball back and forth over a table net, so he wouldn't waste his time now. Just then Simon remembered he was scheduled to take over at guard duty, which wouldn't end until ten o'clock that night. He looked at Warren, nodding his head.

"Good. Then it works out with no hassle. You can take over my shift."

Although Warren hadn't elected to join the activities, Lucas was sure he was looking forward to lying around the house or beach, stuffing himself and getting high. So when he saw the display of outrage on his face in response to Simon, Lucas wasn't surprised. And he couldn't have been more pleased.

"Got a problem with that?" Simon asked, not missing his reaction either.

Warren paused a moment, and though there was always the possibility of him blowing right then and there, Lucas was hoping that he'd be a little more intimidated. He was. Shaking his head, Warren looked at Earl, who was already taking off his holster, gun, and telephone, eager to get rid of them. As he handed them to Warren, Simon sent Haley off to get the paddles and balls from the shed.

So it was not even seven-thirty, still daylight, when the proceedings began. Though Lucas would rather have gone downstairs to the beach, a little nearer to the competition, ready to jump into whatever was to happen later, Simon instructed Warren to remain on the deck with Lucas. It worried Lucas that his leg was getting worse, making it harder for him to navigate with any kind of speed. He wouldn't have a choice when the time came—he would have to move fast.

By nine o'clock they had already put on the outside lights to illuminate the table tennis area, and they were about to begin the seventh game: Cat and Simon, both having played each of the kids and Earl, would now be pitted against one another.

Until this point, being jumpy and apprehensive, Cat hadn't been able to muster much enthusiasm. Still being a competent player, she had managed to pull out the games, albeit with slim margins. Now, however, she was up against Simon, who'd won all his games as well. Though she had known he was good—she'd seen him play before with the kids—he had suddenly become even more proficient. Not surprising, of course—Simon, like Lucas, thrived on competition.

Before she took her position for the match, she looked once again to the deck—Lucas and Warren were still talking. Earlier she had noticed them look down at Simon as though they were talking about him. That meant Lucas was doing his thing, which meant that at any moment, hell could break loose.

Feeling as though she were battling gravity, she forced her eyes from the deck and took her place across from Simon. She picked up the ball and began a volley for serve.

Chapter Twenty-two

A proper round robin with five players would require at least sixteen games to complete—everyone playing everyone else, and if need be, a tiebreaker. Though the entire play-off couldn't be completed in one evening, Simon gave no indication of getting tired. By now Lucas had brought up Simon's name quite a number of times to Warren, actually pointing out his pluses: good physical appearance, leadership qualities, stamina, intelligence. Warren argued with none of this but the reverse psychology increased his irritability.

"Despite the obvious that I'd really relish seeing the guy fry," Lucas said, "I can't help but give him credit. From the little bit he's mentioned, he's had a hard time of it. But look at him—hey, he's your leader, you ought to know. Is there anything he can't do? And do it better than the next guy?" Lucas pointed at the game, which had only started, but Simon had already begun to outplay Cat. Smil-

ing, shaking his head, good-naturedly mocking her.

Maybe the mocking was responsible, or
maybe it was the heat of the competition, but
Cat was suddenly able to push thoughts of all
else aside. Her attitude made a surprising
change. She stopped a moment, took a long,
deep breath. Then, her chin tilted and stiffen-
ing, she backed up about ten feet from the table and took her stance. Cat was a dynamite
player when she wanted to be.

The next five serves came at Simon with
such force and speed, he could barely see the
ball, much less get his paddle to connect with
it. Finally he managed to hit the next serve,
but not taking into account the spin on it, he
totally miscalculated, banging the ball over
Cat's head to the sand. While she ran to retrieve it, he slammed down his paddle on the
table.

Angry.

Lucas glanced at Warren. They now didn't
have just one angry man. They had two.

Was Lucas ready to play his trump card?
The question was, would Warren be angry
enough to finally go after Simon? But he had
no other cards left to play, so he plunged in,
trying to divert Warren's attention from the
game.

"He'll pick up, I'm sure. No one makes a fool of Simon. Usually the opposite, I'd say."

No response—Warren continued to watch the game.

"You know, he's good at repairing things, too," Lucas began. He pointed at the shed. "For instance, right there. He did a hell of a job—the roof, the inside. Not that he isn't pulling in excellent compensation for his time, of course."

Warren finally gave his undivided attention to Lucas. Though Warren had wanted him to shut up before, now he was looking interested to hear more.

Lucas paused, put out his hands as though to apologize. "Look, I wasn't even going to bring it up. So maybe—"

"No, I want to hear. What kind of compensation?"

Lucas sighed, circling closer. "Okay. Just that Simon has not only been living up to the letter of the law, keeping his ass intact while you and Earl are out there taking the chances . . . well, with respect to cash, he's made out fine. In fact, is still making out. And if I might add, like a fucking bandit."

"How much we talking about?"

"See, I figured you and Earl were in on it, taking your cut. In fact, he actually led me to believe . . ."

"Fuck you, asshole!" Warren said, getting

up from his chair. "I asked you a goddamned question. Answer me!"

Fortunately, the cheers from the kids as Cat continued to slaughter Simon drowned out Warren's outrage when Lucas delivered his next jab. "Two grand a week," he lied. "And with no expenses, I would guess that Simon has quite a respectable stash by now. Hey, what did you say your split was for getting rid of the Bronco?"

Right then Warren's blood went from simmer to a full boil. His eyes looked small and red in his swollen face. As he rushed downstairs to confront Simon, Lucas got up fast, the pressure on his leg rocketing pain straight through his hip.

Simon had four points, and she had ten—game was eleven, and he was seriously angry. Slamming his paddle, kicking up sand, he was behaving like a disillusioned child. Although Cat had been prepared all evening, when the time actually came, she was too involved in the game to see the explosion coming.

Suddenly Warren was in Simon's face, hardly able to articulate his complaint, but confronting him anyhow. "What the fuck're you pulling?" he demanded.

Simon, not aware of what he was talking about, but in a surly mood himself, glared at him. "Who in hell let you out? Get back in your cage and stay there!"

Warren followed with a stream of curses enraging Simon still more, until he finally grabbed Warren by the collar. Earl, nervous over what was going on, moved in to try to break it up.

Clumsily yet swiftly, Lucas had made it down to the beach, and now was motioning to Cat. Feeling as though the air were being suctioned from her lungs, she nodded to the children. They started to race toward the Jeep, and then Cat did the hardest thing she had ever done: she turned away from Lucas.

She couldn't believe that she had actually turned the corner of the beach house without Simon having noticed.

He came close to noticing, though, Zack saw, watching from around the corner of the house, waiting for his mother to get there. But just as Simon began to turn in their direction, his father jumped in to grab his attention. Suddenly Daddy was in trouble, right smack in the middle of the fight. Zack cringed as Lucas got two heavy-duty punches in the stomach, one after another taking him partially down.

"Get in the car," his mother hissed, taking his arm and dragging him along.

"But what about—" he started to say, trying to pull back, but she didn't listen.

Instead she lifted him, boosting him through the back window. "Close the window and lock the door," she said, already on her way to the driver's door.

Haley was closing the windows and locking the doors in front as his mother fumbled with the key, swearing softly, breathing heavily, as she tried to get the key in the lock. So neither his mother nor sister noticed when Zack climbed out the rear window and dropped to the ground. Within seconds the car was pulling away and speeding down the road. And Zack was on his way back to the fight. Until the cops got there, his father was going to need all the help he could get.

Zack stuck his hand in his jeans pocket and pulled out the little screwdriver.

It was a free-for-all at first, then they seemed to choose off partners. Simon and Warren were still going at it hard—Simon, physically much smaller, was getting the worst of it. And Lucas was on the sand, trading punches and wrestling with Earl. He was getting the better of him until Earl hauled off and kicked Lucas's cast.

Pain soared through his leg, and Earl seized the moment. He leapt on top of him, both hands wrapped around his throat. Lucas couldn't get enough power behind his arms to budge him, but it turned out he didn't have to: Earl's hands suddenly lifted, seemingly of their own accord. His jaw dropped, his back jerked, then arched as though he were in extraordinary pain.

Lucas grabbed his opportunity and pushed Earl off him. Despite the cast inhibiting him from normal movement, he rolled over onto Earl, then began to pound his face with his fists. Punching and punching and punching until he saw Zack standing over him, watching. Where the help had come from was no longer a mystery.

Lucas, out of breath, dropped his arms and looked at Earl: out, definitely not going anywhere. He glanced over at Simon—he was still fighting Warren, but now had the edge. Lucas quickly raised his arm to Zack, and he helped him up. Holding on to his hand, he began to run with him. He had only one thought: to get Zack the hell out of there, to find somewhere to hide until the police arrived.

But they hadn't gotten a hundred feet into the street when Lucas heard footsteps on the pavement chasing them and Simon calling out, "Stop now, Lucas, or I'll shoot the kid."

Haley couldn't believe they'd actually gotten away from the beach house, away from Simon and the others. Most surprising of all was her mother. Though she was white-faced and afraid, she seemed to know what she was doing. She seemed to have thought about the whole thing beforehand, because when Haley expected her to take the usual road into town, she didn't. She turned off at another street.

"In case they try to follow," Cat said. "There's a bar and grill not far off this road. It's got to be open."

Green Apple Road, Haley remembered. Only a mile and a half from the house, a place where they could stop and phone for help. That would be quicker than driving all the way to the police station in Clinton. Mom told Haley and Zack to watch carefully for the road sign so she wouldn't miss it in the darkness. So it wasn't until Haley saw it and shouted and pointed it out to her mother that she turned in her seat to look at her brother. He wasn't there!

Her mother gasped, her mouth dropped as Haley told her. But she took the turn onto Green Apple Road. "No!" Haley insisted. "We've got to go back to get him."

"It's too late for that now, honey. Daddy is there, he'll take care of him."

Another three hundred feet and they were pulling into the nearly full Apple Bar and Grill parking lot. Her mother pulled up to the door, blocking it, and was out of the Jeep almost before it stopped with Haley racing in after her.

* * *

Just the three of them were walking down to the dock. Because of Lucas's leg, which had begun to tingle and grow numb rather than hurt, they were moving slowly, painstakingly. Certainly they were taking more time than Simon would have liked. But he didn't show any temper. Quietly, calmly, he walked in back of Lucas, keeping the gun dug tightly into his ribs. They passed Warren and Earl, both spread-eagled in the sand, unconscious. Or dead.

"Where're we going?" Zack asked as they got down to the dock and he saw Simon untie the boat. The fear in his voice at the prospect of going out to sea was nothing compared to the fear Lucas had of what Simon had in mind for them.

"Please let Zack stay, Simon," he pleaded, his mind racing, trying to come up with an offer, any offer. But how do you make an offer to a guy when you don't know what he wants? "Please. You've got me. What's the point in taking him?"

Simon didn't answer—he looked at Zack. "Hey, *kemosabe*, double-crossed me, huh?"

"You've got it all wrong," Lucas said. "He panicked, got scared for me. I know you're gutsy, Simon, but even you must have gotten scared at one time or another."

Simon flinched, but didn't answer right

then. Still he put the gun to Lucas's head and ordered Zack on the cabin cruiser. Though the boy looked ready to faint at any moment, he did exactly what he was told. After him went Simon. And then Simon reached out one arm and helped Lucas on board.

Cat didn't waste any time looking around for a public phone. Instead she ran up to the bar and loudly demanded that the bartender phone the police.

The barman took a telephone from beneath the bar, lifted it onto the counter. He dialed the police, then handed her the receiver. An officer came on, listened to what she was saying, and assured her they'd be on their way. Then Cat looked around at the faces at the bar—everyone had since stopped talking to listen to what she was saying—and asked, "Is there anybody here with a gun?"

Two takers. Both stepped forward, and one said, "Whad'ya have in mind, lady?"

"You just heard me—my husband and son are in danger. I can get there quicker than the police."

"Three guys?"

"Two in mid to late twenties, the other's nineteen. One's big."

She pulled out of the parking lot first, and the two men followed in their truck. As they shot down the road, Haley said, "Simon's not nineteen, he's twenty-one."

"But he said—"

"I know, he lied. Once when we were on the island, he went in swimming, and I looked through his wallet. I saw his birthdate on his driver's license."

Simon sat on the circular bench behind the controls and told Lucas and Zack to sit on the other end. He started the boat, then eased it away from the dock and, with just the lights from the boat, headed to sea. They motored in the direction of Mirra's Island. What was he going to do, take them out to the island to execute them?

Lucas looked back to shore, but was unable to spot any sign of police. Any sign of anyone. Then he looked down and put his arm around his young son. He had never prayed before— hell, he didn't even know if he believed in God. But if there was one, Lucas was asking . . . Not for himself, he'd had it good. For Zack.

They hadn't gone far when Simon lit up a joint and took a couple of hits. Soon he started to relax. "I used to be scared to sleep in the cellar," he said, "but that's a long time ago."

At first Lucas thought he was talking about sleeping in the tool room. But then he realized he was talking about when he lived at home with his aunt.

"Your aunt made you sleep there?"

He nodded. "She didn't want me upstairs to dirty things up. I used to pee my bed as a kid. Remember I told you, Zack?" The boy nodded. "Well, I'd stink up the whole lousy room. So it was that or put me out in the garbage shed. The old loon gave me a choice." He shrugged, chuckled, put the gun down on the bench, and took another hit. He drew it way deep into his lungs. And he didn't pick the gun up again. "I got used to it, though. Even began to like it."

"I'm sorry," Lucas said, not knowing what else to say. He was reminded of being at a funeral and being confronted with the grieving party. In this case the grieving party was a seriously sick kid about two steps from killing him and his son.

"Of course, if my mother were alive, it would have been different," Simon said. "It would never have happened like that. Keep in mind, she could have aborted me easy. Or even had me adopted out. But she didn't do either. She must have wanted me. Right, Lucas?"

While he was reminiscing, Lucas had taken his arm from Zack and inched it down the bench. Now he was within arm's reach of the gun. Just as he was agreeing with Simon's analysis, he snatched the gun and jumped up.

Simon lunged for it, and Lucas was taken by surprise. Before he could squeeze the trigger, Simon grabbed his wrist in a vise grip. They fell to the floor, struggling. Simon couldn't dislodge Lucas's finger from the trigger, but twisted Lucas's hand and wrist, twisting the direction of the gun. Lucas felt his finger being pushed even tighter over the trigger—until suddenly the gun roared.

The pistol went flying across the deck. Lucas, stunned, looked at Simon, who was now lying there, his features twisting, his hands clutching his stomach. *Had Simon pointed it at himself deliberately?*

Blood was pouring out of the stomach wound. "Get me the sheet off the bed in the cabin, Zack." Lucas reached up and temporarily stopped the boat. Eyeing Simon, he said, "Listen to me, it's going to be okay. I'm going to stop the bleeding, then get you to a hospital."

Lucas's thoughts flitted back to the night when Simon had helped him, making him comfortable, calling an ambulance. Of course, Lucas hadn't known then that Simon was the one responsible for him needing an ambulance.

"Yeah, sure," Simon said, not seeming to care, or perhaps not believing him. But then he asked him again, "Hey, Lucas, did you love her?"

It was all insane—the kid was lying there with a hole in his stomach. What difference did it make? Zack came back with the sheet and Lucas ripped off strips, tied the strips around him. But the boy's pressure was dropping, his pulse was weakening.

Lucas looked at Zack, who was crying silently. "Think you can drive this boat, son?"

He nodded. "If you tell me which way."

As Zack sat at the controls, Lucas released the brake and headed him to shore. Then he pressed Simon's head to his stomach, cradling his face. For those next few moments, the horror of Simon, the accidental shooting, faded to the background. Lucas thought about a little boy kept in a cellar, wetting his bed, befriending a bull snake.

Simon's eyes were closing, as though he were giving up. "Simon?" Lucas called. Then he called again, this time louder. And his eyes opened. "About your mother?" Lucas said, and he nodded, waiting. "I loved her."

Simon smiled and shut his eyes.

The Coast Guard apparently had been called—other men, too, Lucas could see them out on the beach with Haley and Cat. But Zack and Lucas pulled to shore by themselves. Zack, red-eyed and in shock, handed

Lucas a wallet. "Daddy, it's Simon's," he said. "It came out of his pocket when you were fighting." The boy jumped to the dock, eager to get to his mother and sister waiting there for him.

But Lucas held back, not yet ready to disembark, his mind going back to the shooting. He stood holding the wallet, looking at it, feeling the worn leather, knowing he had to look inside. It was all starting to make sense.

Finally he opened the wallet, took out Simon's driver's license, and looked at his age. He gasped. Though he thought he was prepared, he wasn't really. Nothing in his entire world could ever have prepared him for that.

Tears blurring his vision, his eyes moved to the picture of his firstborn son.

Epilogue

They still hadn't decided what to do with the beach house. They weren't ready to return next summer. The fact was, they might never be ready. But they didn't want to sell it either—at least not without giving their feelings more time. Next summer they would travel instead, play it by ear. So this late February trip was just a simple overnighter, mostly to pack up a few things to take home with them.

After putting away the two bags of groceries which they had bought on the way, Lucas and the children bundled up and went down to the dock. Cat headed to the bedroom closet with a cardboard box. When she reached up on the shelf to get the camcorder, a dozen papers came flying down, scattering to the floor.

She put the movie camera down, stooping to pick up the papers, and when she saw they were composites of Warren and Earl, she sat down and looked at them. Of course, she had learned about the private investigator Lucas had hired at just about the same time she had learned he was in the cellar dead.

Warren and Earl were quite alive when she got back to the house that night. The men from the bar and grill saw to it that they didn't go anywhere until the police arrived. Though they were indicted for the murders of Winnie Rawson and Roger Davidson, and were being held without bail in a Danbury prison, the trial wasn't scheduled until late spring. At that time Lucas and she would testify.

According to the District Attorney, though, their defense would be Simon. The bright young attorney who was handling their case was planning to allege that Simon mesmerized a couple of decent, well-meaning but not tremendously bright young men. So the nightmares were not yet put to rest. Still lingering was the threat that they might get off with an easy sentence.

Or get off entirely.

Lucas stood back some from the dock, his hands in his parka pockets, not as willing as the kids to get sprayed by the crashing waves. As he gazed out into the water, he couldn't help but get images of Simon: as he was when they first met, as he was when he died only three weeks later in his arms.

Had Simon wanted more than revenge from Lucas? Might there have been some way to reach the boy if Lucas had been a little smarter, a little more intuitive? Or had Simon just determined it was too late? He was responsible for two murders here. Had there been more?

Now came the pain and, along with that, the guilt. Suddenly Lucas's life had been weighed in the balance and he hadn't been ready. He had prided himself on being fair, responsible, honorable, all those fine traits a man likes to think he possesses.

Yet what kind of life had his own son had?

If he had only known there was a Simon . . . but then, hadn't he made it clear then that what he really wanted was for Pamela and her problem to disappear?

When the authorities notified Simon's aunt of her nephew's death, she was aloof, claiming she had done her job to the best of her ability, but had given up on Simon years before. So Lucas made arrangements to have his body taken back to Massachusetts with them. They had a family funeral, burying him in a cemetery near their home. Simon—his son, Cat's stepson, Zack and Haley's big brother—even thinking about it now, as he had so often, stunned him.

But most of all saddened him. And always

when he got this way, the person he gravitated to was Cat.

Lucas called out to the kids that he was heading back to the house to help their mother pack. Haley smiled, that sweet radiance having left for some time had finally begun to return. But Zack's glance seemed a bit concerned. Lucas had suffered nerve damage in his right leg, causing a permanent limp. Nothing too painful or incapacitating, but these days Zack had a habit of worrying about his dad.

They were pretty thick now, able to get through to each other, cherish each other. Like a father and son ought to do. For that, he thanked Simon.

"Taut, highly literate ... Barbara Parker is a bright new talent."—Tony Hillerman

"Superb ... masterful suspense ... hot, smoldering, and tangy."—*Boston Sunday Herald*

SUSPICION OF INNOCENCE

by Barbara Parker

This riveting, high-tension legal thriller written by a former prosecutor draws you into hot and dangerous Miami, where Gail Connor is suddenly caught in the closing jaws of the legal system and is about to discover the other side of the law. . . .

"A stunning, page-turner!"—*Detroit Free Press*

"A fast-moving thriller . . . charged Florida atmosphere, erotic love and convincing portrayals make it worth the trip."—*San Francisco Chronicle*

Available now from **SIGNET**